THE
ICE-CREAM
HEADACHE
&
OTHER STORIES

by James Jones
with a new preface by Kaylie Jones

Akashic Books
New York

Also by James Jones

From Here to Eternity
Some Came Running
The Pistol
The Thin Red Line
Go to the Widow-Maker
The Merry Month of May
A Touch of Danger
Whistle
World War II
Viet Journal

Published by Akashic Books

©1948, 1949, 1951, 1952, 1955, 1957, 1958, 1963, 1968, 2002 by Gloria Jones, Kaylie Jones, and Jamie Jones

Acknowledgment is made to the following magazines in whose pages these stories first appeared:
The Atlantic Monthly for "Temper of Steel."
Collier's Magazine for "Greater Love."
Esquire for "The Tennis Game" and "Two Legs for the Two of Us."
Harper's Magazine for "The Way It Is."
New American Library of World Literature for "A Bottle of Cream" and "None Sing So Wildly."
Playboy for "The King" and "Just Like the Girl."
Saturday Evening Post for "Valentine."

ISBN: 1-888451-35-1
Library of Congress Control Number: 2002106361
All rights reserved
First Akashic printing

Akashic Books
PO Box 1456
New York, NY 10009
Akashic7@aol.com
www.akashicbooks.com

Printed in Canada

This collection is 'dictated' to my 7-year-old son, Jamie

CONTENTS

PREFACE
by Kaylie Jones

My father had mint-condition first editions of all of his books leather bound with gold lettering—blue for my brother Jamie and brown for me. He signed each volume on birthdays and other holidays, an extra little gift from him. In my volume of *The Ice-Cream Headache,* he wrote: "To Kaylie—on her ninth Birthday. Hoorah! A new one is almost finished! And so am I." In Jamie's—to whom the book is dedicated—he wrote: "To Jamie—this is the one I promised you two years ago. Sorry it is a year late. Still, it's better than nothing. Anyway, it's your own." Rereading his inscriptions, I see a recurring theme: The next one is almost done . . . and the next one . . . and the next one . . . As if he were already concerned about running out of time; feeling guilty for not having met some harsh, self-imposed deadline. We had no idea that within a year he would suffer his first bout of congestive heart failure, the disease that seven years later would take his life.

In his introduction to *The Ice-Cream Headache,* James Jones compares writing stories to "having a series of high-fever ailments," while writing a novel "is like having t.b. or some such long term chronic ailment with a low grade fever." Typical of his sense of humor, the point he's making is that writing is painful as hell on the best of days. My brother Jamie and I would watch him come downstairs from his office in the late afternoons, and it was not unlike witnessing a champion runner a few minutes after he's crossed the finish line. If writing a novel is a marathon, then the short story is a sprint. But even while James Jones was putting together these stories, he was thinking of the book as a whole, and still suffered all the pain and loneliness of a long-distance runner. What amazed my brother and me as children was how, even on the most beautiful summer day, he'd climb those stairs, lock himself in, and write. No one was making him do it, and we found this astounding.

His novels were big and fat and frightening. My bound editions went high up on a shelf next to my brother's, for when we "grew up." His books in progress lived with us like some strange relative in the attic. He'd talk about them, the problems he was having, and when he finished one, it was a celebration as big as a national holiday. Upon receiving *The Ice-Cream Headache* on my ninth birthday, knowing already that it contained short stories, I asked my father if he thought I was old enough to read it. He thought about it for a moment and said, "Sure—go ahead and start with the childhood stories." And he told me their titles: "Just Like the Girl," "The Tennis Game," "A Bottle of Cream," "The Valentine," and "The Ice-Cream Headache."

My father had never talked much about his childhood. I gathered it had not been a happy one. I knew he'd been a boy through the Great Depression. He was eight years old in 1929, when his family lost everything, including their high standing in Robinson, the small southern-Illinois town where he was born and raised. Now, in preparation for my reading of these childhood stories, he told me that they were based on his own life, that the grandfather in "The Ice-Cream Headache" was his own grandfather, George Washington Jones, a lawyer who was a quarter Cherokee and had written a book himself, based on the trial of Christ. James Jones had loved and admired his grandfather, had adored his own drunken father Ray Jones, a dentist, whose best advice had been to always tell the truth, and he'd hated—passionately hated—his mother Ada, on whom the mother in the stories is based.

When I turned nine, we were spending the summer in Deauville, France. I was taking riding lessons and swimming in the ocean every day. I lived a dream life of privilege, far from Robinson, Illinois, where I'd never been. I'd never met a single relative on my father's side. His childhood was far removed from anything I knew, but his writing was so straightforward, so honest, the details so clear—the Midwestern summer heat, the small backyard, the public school's hallways, the mother's sweating back as she toils over the kitchen stove—that I felt I was there with him, witnessing his childhood as a powerless onlooker. My father was a romantic child, with an inquisitive, wide-open mind, and he was misunderstood, misinterpreted, by the adults entrusted with his care. They were no help at all to him in figuring out the ways of the world. The injustice, the cruelty, the absence of understanding he suffered as a child made me, at nine, sick at heart. And I knew that even if some of the details were changed— my dad often said that's what a novelist did, fool with the facts—the little boy was my father, and he'd lived through these terrible things. It was almost impossible to imagine this strong, powerful, decent man at the mercy of such bungling, self-centered adults.

In 1982, five years after his death, I visited Robinson for the first time. I learned that James Jones had had a helper in his young life—the librarian at the public library. He'd been a child who read voraciously, and by the age of eight, he'd read every book in the children's wing of the Robinson library. He begged the librarian for permission to read the adult books. Concerned about what terrible lessons the little boy would learn, the kind lady supervised his reading until his high school graduation. But in school, he was a mediocre student, even in English—his best subject. According to his report cards, he was often bored and angry in class, argumentative with the teacher, who in his opinion didn't understand the first thing about the books she was teaching. Following graduation, with few options, he joined the Army. This was in 1939. At his father's suggestion, he went to Hawaii, where my grandfather was certain Hitler's war would never reach.

My father never saw his parents again. His mother, Ada Blessing Jones, died shortly before Pearl Harbor of diabetes, which she refused to have treated because she'd become a Christian Scientist. After Pearl Harbor, his father, Ray Jones, tried to enlist. He showed up stinking drunk at the recruitment office and was laughed out the door. He went back to his office, sat down in his dentist's chair, and shot himself through the mouth.

It was not until my first trip to Robinson that I tackled the rest of *The Ice-Cream Headache*, the stories about love and war. I'm still struck by their brutal honesty. James Jones doesn't gloss over the ugliness, and yet, he handles his characters, adult and child, with infinite delicacy and compassion. He was ahead of his time in every way, addressing issues such as the plight of single women trying to make it on their own in New York City, and young men returning from WWII with Post Traumatic Stress Disorder, which the soldiers called combat fatigue, and were expected to recover from by the sheer force of their will. He never treated his characters with condescension, instead with epic compassion and a straightforward language that reflects the very nature of who they are. James Jones paints a devastatingly clear and poignant picture of a time and place, of a young artist's struggle to break free, not only of his past and his prohibitive culture, but of the scars left upon his psyche by the horrors of war, and the horrors of childhood.

It is no surprise, then, that he dedicated the book to his only son, Jamie. Just as Jamie and I were under the impression that we were "one nation *invisible*, with liberty and justice for all," we believed our father *dictated* his books to those he loved, and thus the dedication, a testament to his unique sense of humor.

With another novel almost done, indeed, so was he. In 1977, fighting against time, writing twelve to fourteen hours a day in order to finish his last novel, *Whistle*, the last of the trilogy begun with *From Here to Eternity* and *The Thin Red Line*, he died, four chapters from the end. Willie Morris put my father's tape recordings and notes together and finished the novel for him.

I feel sad to this day that I never got the chance to discuss his larger works with him. But I do have the memory of that one day, when at nine years old, in France, I ran to him in tears and threw myself into his arms.

"But, Daddy, these stories, they're not true, right? They're not really true?" I wanted him to reassure me.

"They're all true," he said in a quiet tone, "I just had to change things sometimes, you know, lie a little, to make them better stories."

I remember crying in his arms, unable to stop, and his calm and even voice as he explained to me that the world was not always a nice place and that people were sometimes quite terrible, even though they usually thought they were doing the right thing—and he wished it could be otherwise and that he could tell me it wasn't so, but there it is.

I felt so guilty for every cruel thing I'd ever done to anyone smaller or weaker than myself. And I blurted this out to my father:

There was a little girl in my class—a chauffeur's daughter who was on scholarship. She was small for her age and her clothes were too small and stained. I admitted forlornly that I'd been mean to her and I vowed never to laugh at her, or mistreat any other fragile soul ever again.

My father chuckled good-naturedly at my solemn vow and told me not to be too hard on myself, but he was proud of me, he said, for telling the truth.

"What happened to Chet Poore?" I asked him. I was referring to the magnificent outlaw in "A Bottle of Cream"—to this day one of my favorite short stories.

"Oh, he died in jail, I guess," my father said wistfully. "That wasn't his real name."

"What was his real name?"

"I don't remember," my father said. "I don't remember if it really happened that way at all."

INTRODUCTION
by James Jones

In planning this book of stories I decided against any rewriting or revising. So these are presented to you just as they were when they were first finished no matter how long ago and then published, or in the case of two, not published at all. Mainly this is because I felt that to revise them at this late date instead of helping them might very well take away from them the very thing I like about them most which is their flavor of "youngness", of emotional freshness of "Then," of emotional immediacy according to the time and place in the progression of a writer's life when they were written. The truth is, I don't think I could revise them, because I am no longer the man who wrote them. As a matter of fact, the man who wrote each story probably ceased to exist after that story was written and finished, by the mere fact of having written it.

Particularly the first story I find "young" in the technical sense of writing technique. It makes its effects well, I think, but in a way which is a little bit too obvious, too heavily pointed, too easy for the reader to see behind. This is a little embarrassing, but not very much so, since I was "young" myself then. I find the story amusing for this, perhaps an interested reader will also, but I think the story's point is as valid today as it was then, if perhaps (with the Special Forces soldiering of today) not even moreso.

Anyway naturally I got older. I think a reader who is interested will find that the stories get older too. This is not to say that each story is conclusively and positively better than the last one! How I would like to be able to say that! How any writer would! But I find it interesting to follow the changes and progression, the various experiments successful or less successful. Perhaps the interested reader will also. There are a number of moods, several different styles, several different attacks. They begin with five stories written in 1947, when I was 25 (My God, is that possible?!) and run through a period of ten years to four written in 1957 when I was 35, which are the last stories I have written.

Probably one of the reasons I've written so few stories is that I've almost always been involved with some damn novel or other. Also, it's often hard to get them published in the magazines, even if you're not young and unknown. Certainly, unless you want to turn yourself into a story hack, you cannot make a living off them. Then too there is the question of self-imposed censorship. One simply can't write anything outspoken about sexuality and get it published in any magazine printing today. This automatically rules out a whole raft of subjects. If sexuality and an interest in it is one of your main themes, as it is with me, this takes away from what you can write a very large chunk of what you'd like to write. You find yourself pre-censoring from your material much of what you'd like to write according to what you know you can get printed, or else you just lay the idea away and never do it at all. I can do better with novels.

But perhaps some gossip about the stories would be interesting. The first batch of five was written in the summer of 1947 just after I had sent in to Maxwell Perkins the first two hundred pages of the first draft of *From Here to Eternity*. I had begun it in March. Before that I had written an entire novel and then rewritten it twice, once in New York and once while working on a commercial fishing boat in the Florida Keys, and had tried my hand at innumerable stories. I was pretty discouraged about my two hundred pages and while waiting to hear from Perkins, unable to continue with the novel until I did, I hauled out some old story attempts (only one of them even finished) and had a go at rewriting them. I finished five of them before a letter came from Perkins; and in doing so suddenly and for no reason that I could find I began to write well, in my own voice and in my own way, with a sense of timing and with rhythms that suited my ear and my emotion. These five are reprinted here in the chronological order in which they were written from first one to last one, beginning with THE TEMPER OF STEEL and ending with SECONDHAND MAN. And when Perkins' cautiously and politely critical letter came back, I knew what he was talking about. I put the two hundred pages away and without looking at it began to write the version of *Eternity* which exists today, chapter by chapter without ever going back. That early two hundred pages, now lost or destroyed, gone anyway, had a rudimentary version of the 'bugle scene' where Prewitt blows Taps, a very poor version. Perkins did not live to see the final version because he died that fall in 1947.

I worked hard all that year on *Eternity*. Then in the winter of 1948 while living in Naples, Florida, after sending in the second section of it to my new editor Burroughs Mitchell in the hope of a further advance, I was so written out, busted up and worn down I decided to take some time off and began a story concerned with some events of the previous summer. This became NONE SING SO WILDLY, more a novella or novelette than a story. It took me three months to write. I had never meant to spend that much time on it. After I finished it, I rewrote the story SECONDHAND MAN which had never satisfied me, expanding it from a mood piece about the North Caroline mountains into the character study it is today. I sent both of these all over, to just about everybody, but could not sell them. But I was getting used to that. I had sold one story the year before to the *Atlantic*, and after the first flush of joyful disbelief, found it changed my life almost not at all.

The next summer, in 1949, found me living in a house trailer in Memphis, Tennessee. It was very hot and I remember I had reached and was working on The Stockade section of *Eternity*. I had just introduced the character of Jack Malloy and was forced to bone up and reread everything I could about the Wobblies, and could not continue the book until I had. The story I began then, just to have something to do, became GREATER LOVE and my first real attempt at writing seriously about combat. A new guy had moved in with a trailer down the street in the trailerpark, and it turned out that although I had never known him, he too had spent time in Guadalcanal and in New Georgia. I'm sure that our talks, sitting out at night on the porch beside his trailer or mine, breathing the night air and drinking beer, had something to do with that story being written when it was. I sent it all around too, with the usual result.

THE KING was written in the summer of 1955. By then I had finished *Eternity* and it had become a bestseller and famous and I was deep into the writing of *Some Came Running*. I had lived several months in New York that year, working on the novel, and while there I had returned often to an old haunt from poorer days at NYU: Jimmy Ryan's on 52nd St. Jimmy claimed he remembered me from the "old days", whether he really did or not, and we talked a lot about those "old days" back in the '40s before Sidney Bechet moved to France. THE KING grew out of all that. I wrote it sitting in my housetrailer under the shade of three big soft maples on a grassy hillside in Marshall, Illinois.

Some Came Running was coming on toward being finished by this time. Whatever the critics thought of it (which was damned little!) it had nevertheless kept me occupied for six whole years. During that time I took time off to do only that one story, THE KING. But I made notes from time to time on story ideas and various approaches to them. Then in 1957, *with the book in hand* (that magnificent phrase!), I met my wife, married, spent half a summer in Haiti, learned skindiving. Perhaps this huge change in my life, this half a year spent in the middle of an "expanding universe" so to speak, influenced me. In any case when my wife and I returned to Illinois in the summer of 1957 I found myself aware of the Middlewest and its ambiance in a way I had not been since probably my twelfth or thirteenth year. Also I wanted to do some stories before tackling the next novel on the list. I had always meant to do a novel on childhood in the '20s and '30s set in that beautiful, grim, frightening, land- and spirit-locked part of the world. Ergo, why not do a book of childhood stories on it instead?

I thought it was a great idea. Novels on childhood, particularly Middlewestern childhoods, were dime a dozen. It would be a fresh approach. I already had one finished childhood story (JUST LIKE THE GIRL) which would fit right in, and I had notes on a whole flock of others, twelve or thirteen. I attacked this project. Three of the last four stories here are the result of that. SUNDAY ALLERGY is the result of a break taken off from childhood stories.

Then, after finishing THE TENNIS GAME, I took another break from childhood stories to write another short story, one I had made notes on for a long time. It was an Army story and was to be called THE PISTOL. And, of course, somewhere about five or ten pages into it I suddenly realized I didn't have a short story here, I had a short novel. Moreover, I had something I had been looking for for a long time: namely, a subject around which to construct a deliberately, consciously *symbolic* novel; one in which the symbol is deliberately imposed upon the material from outside, beforehand, more in the European manner. But I wasn't sure I had enough material to flesh it out. Should I try it or not? I discussed it with my wife. "Write in a fight," she suggested. "You write fights marvelously." So I did.

And, I haven't gotten back to my book of childhood stories since.

They're still there though, waiting. I have the notes, and I have the titles for most. Maybe I'll get to it after I finish the current novel. If I do, all of the childhood stories in this volume will be included in it.

Writing short stories has a totally different feel from writing novels. I'm not sure whether I like it better or less. There isn't that long haul ahead of you staring you in the face: this year, next year, the year after. By the same token the anguish of creative decision is much sharper writing stories. The particular point at which you must decide on the structure to point the ending you have finally discovered, comes much quicker. But then too it's decided and over and done with much quicker. Writing stories is like having a series of high-fever ailments in which the crisis comes soon and either passes or doesn't. Writing a novel is like having t.b. or some such long term chronic ailment with a low grade fever that takes a long time to cure. Take your choice. It's six of one, half a dozen of the other.

As a postscript, it might be interesting for a writer—if not for a reader—to note the following statistic. In 1951 when *From Here to Eternity* was published I had five unpublished stories on hand. Within four months I sold four of the five, and sold them in every case to a magazine which had previously turned all five stories down at least twice. I don't know what this statistic signifies. But I'm damn sure not going to knock myself off over it like Martin Eden did.

J.J.
Paris, October 1965

THE TEMPER OF STEEL

Edward Weeks chose this story from among the first five to print as an "Atlantic First" in the March 1948 issue of *Atlantic Monthly*. It seems young to me today, but I think it makes a good and serious point. The point however is well concealed. See if you can find it. In case you can't, I'll explain it after the story. It's possible I didn't point it up enough, but at the time I believed with Hemingway that one should not point one's story points up.

K nives," the tall man said, looking down at the gate-leg table. "They are truly ingenious things, are they not?"

Johnny moved his cocktail glass and followed the tall man's gaze down.

Their hostess smiled brightly. "Yes, aren't they? So gruesome." She spared the table one polite glance from her quick peerings about the room at her other guests. Her short hair, feathered about her ears and forehead, heightened the effect of a sparrow looking for bread. "Oh," she said. "I see someone I must speak to. You two know each other? You won't mind?"

"No," Johnny said. He looked at his drink and decided he needed it.

"My dear lady," the tall man said. "We met here in your home, at dinner. Don't you remember?" He eyed Johnny. "Did we not?"

"Yes, Lon," Johnny said. "Yes, we did."

"But of course." Their hostess smiled brightly. She put her frail hand on Johnny's arm. "I want you to relax and just make yourself at home here. Another cocktail? These affairs are really nothing." She brought the cocktail and flickered away after new crumbs.

The tall man picked up one of the knives and his eyes burned down into Johnny's face. He tugged abruptly. The sheath embraced the knife, surrendered it only under pressure and with a squeak of protest. He held the knife with its tip pointed at Johnny's chest and looked at him with that bright hard stare.

"Truly," he said, "they are ingenious. Now you take these: there are none of the too heavy, too chrome, too fine-lined characteristics of mass production about these."

Johnny looked at him and did not say anything. There were two knives in their embossed sheaths on the small table. Both knives had come from Africa in the hill country. The tall man had picked up the smaller one. The frantic buzz of conversation by which people earned their way at cocktail parties was incessant, fearing a letdown.

"These are individual pieces of work." The tall man spoke authoritatively and gestured toward Johnny with the knife in his hand. "The savage who made this tried in his dim ignorant way to express himself, to put some of his knowledge of life and living into the making of it. To him, probably, it was truly beautiful. In fact, it is beautiful, because of its very crudeness, in the sense of being directly the opposite of our smoothly machined knives. Don't you think so?"

"Yes, Lon," Johnny said. "I guess that's right." It was his own fault for coming to cocktail parties. He had only met Lon twice. Lon had lived an adventurous life. That was all right, he liked Lon, but he did not want to talk knives.

Lon tossed the knife into the air and caught it deftly by the blade as it flickered down. His eyes glittered an answer to the knife's flicker of light.

"Yes," he said caressingly, "this is a nice knife."

Lon swung the knife up and down lovingly, as if tentatively measuring the weight for throwing. He looked almost as if he would throw it through the cocktail party to stick it quivering in the wooden door. His hatchet face turned toward Johnny, stabbing at him like a knife itself, like the killing knives Lon knew, and used, and loved.

Johnny could hear the unending slur of voices around the large room playing Lon's accompaniment. All of them knew of Lon's achievements. He knew them too, and he wished that Lon would drop it.

"The wide part of the blade," Lon explained technically, "that is for cutting. You can slash a man to ribbons with this one—in spite of its crude workmanship. Knowing where our host got it, I don't doubt that the lifeblood of a number of men has flowed along this blade, right where my finger is. Does that not evoke a peculiar emotion?"

"Yes."

Johnny could tell what he was doing but he was not angry, he was only tired. He wondered abstractedly if Lon knew why he avoided knives, or if Lon knew that there was a memory struggling to crawl up from the bottom of his mind.

"The point is also very sharp," said Lon. "Not much power would be needed to push this knife through the thick outer epidermis of a man."

"That's right," Johnny said wearily. "But the trouble with a long thin point like that is if it hits a bone, it's liable to break or bend and then your beautiful knife is ruined."

Lon nodded approvingly. He squinted down the thin length of the blade, holding the point with his thumb in the old practiced manner.

"That is true. Still, this is a fine knife. Better than the other, which is too long. One wants a short knife. Knife fighting is a lost art, just as the making of fine knives is a lost art."

"You must have had an adventurous life," Johnny said. He could feel the memory climbing the ladder of his spine into his brain.

Lon looked at him quickly. "Well," he said. He pinged the point with his thumbnail. "Most of my knife experience came after the *first* war. In Spain and in northern Africa when I was wandering around. Of course, I had already learned my technique in Mexico, but the Mexican has not the finesse of the Spaniard, in knife fighting or anything else.

"Alley fights were the best. You have to learn to be quick and clean, or you do not get to use your technique very long. *N'est-ce pas?*" His hatchet face grinned. His bright eyes commanded Johnny as he jammed the knife back into its sheath. His bright eyes commanded everybody.

Johnny stood quietly wondering when he would finally shut up. Perhaps he did not know left hooks as he knew knives? He drew a deep breath and let it out slowly but the other would not go out with it. It was like a cat on the ladder and would not come down.

"I think I will go and find our host," Lon said. "It is about time I was leaving."

He stuck out his hand. Johnny shifted his glass to his left hand and took it. There was a heavy, smooth, clean pressure in Lon's handclasp.

"I hope I have not upset you by my bloody talk," Lon said.

"No. It didn't bother me." The knife was lying sheathed upon the table as before.

When Lon left him, he sat down in the nearest chair. He could feel the memory rising, as a gas-filled corpse rises to the surface of the sea. He tried listening to the conversation near him. His jaws tightened in the struggle.

2

They had conversed little and softly, lying in a slit trench three feet by seven feet by two feet. Most people did not know the difference between a slit trench and a foxhole since the famous chaplain said there were no atheists in foxholes. You could not lie down in a foxhole and they were harder to dig and they were only for special cases. Even after digging a slit trench a man would be exhausted and drenched with sweat. And that when they were not even under fire.

On the line they never dug them any closer than five and it was often ten or fifteen or even twenty yards, when the line was too great for the number of them as it so often was in the early days of the 'Canal.

It was so different, this war, from the other, it was not like you read. Archie Binns did a good job of showing what it would come to be, next time, with his Japanese and Russians in Siberia in *The Laurels Are Cut Down*. Chivalry Was Dead, he said. Long live chivalry, I said, it all was dead. That trick of crawling in between the slit trenches at night, then jumping in from behind. Probably some point of *Bushido* honor: come back with a souvenir of a kill. Apparently honor also is subject to the Law of Relativity. But then they did not mind dying. Or maybe it was just that they were so hungry and they did it to get the luxurious cans of C ration each Yankee carried. You never knew, not any more.

He was terribly sleepy. After a certain point you were always terribly sleepy. Even if the guy in the next slit trench had the watch you did not sleep. How could you sleep? It was an all-out war, they said, twenty-four hours a day, seven days a week, no time off for good behavior. Paydays used to be a half holiday, back in peacetime. This was it, they said, this was really the war to end war, this time we mean it, no crap, this is the one that counts, think of your sons. Probably the Russians said the same thing. But apart from that your ears and your nerves were always wide awake anyway, for a sound or a feel, always reaching, reaching out.

He heard no sound. Or felt anything either. He just knew it was there, suddenly. The hairs on the back of his neck rose up and prickled. Somewhat the same feeling you get when you suddenly know somebody is staring at you from behind and you turn around and sure enough there is somebody staring at you. Only this, of course, was greatly enhanced. When it hit him it shot clear through like an electric shock and he was wide awake. Yet he heard nothing.

He was lying on his belly with the brim of his helmet dug into the dirt to keep his face out of the mud. This slit trench was not really wet. It was only muddy with that thin film clay gets when the dew is mashed into it. Oh, it was a slick war all right, they said, it was a slick war.

He always lay on his belly with his back up. Really comical how hard it is to lay on your back. You can't do it. Whenever you heard one coming you always lay on your belly while you waited. Maybe you dug your fingernails into the slick too, but then that was different. They will always flop over on their belly when they hear one coming if they are on their back. You just can't help it. Like a fish or a porcupine.

He turned his head to the left very slowly to look back. He could see nothing. The sky was clouded and there were no stars to outline a figure. He strained his eyes until he felt their muscles would crack and curl up like springs. Nothing.

Still, he knew it was there. He could tell. The instinct told him. It was invari-

ably right. He had developed it over a period of weeks. It was what they did not
teach you in the field manuals.

It was very quiet and his eyes rolled in his head. Somewhere in the silence a
grenade popped, fizzed, went off, sending a shower of little screamings outward.
This was too close for a grenade and you could not fire without the muzzle blast
betraying you. At night it was always the knife. This was his first.

The thought of it there sent a spasm of refined terror through him. A terror
of hopelessness that made him want to shrug and turn his head back and close
his eyes and simply wait. Waiting for it dejectedly, yet hoping all the time the instinct was wrong, and knowing at the same time the instinct was never wrong.
He felt, then, it was not worth the trouble. There were a lot of things worse than
dying. Slowly disintegrating day by day was worse than dying.

He did not know, you never knew any more. When you looked back and you
saw how it all came about, it was so logical. How, in the beginning, it was not at
all necessary. Just simply cause and effect that, in the beginning, was not at all
necessary. It was not that people did not see it, everybody saw it. Everybody always saw it. That was why it was so hard to know. It was like the being always
terribly sleepy. Just to relax, to sit quietly and not be sleepy, maybe then you
could know. Just to relax was all. It was really very simple. It was not a question
of being paralyzed with fear, it was simply having to decide. He was wide awake
and terribly sleepy and he could not decide.

While he lay in the mud-slick fatigues, unable to decide, his hand with the
rolls of dirt under the cracked and crusted nails decided. It slid down over the
cloth made waterproof by weeks of soaking up his body oil. Quite silently it un-
fastened the snap and freed the knife from the sheath strapped to his leg. Then
it relaxed full length along his side, cunning as animals are cunning. Perhaps in
the end that was all it was.

Over the luxurious feeling of resignation was something else apparently, a
flame over the sour damp ashes; a flame, now, that never came alive until there
was no other thing, burning strongly in a wind of death. The hand and this prim-
itive flame worked together leaving him out of it.

He was astonished to realize it was not five seconds since the hair first rose.
He felt like he had just carried three thousand pounds a couple of miles.

The hand jerked sideways when the nothing jumped, flopping him over on
his back and raising the knife in an arc until it was sticking straight up. The knife
in the hand made of the arm the sharpened spike of the elephant trap. The nothing impaled itself by the weight of the body. The falling body jarred through his
arm releasing the hand from its responsibility, pushed his arm down till the knob
on the knife hilt ground against his pelvic bone.

The Jap's knife struck his helmet slitheringly and stuck itself into the clay without power. The Jap hardly made a sound, only a sharp "unh" as the knife went into him. Such a silent war this one was.

There was a little struggle when he grabbed the Jap's wrist with his left hand. But not much. The Jap's hand came away from the hilt of his knife fairly easily. The knife had gone into him just under the breastbone. Sort of a solar plexus punch you might say, and it took his wind.

Blood ran distastefully over his hand and he pushed the Jap's leaden weight away from him and pulled his knife out. He could see him now, the inscrutable almond eyes and the funny bell-shaped helmet, like a woman's 1920s hat. The Jap put both hands over his belly where the knife had been. The Jap lay on his back, eyes watching, chin pulled down against his chest, breathing with a kind of grunt.

Johnny heard the breathing above the explosions of his own heart and knew he had nothing more to fear from this one.

They looked at each other for a little while, both breathing softly. Then Johnny put his hand over the Jap's face, the heel of his palm on his chin. The Jap did not shut his eyes and opened his mouth and bit at one of the fingers. Johnny moved the finger and thrust it up the Jap's nose, the Jap still trying to bite it. Then he pulled his knife across the Jap's bent throat, downward and away. The Jap quit trying to bite. He had not moved his hands from his belly.

Johnny grabbed him and rolled him out of the slit trench on the downhill side. His right hand had escaped, but he had not jerked his left hand quick enough and the geyser pumped against his arm. He wiped his hand vigorously and then lay in the slit trench, trying to keep out of the blood, waiting for morning to come. Somewhere in the silence a grenade popped, fizzed, went off, sending a shower of little screamings outward. A Nambu MG chattered in its falsetto foreign tongue. And him wishing to relax, just to relax, lying slow and easy, maybe under a tree, on a creek.

3

Johnny took a sip from his fresh martini. The olive oscillated slightly and a few drops sloshed over his fingers. People nearby were laughing at some quip of a Successful Author. He had missed it. The woman next to him offered to explain it, so that he could laugh too. He thanked her, seeing Lon coming toward him across the room with their hostess. Lon was wearing his rakish trenchcoat and carrying his slouch hat.

Lon shook his hand again. "Do not let my talk of knives get on your nerves. It is only that knives fascinate me."

"No," he said. "Forget it, Lon. Do you remember the scene in *All Quiet* where Paul kills the Frenchman in the hole and then begs his forgiveness?"

Lon looked at him curiously. "Yes. That scene. Highly sentimental stuff."

"That's what I mean. It's outdated, isn't it? You couldn't write it that way now, could you?"

"No," Lon said. "You couldn't write it like that now. Pointlessly hysterical. What they call a chaotic reaction."

Johnny nodded. "Chaotic reaction. Psychological? That's good. In other words, they had not developed the high art of proper indoctrination in those days."

"Yes. That's it."

"But this war was different, wasn't it, Lon?"

"Yes," Lon said. "This war was different. I must go." He shook Johnny's hand again. "I hope I did not upset you with my bloody talk."

"Forget it, Lon. I've got a couple knives you might like to see. I took one of them off a dead Jap."

Lon was interested. "What kind of knife is it?"

"American-made. The Jap probably took it off a dead American."

"Oh," Lon said. "I thought it might have a story behind it. . . . Well, good-bye."

"So long." He watched Lon stride to the door, the trenchcoat ballooning about his legs, the high collar covering his ears.

"I must see him out," their hostess whispered. "Isn't he fascinating? He has been everywhere and done everything."

"He must have led a truly adventurous life."

"Oh, you can't know. Truly incredible. Do you want another cocktail? You are enjoying yourself? You veterans, you who have done so much, you need to relax."

"Excuse me, my dear. I must really see Lon out. I was very lucky to get him. He abhors cocktail parties, you know. Truly an amazing personality."

"Yes," Johnny said. "I can see that. Truly he is."

AUTHOR'S NOTE:

The point is in the reference to Archie Binns and the quote about chivalry being dead, and in the boy's comparison of his own coldblooded killing of the Japanese to the comparable scene in *All Quiet*. This is what modern warfare has come to be, with all of our blessings, and God help us for it.

JUST LIKE THE GIRL

This one was sold to Frederick L. Allen of *Harper's* with the story following but was never printed for reasons described below. It was later sold to *Playboy* and printed in 1958 after Hugh Hefner suggested I make it a little plainer that the mother was the villain. I once showed this story to a newspaper editor in my hometown of Robinson, Illinois, who had known and admired my mother. The strange, guilty, upset, almost disbelieving look on his face when he handed it back, which seemed to say: "Even if it's true, why *do* it?" was worth to me all the effort I put into writing it.

> *"I want a girl, just like the girl*
> *that married dear old dad."*
> —Old Popular Song

Now listen carefully," John's mother said, and her voice was rushed and breathless.

She took him by his left arm, and her skin-flaky hand—which, as she said, was "rurned" from washing dishes—went clear around the thinness of his arm. She pulled him close to her and talked into his ear as if they were not alone in the house.

"He'll be home in a minute," she said to him, her eyes bright and nervous. "It's after six now and he never stays at the office later than five. He's been somewheres drinking. I could tell by his voice over the phone. He'll come home with that great big ugly nasty belly tight as a drum with beer again."

"Yes, Ma'm," John said. He was scared by the intensity of her voice, and she was gripping his arm so hard he could hardly keep from wincing.

"Here is what I want you to do for me, John. I want you to do this for your mother who loves you. When he brings the groceries in, you run out and get in the car. You understand?"

"Yes, Ma'm," John said. "All right, Mother." He knew this was important, because she was shaking his arm hard. "But what for?"

"Be still. Listen to me. I asked him please not to go back downtown in his condition. I asked him to stay home. I only just hope the operator was listening. Mrs. Haddock says they always do. God knows I've lived with it long enough and tried to hide it and hold our heads up," she said. "And he just laughed at me. Like he always does. But I've always done my duty, in the eyes of God and society. I've done all I could be expected to do."

John was nodding his head. His arm hurt and his mother was still shaking him; he was wondering how, if he was to go in the car, they would be able to go to the Sugar Bowl and the show. This was Saturday and Saturday night his mother always took him and Jeannette to the Sugar Bowl and they ate coney islands or barbecues and they had a malted and then they went to the show. And the malt-eds at the Sugar Bowl were thick, boy. It was their Saturday treat and he hated to miss it, even if his mother always did make them sit with her at the show instead of down front with the other kids and she stopped outside the show to talk to the other ladies and always made them stand right beside her because, as she told the ladies, John was grown up and taking his father's place like a little man. But then that was what you had to do if you wanted to go.

"Aren't we going to the show tonight, Mother?" he said.

"No we're not going to the show tonight, Mother. Aren't you listening to me? I want you to go in the car with your father. I want you to get in the back seat and keep out of sight. Get down on the floor and stay hid. You watch where he goes and when he comes home you tell me every place he went. I want you to do this for me."

"I don't care about the show, Mother," John said.

"Maybe we'll go tomorrow. If you love your mother like you say, you'll do this for her. You'll hide in the back of the car and find out who it is your father meets, and find out what her name is if you can, and then when I go away I'll take you with me and we'll go away forever."

"Will Jeannette go too, Mother?" John said.

"Yes. We'll take Jeannette with us too," she said to him and there were tears in her bright eyes. "He isn't fit to have children. Him with those great big arms and strong as a bull. He hurts everything he touches, he'd kill any woman. We'll go far away where he can never find us, with his big talk of education and making fun of my Science and Mrs. Eddy, making everybody think he's so intelligent and saddled with a dumb wife."

"You're not dumb, Mother," John said. "You're smart. You're my mother." He blinked tears from his own eyes, he felt very sorry for his mother. A divorce, he thought, we're going to get a diworce.

"I've given my whole life to you children." His mother let go of his arm and he was glad of that. It was a little numb, but he didn't rub it because his mother put her hands on his shoulders. "You're all I have left now. You and Jeannette. Since your brother Tom grew up and left me. Everybody said I was the most beautiful woman in this country and he was lucky to get me. Now he's cast me aside, for any hotassed bitch that walks the streets."

John nodded, memorized the phrase. He learned lots of good swearwords the other kids never heard, listening to his mother and dad when they were mad, although he never said them around her, except when he forgot, because she always washed his mouth out with soap, holding him by the back of the neck, and turning the washrag around wrapped over her fingers and rubbing it hard over his tongue and the roof of his mouth, whenever she heard him swear.

"Someday women will be free," his mother said. She knelt down on the floor beside him and put her arms around him. "Your mother loves you, Johnny, even if she is the ugliest old hag in town."

"You're not ugly, Mother," John said. "You're beautiful and you're my mother." He patted the cook-sweating broadness of his mother's back. It was almost like the game where someone asks the question and you have to give the right answer or pay a forfeit, except he always got so scared it wasn't any fun.

"If you really love your mother, you'll stand by her."

"Sure I will, Mother," John said. "I'll do anything for you. Someday, Mother, I'll make a million dollars and I'll give it all to you."

"No," his mother said. "No, you won't. Someday you'll do just like your brother did. You'll grow up and forget all your mother ever did for you. You'll remember the money your father gives you and I don't have to give you and you'll turn on your ugly mother just like your brother did and go over to your father."

"No I won't either," John protested, feeling guilty. He knew his mother didn't have the money to give him quarters and half dollars like his father did. He knew how hard up they were because his father threw so much money away on beer and whiskey, and then tried to buy his son's affection with quarters and half dollars. Every time he sneaked up in the garage loft to play with his secret collection of extra soldiers and guns, he felt guilty.

"I'll always stand by you, Mother," he said. "I won't be like Tom. Honestly I won't. I'm not like Tom."

"Will you prove it to me? Will you find out who your father goes out with tonight?"

"Sure I will, Mother. Didn't I say I would?"

His mother stood up. "All right. You wait out on the front porch where he won't see you. When he brings the groceries in you run out and get in. But be careful: He bought groceries for over Sunday and he'll probably have to make two trips to the car."

"All right, Mother," John said. "You can trust me, Mother."

His mother was on her way back to the kitchen. "Don't let him see you out on the porch."

"OK, Mother," John said.

He went out the front door and sat down in the porch swing to wait for his father to come home. The moon was full, and reminded him of the quarters and half dollars his father tried to buy his affection with every now and then. It was so bright it made shadows under the trees just like daytime. It made everything hazy like a lace curtain. He sat and swung the swing and listened to the chain creak and rubbed his arm where it still hurt and watched the lace curtain of moonlight.

I'll fool him, he thought. I won't let him buy me away from mother with quarters and half dollars like he did Tom. I'll take the quarters and half dollars, but I won't let him kid *me*. It made him feel a little better, a little less guilty, but still he knew, guiltily, that he shouldn't take them, any of them.

Once his father had given him a half dollar right in front his mother. It was the time she hit him with the kitchen fork when she was frying chicken. He was standing by the stove bothering her with questions and making a nuisance of himself, and it was a hot day long, long years ago, and she just got mad and hit him with the fork. The fork cut his forehead and broke his glasses and the blood ran down into his eyes. It did not hurt much but the blood in his eyes scared him because he couldn't see and thought maybe he was going to die. His mother threw the fork down on the floor and started crying and that scared him worse because then he was sure he was going to die and he did not want to die yet, when he was still just such a little boy. She phoned the doctor and his father, and she kept wringing her hands and crying "O what have I done! My poor little boy! My darling son!" and he had felt very sorry for her and put his arms around her and told her it was all right and it didn't hurt much and for her not to worry, he did not really mind dying when he was still such a little boy, but it only made her cry worse. He knew she did not really mean to do it because she cried so much and she sacrificed everything for him and Jeannette and loved them better than anything in the world. So when the doctor and his father came, he and his mother told them he fell down and cut his forehead on the edge of the table. His father gave him a half dollar right in front of his mother and squatted down and put his arm around him. If he had been cut over both eyes he bet his father would have given him a whole dollar.

Other kids' fathers didn't give them whole dollars when they got cut over both eyes, and his father really looked tough when he got mad. He bet there wasn't anybody would tackle his father when he got mad, even if he was a drunkard and ran around with hotassed bitches and had those great big arms and belly and strong as a bull and would kill any woman. Sitting in the swing he wondered what the hotassed bitch looked like. He hoped he would get to see them doing it.

Suddenly in his mind he saw his father sitting at the kitchen table, all alone, holding the diworce, drinking a bottle of beer, playing with a pile of quarters and half dollars that he did not have anybody to give them to, that was the way it would be when they were gone. He blinked tears from his eyes, he felt very sorry for his father. A divorce, he thought, we're going to get a divorce.

When his father drove in the driveway he got down on his hands and knees behind the brick railing and watched through the four-cornered hole like a diamond while his father opened the back door of the big square Studebaker and took two huge paper sacks of groceries in his big arms and carried them to the back door. Looking through the trees into the clearing, Hawkeye leveled his cap-n-ball-long-rifle and let the big Indian have it, right in the chest, and the two big paper sacks of dynamite tumbled unhurt to the ground; Hawkeye had fired between them carefully because the dynamite was needed to blow the Indian village up the river. He aimed over his finger and fired; and his father walked on to the house.

Then he waited, just as his mother had told him, grinning at how he was outsmarting his father. After the second trip he ran lightly out into the yard, carrying his rifle at trail and loading her as he ran, the Indians called him The Man Whose Gun Was Always Loaded, opened the back door of the car and hit the dirt. It was dusty on the floor and the dust got in his nose and choked him up but he did not mind because he had made it across the clearing unseen and had slipped into the enemy general's limousine.

He heard them talking loud in the kitchen and guessed they were having another big argument. His father came out and slammed the door and got in the car and he lay, laughing to himself, very excited.

His father drove down toward town and every corner John concentrated hard on which way they turned and tried to see the corner in his mind. There was a place on the road through the forest the enemy general's truck was following that it was of the greatest importance he jump out the back of the truck unseen. Some enemy soldiers were holding Priscilla Jenkins captive and going to torture her with red-hot irons. In his mind he saw Priscilla, a great lady now, standing tied to a tree, her clothes torn clear off of her and the enemy soldiers stepping up to put a red-hot iron against her thing—just as he leaped into the circle of firelight wearing his fringed buckskins of a scout and the two enemy soldiers were deaders and Priscilla was very happy to be saved from a fate worse than death and they did it there in the firelight with the two deaders staring open-eyed at the sky.

When his father stopped the car it was the spot, and it was of the greatest importance that he know where it was, and he picked Meeker's Restaurant. He waited till his father got out and was gone and then peeked over the bottom of the window. Instead of Meeker's Restaurant they were in front of the old American Legion. It was very bad, because Priscilla was a deader unless he could figure something out.

He lay there on the floor a long time, wishing his father would hurry up and come back with the hot-assed bitch so he could see them do it, he had never seen anybody do it, but he was tired of laying on the floor and he was getting sleepy. He lay with the sleepiness and the Saturday night noises coming loud suddenly, then going far away, and coming and going and coming and going and he heard his father speak from behind a curtain and far away the car doors opened and his father and someone else got in. Then suddenly he was back inside himself again and listening hard. None of the kids had ever really seen anybody do it. They wouldn't care if he was a drunkard's son or not, if he told how he had seen them do it and just what they did.

"Give me the bottle," he heard his father say. "You mark what I'm saying, Lab. It won't be ten years."

John recognized with disappointment the other voice that answered. It was no hot-assed bitch at all, it was only old Lab Wallers from the American Legion, and he felt he had been cheated of a great adventure.

"I still say she wouldn't want you to go, Doc," it said.

"I don't know," his father said. "Sometimes I think she would. I know she would. She'd be damned glad to get rid of a no-good like me. And I guess I don't blame her any. Anyway," he said, "I'll be too old."

"There won't be another war anyway," Lab Wallers said. "Thas why we won the last one, so there wouldn't be no more. Wilson was a good man, and he knew what he was doin'."

"He couldn't do anything with a Republican Congress," his father said.

"Well, he was smarter than this Coolidge. Doc, you don't want your boys to grow up and get drug into something like we did," Lab Wallers said.

"Hell, no," his father said. "But there's no way out. Give your son luck, and throw him into the sea. That's what the Spaniards say. That's all any man can do. I tell you it won't be ten years."

That's me, John thought, they're talking about me. He was a little surprised because everybody knew there wouldn't be any more war. He had always been sorry when he thought how he would never get to be in a war like his father. He lay there, excited, thinking how he would save Priscilla Jenkins from the enemy just as they were about to burn her thing with the red-hot iron. He would come home a great hero and everybody would think he was a fine up-standing man. He wouldn't drink at all, and maybe he would marry Priscilla Jenkins.

Following the pictures in his mind the sleepiness came back and the voice talking began to come and go, loud and faint, like the band concert across town sounded in a shifting summer wind.

"She's a fine woman, Doc," Lab Wallers said. "They don't come any finer. My wife's always talkin' about how fine she is."

"I know she is," his father said. "Everybody knows it. Nobody has to tell me that. I know it's my fault. I know I'm a bum and a drunk."

"We don't deserve the women we got, Doc," Lab Wallers said, his voice thick. "Neither one of us. *None* of us."

"If it wasn't for the kids I'd light out tonight," his father said. "Give her a chance. But it's awful hard to leave your kids, your own kids. What you've done lives on in your kids, if nowhere else."

"She loves you though," Lab Wallers said. "Don't you forget it."

"No she doesn't," his father said, "and I don't blame her. I know what I am," he said. "I know what I've done."

"Give me the bottle," Lab Wallers said. "I don't know where I'd be if it wasn't for my wife. Or you either. Where would the world be, without the wives? Where would our kids be, if it wasn't for their mothers? Where would this nation be, if it wasn't for the women?"

"She was the most beautiful woman in this part of the country when I married her," his father said. "I was lucky to get her. Everybody says so. If she just wouldn't devil me so. Goddam it, Lab, someday the men will be free.

"What time is it? I have to be back in town by ten. I have to see somebody. Goddam it, a man has to live, Lab . . ."

John didn't hear the rest. He was very sleepy and none of it made sense. He just shut his eyes for a minute, only a minute, because he really had to stay awake.

He woke up surprised, because he wasn't in the car any more. As he came awake he realized he was being carried. His father was carrying him in his arms. John noticed sleepily that his father was wearing some funny kind of sweet shaving lotion. He did not know where they were at first, but then he saw they were at home at the house. His father carried him inside.

Upstairs, his father laid him down on his bed in his own room and began to undress him, fumbling the buttons. He lay very still, his eyes shut, letting his father undress him and put him to bed. It made him feel good. When he was under the covers, he opened his eyes and smiled at his father. His father smiled back, and John could tell by his eyes that he was pretty drunk.

"Here," his father said, reaching in his pocket. "Put this under your pillow. You earned it. You're a damned good man. You've got a lot of guts and I'm proud you are my son."

John reached out his hands and took it. He rolled over sleepily in the bed. Gee, he thought, a quarter and *two* half dollars *both*. Gee. But he held them in his hand and did not put them under his pillow, because he was suddenly think-ing of his mother. I really oughtn't to take them, he thought, thinking guiltily about his brother Tom. I ought to give them back.

"Guts are what a man needs," his father said. "You're going to need a lot of guts, Johnny boy, someday. Someday you'll need guts bad."

His father paused and patted him on the head and then he rubbed his strong stubby-fingered hand over his chin that needed a shave. He got up from the bed slowly. "Always remember: If a man's got guts, he'll come out all right. You got to have the guts to stand up for yourself, even when you're bad and wrong," he said, "or you're dead. You'll never be a man again." He stood beside the bed looking down and smiling sadly.

There was Priscilla, the soldiers getting ready to put the hot iron against her thing, in her thing, hard; and there was the general and he was handing him $2,000, to go away and forget he seen it, like every good spy should. And it wasn't even Priscilla. It was just some woman. And a good spy had work to do at the front.

But this time it didn't work, because over the scene in the forest John could see his mother's face with her bright bright eyes looking at him. He wished it *would* work, because he wanted to keep the money. But this time it was not real. It wasn't a real game at all. It was only playlike. It wasn't $2,000 at all, it was only a quarter and two half dollars both.

And there was Mother watching him who didn't think he loved her anymore. He could almost see her. Mother thought he was going to be like Tom. He could almost see her looking at him if he took the money.

"Dad," John said, looking at the silver moons. "Here, Dad," he made himself extend his arm. "I don't want your money."

His father stood looking down at him, his big face and the muscles around his eyes getting a crinkledy look that frightened John, and his eyes seemed to go out of focus and swing around back and forth behind themselves, from one side of John to the other. Then he took the coins and looked at them and put them in his pocket.

"All right, buddyboy," he said in a voice John could hardly hear. "Good night, old man." Carefully with his big hands, gently, he turned off the light and went out of the room and slowly shut the door.

That look on his father's face still scared John a little, but it gave him great pleasure to know he was not like Tom. Mother would be proud of him. He can't buy my affection, John thought proudly. I'm not like Tom.

THE WAY IT IS

Frederick L. Allen printed this one in the June 1949 *Harper's*. We argued so much over it that Allen sent me back free the ms of the other story he bought, "Just Like the Girl," saying he wasn't up to it a second time. We argued over things like the fact that Allen wrote into my story a paragraph explaining it was Hawaii and Pearl Harbor. I refused to allow this. We argued over things like the abbreviation of lieutenant. I didn't want a period after it. Allen wanted a period after it. We compromised by spelling it out.

I saw the car coming down the grade and got up from the culvert. I had to push hard with my legs to keep the wind from sitting me back down. I stepped out into the road to stop him, turning my back to the wind, still holding the mess kit I had been scouring. Some of the slop of sand and grease dripped out of it onto my leg.

Then I saw Mazzioli was on the running board and had his pistol out and aimed at the driver's head. I tossed the mess kit, still full, over against the culvert and got my own pistol out.

I couldn't see the driver. It was hard to see the car in the red air of the dusk against the black of the cliff and with the cold wind pouring against my eyes. It was a foreign make, a runabout with strange lines and the steering wheel on the right-hand side. When it stopped Mazzioli jumped off the running board and motioned with his pistol.

"All right," he said in that thick voice. "Get out of there, you."

I knew the man when he climbed out. He used the road every day. He could have passed for a typical Prussian with his scraped jowls and cropped bullethead. He wore a fine tweed jacket and plus-fours, and his stockings were of ribbed wool and very fine. I looked down at my legging and kicked off the gob of sand and grease. It didn't help much. I hadn't even had my field jacket off for three weeks, since the bombing.

"What's up, Greek?" I said, peering through the deepening dusk. I had to yell to make it heard above the wind.

"I hopped a ride down the hill with this guy," he said woodenly. "All the way

down he was asking me questions about the position. How many men? How
many guns? Was there a demolition? What was the road-guard for? I mean to
find out what's the story." He looked offended.

I walked over to him so I could hear above the wind. He was a little Wop but
very meaty. His father ran a grocery store in Brooklyn.

"What do you figure on doing?" I asked. I thought I had seen the Junker before someplace, and I tried hard to make my mind work.

Mazzioli waved his pistol at the standing man. "Git over there, you, and put
your back to the cliff," he said ominously. The beefy Junker walked to it slowly,
his steps jerky from rage, his arms dangling impotently. He stood against the
black, porous cliff and Mazzioli followed him. "Where's the men?" Mazzioli
shouted to me above the wind. "I want a man to stand guard over this guy. You
git a man and have him . . ."

"There's nobody here but me," I called back. "I let them go up to the top of the
hill. Two of them didn't get any chow tonight. They went up to number one hole
to listen to the guitar a while." I walked over to him.

I could see him stiffen. "Goddam you. You know there's always supposed to
be three men and one noncom here all the time. That's the orders. You're supposed to be second in command. How do you expect to handle these men when
you don't follow the orders?"

I stared at him, feeling my jaws tighten. "All right," I shrugged. "I let them go.
So what?"

"I'm turning this in to Lieutenant Allison. The orders are the orders. If you
want to be on this road-guard to do your duty, okay. If you want to be on this
road-guard to stop Coca-Cola trucks you can go back upstairs to the position.
This road-guard is vital, and as long as I'm in charge of it everybody does like the
orders says."

I didn't say anything.

"You're a rotten soldier, Slade," Mazzioli said. "Now look what's happened. I
wanted you to help me search this guy's car. Now there's nobody here to guard
this guy."

"Okay," I said. "So I'm a rotten soldier. My trouble is I got too many brains."
He was making me mad and that always got him. Ever since I went six months
to the University downtown in Honolulu.

"Don't start giving me that stuff," he snarled.

The Junker against the cliff stepped forward. "See here," he said. "I demand
you stop this bickering and release me. You're being an idiot. I am . . ."

"Shut up, you," Mazzioli snarled. "Shut up! I warned you, now shut up!" He
stepped to meet him and jabbed the muzzle of his pistol into the Junker's big

elly. The man recoiled and stood back against the cliff, his beefy face choleric.

I stood with my hands in the pockets of my field jacket, my shoulders hunched down against the rawness of the wind and watched the scene. I had put my pistol away.

"All right," Mazzioli said to me. "The question is what're we gonna do now? If there's nobody here but you and me?"

"You're in command," I said.

"I know it. Keep quiet. I'm thinking."

"Well," I said. "You could have the guy drive you up the hill to the lieutenant. You could keep him covered till you turned him over to the lieutenant. Then you would be absolved," I said. Big words always got him.

"No," he said dubiously. "He might try something."

"Or," I said, "you could search the car and have me watch the guy."

"Yeh," he admitted. "I could do that . . . Yet . . . No, I don't want to do that. We may need more men."

It was dark now, as black as the cliff face, and I grinned. "Okay," I said, telling him what I had in my mind all along, "then I could call Alcorn down from up on the cliff and he could watch the guy."

"Yes. That's it. Why didn't I think of that before?"

"I don't know. Maybe you're tired."

"You call Alcorn down," he commanded me.

I walked toward the cliff wall that reared its set black face up and up in the darkness several hundred feet. The wind beat on me with both fists in the blackness.

"Wait a minute," Mazzioli called. "Maybe we shouldn't call Alcorn down. There's supposed to be a man up there all the time."

"Look," I said. "I'll tell you what I think. Before you go ahead, you better get the lieutenant's permission to do anything with this guy. You better find out who this guy is."

"I'm in charge of this road-guard," he yelled into the wind, "and I can handle it. Without running to no lieutenant. And I don't want back-talk. When I give you an order, you do it. Call Alcorn down here like I said."

"Okay," I said. I leaned on the culvert and called loudly, my face turned up to the cliff. There was no answer. I flashed my light covered with blue paper. Still no answer.

For a second I couldn't help wondering if something had got him. The Japanese invasion of Hawaii had been expected every day since Pearl was bombed. It was expected here at Kaneohe Bay on the windward side where the reef was low and there was good beach. Nobody doubted they would get ashore.

"What's the matter?" asked Mazzioli sharply from the darkness. "Is Alcorn asleep?"

"No," I said. "It's the wind; it carries off the sound. The light will get him." I picked up a handful of pebbles and threw them up the cliff with all my strength, trying to make no noise the Greek could hear.

Sixty feet up was a natural niche and the BAR man was stationed there twenty-four hours a day. It was a hidden spot that covered the road and the road-guard. In case of surprise it would prove invaluable. That was Lieutenant Allison's own idea. The road-guard was Hawaiian Department's idea.

Alcorn had stayed up there alone for the first four days after the bombing. In the four days he had one meal before somebody remembered him. Now he and the other man pulled twelve hours apiece.

The road-guard was part of the whole defense plan. It was figured out in November when the beach positions were constructed. The defense was to mine the Pali Road and Kamehameha Highway where it ran up over this cliff at Makapuu Point. It was planned to blow both roads and bottle them up in Kaneohe Valley and force them north, away from Honolulu. They were great demolitions and it was all top secret. Of course, in December they found maps of the whole thing in the captured planes. Still, it was very vital and very top secret.

A rock the size of my fist thumped into the sand at my feet. I grinned. "You missed me," I called up the cliff. "Come down from there, you lazy bastard." I barely caught a faraway, wind-tossed phrase that sounded like "truck, too." Then silence, and the wind.

The machinegun apertures in the pillboxes up the hill all faced out to sea. Whoever planned the position had forgotten about the road, and all that faced the road was the tunnels into the pillboxes. To cover the road the MGs would have to be carried up into the open, and it was a shame because there was a perfect enfilade where the road curved up the cliff. But they couldn't rebuild the pillboxes we had cut into solid rock, so instead they created the road-guard.

The road-guard was to be five men and a BAR from up above. That was us. We were to protect the demolition when the Jap landed. It was not expected to keep him from getting ashore. We were to hold him off, with our BAR, till the demolition could be blown behind us. After that we were on our own. It was excellent strategy, for a makeshift, with the invasion expected truly every day. And the road-guard was vital, it was the key.

Every man at Makapuu volunteered for the road-guard. The five of us were lucky to get it. The job was to stop and search all vehicles for anything that might be used to blow the demolition. The Coca-Cola trucks and banana trucks and rocery trucks and fruit trucks used this road every day to get to market. We topped them all, especially the Coca-Cola trucks.

In a couple of minutes I heard a scrambling and scraping and a bouncing fall of pebbles and Alcorn came slouching along the sand at the road edge, blowing on his hands.

"The Greek wants you, Fatso," I said.

He laughed, low and rich and sloppy. "I think I'm deef from this wind, by god," he said and scratched inside his field jacket. "What's he want now?"

"Come over here," Mazzioli ordered. We walked over through the blackness and the wind and I felt I was swimming under water against a strong current. The Greek swung his blue light from the Junker onto us. Alcorn's clothes hung from him like rags and on the back of his head was a fatigue hat with the brim turned up that defied the wind. He must have sewed an elastic band on it. Beside him I looked like I was all bucked up for a short-timer parade.

"Where's your helmet?" Mazzioli said. "You're supposed to wear your helmet at all times. That's the orders."

"Aw now, sarge," Alcorn whined. "You know the steel band of them things gives a man a headache. I cain't wear one."

I grinned and gave the brim of my own inverted soup-plate helmet a tug. Alcorn was a character.

"When are you men going to learn to obey orders?" the Greek said. "An army runs by discipline. If you men don't start acting like soldiers, I'll turn you in."

"Off with his head," I said.

"What did you say?"

"I said, coffee and bed. That's what we need. There's not a man on this position who's had three good hours sleep since this bloody war started. Putting up barbed wire all day and pulling guard all night. And then putting up the same wire next day because the tide washed it out."

Alcorn snickered and Mazzioli said nothing. The Greek had had charge of a wire detail that worked one whole night to put up three hundred yards of double apron wire on the sand beach below the road. In the morning it was gone. Not a single picket left.

"Alcorn," Mazzioli ordered, "get a rifle and keep a bayonet against this guy's belly till I tell you not to."

"I don't know where the rifles are down here," Alcorn said.

"I'll get it," I said.

I walked to the culvert and climbed down around it. The wall made a protection from the wind and I felt I had dropped into a world without breath. The absence of the wind made me dizzy and I leaned my face against the concrete. I felt the way you feel when you look out the window at a blowing rainstorm. All our blankets and stuff were down here. Against the wall of the culvert lay four rifles with bayonets on them, wrapped in a shelter-half. I pulled one out and made myself climb up into the wind again.

Alcorn took the rifle and kept the bayonet against the Junker's paunch. Every time the Junker moved or tried to speak Alcorn jabbed him playfully in the belly. The Junker was getting madder and madder, but Alcorn was having a fine time.

I knew the lewd nakedness of that scraped face someplace before. I went over in my mind all the people I had seen at the University.

The Greek was doing a bang-up job of searching the car, he even looked under the hood. I sat on the culvert and got my mess kit and put a handful of fresh sand in it from beside the road and rubbed it around and around. The dishwater that got out to us from the CP at Hanauma Bay gave us all the dysentery until we started using the sand.

I tried to think where I'd seen him. It wasn't the face of a teacher, it had too much power. I dumped the greasy mess from the mess kit and poured in a little water from my canteen. I sloshed it around to rinse the sand out, listening vacantly to the Greek cursing and fidgeting with the car.

Just three days ago a two-man sub ran aground off Kaneohe and the second officer swam ashore, preferring capture. It was expected the sub was scouting the invasion that was coming truly any day.

They said he was the first prisoner of the war. I got to see him when they brought him in. He was a husky little guy and grinning humbly. His name was Kazuo Sakamaki. I knew a girl at the University named Harue Tanaka. I almost married her.

It seemed like the wind had blown my mind empty of all past. It had sucked out everything but Makapuu and the black rocks and blue lights and the sand-choked grass. The University with its clear, airy look from the street, its crisp greenness all hidden away in a wind-free little valley at the foot of rocky wooded Tantalus, it was from another life, a life protected from the wind, a life where there were white clouds in the sun but no wind, just gently moving air.

I wiped the mess kit with the GI face towel I kept in it and clamped it together and stuck it back in my pack that lay by the culvert, wanting to go down behind the culvert and light a cigarette.

Maybe the Junker was one of the big boys on the University board. The big boys always sent their kids to Harvard or some school on the mainland, but they were the board. The only white faces you saw were the instructors and the haoles who didn't have the dough to send their kids to the mainland—and an occasional soldier in civvies, looking out of place. Only these and the board. And the tourists.

Then I remembered the scraped face, coming out of the main building on a hot still August day, wiping the sweat from the face with a big silk handkerchief.

"Couldn't find a thing," Mazzioli said, coming up from the car. "I don't know what to do. This guy looks like a German. He even talks like a German."

"Listen," I said. "No German who looks like a German and talks like a German is going to be a spy. Use your head. This guy is some kind of big shot. I seen him at the University."

"To hell with you and your University."

"No," I said. "Listen."

"Why would he ask me questions about the number of men and guns and pillboxes?"

"Hell, I don't know. Maybe he wanted to write an editorial for the *Advertiser*."

"I can't let him go," he said.

"All right. Send Alcorn up for the lieutenant and let him handle it. You worry too much, Greek."

"Yeh, I could do that." But he was dubious. He walked back to the car for a moment and then went over to Alcorn. "Alcorn, you go up and get the lieutenant down here. Tell him we got a suspicious character down here." He turned to me. "Slade, you watch this guy and don't take any chances with him. I'm going over this car again."

Alcorn handed me the rifle and started off up the road. Through the darkness Mazzioli hollered after him. "Double time and jerk the lead," he shouted. The wind carried it away. The wind carried everything away.

To me Mazzioli said, "If he tries anything, shoot the bastard."

"Okay," I said. I set the rifle butt on the ground and leaned on it. "Take it easy, mister," I said. "Remember there's a war on. The lieutenant's coming down, and you'll be on your way home in a little bit."

"I am not accustomed to such treatment," he said, staring at me with flat eyes, "and I intend to see somebody pays for this indignity."

"We're only doing our duty," I said. "We got orders to stop all suspicious persons. This is important to the defense plan."

"I am not a suspicious person," he said, "and you men . . ."

I interrupted; it was probably the only chance I'd ever get to interrupt a big shot. "Well," I said, "you were asking suspicious questions about our position."

". . . and you men should have something better to do than hold up citizens."

Mazzioli, looking harassed, came over from the car. "What's that?" he snarled. "What's your name?"

The Junker stared at him. "My name is Knight," he said, and waited for it to sink in. When Mazzioli's face was blank he added, "Of Knight & Crosby, Limited." His voice was cold with rage and hate.

Above the wind we heard the voices of Lieutenant Allison and Alcorn on the road.

I looked at the Greek but he showed nothing. Nobody could live in Hawaii without knowing Knight & Crosby, Ltd. The Big Five were as well known as Diamond Head.

Lieutenant Allison put one hand on Mazzioli's shoulder and the other on mine. "Now," he said paternally. "What's the trouble?"

Mazzioli told him the whole tale. I went back to the culvert and listened to the wind playing background music to the double tale of woe. After both stories were told, Lieutenant Allison escorted Mr. Knight to his runabout with extreme courtesy.

"You can appreciate, Mr. Knight, our position." Lieutenant Allison put his foot on the running board and rested his hands on the door. "You can understand my sergeant was only doing his duty, a duty conceived to protect you, Mr. Knight."

Mr. Knight did not speak. He sat with his hands gripping the wheel, staring straight ahead.

"I'm sorry you feel that way, Mr. Knight," Lieutenant Allison said. "These men were carrying out orders we have received from Hawaiian Department Headquarters."

Mr. Knight made no sign he had heard. He gave the impression he was suffering this association under duress and was fretting to have done and be gone.

"A soldier's duty is to follow out his orders," Lieutenant Allison said.

"All right," the lieutenant said. He took his foot off the running board and dropped his hands. "You may go, Mr. Knight. You can rest assured such a thing won't happen again, now that my men know who you are."

"It certainly won't," Mr. Knight said. "Bah!" He started his runabout with a roar and he did not look back.

I watched from the culvert and grinned contentedly. "Now there'll be hell to pay," I told Mazzioli.

After Knight was gone, Mazzioli called the lieutenant over to the other side of the road and spoke earnestly. I watched the excited movement of his blue light and grinned more widely.

Lieutenant Allison came over to me with the Greek following close behind. "Alcorn," he called. Alcorn shuffled over from the base of the cliff.

"I've been having bad reports about you two men," Lieutenant Allison began. "Where's your helmet, Alcorn?"

Alcorn shuffled his feet. "It's up the cliff. I cain't wear one of them things more'n a half hour, Lootenant," he said. "I get a turrible headache if I do. When Corporal Slade called me down, I clean forgot all about it."

"You're all through down here," Lieutenant Allison said, "Get back up there and get that helmet on. I'll be coming around inspecting and I don't want to catch you without a helmet. If I do there'll be some damned heavy details around here, and if that don't stop your headache, by god, maybe a court-martial will.

"You're no different than anybody else. If I can wear a helmet all the time, then you can do it. I don't like it any better than you do.

"Now get the hell back up there."

Alcorn saluted and started for the base of the cliff.

"Alcorn!" Lieutenant Allison called after him in the darkness.

"Yessir?"

"You don't ever go to sleep up there, do you?"

"Oh, no sir."

"You'd better watch it. I'll be inspecting tonight."

I could hear the scrambling and falling of pebbles and I thought it was a very lonely sound.

"Come over here, Slade," Lieutenant Allison said. He walked away from Mazz-ioli and I followed him, pleased the calling-down would be in private instead of in front of the Greek. It was a luxury.

"I'm going back up the hill," Lieutenant Allison said. "You walk part of the way with me. I want to talk to you." The two of us started up the road. "I'm going to send those men back down here when I get to the top," Lieutenant Allison said. "You won't need to go up."

"Thank you, sir," I said.

"Why did you let those men go up the hill tonight, Slade?"

"They didn't get any chow tonight, sir," I said. "I felt sorry for them."

"You're not supposed to feel sorry for anybody. You're a soldier. You enlisted in the Army, didn't you?"

"Yes, sir," I said. "But it was because I couldn't get a job."

"A soldier's job is to feel sorry for nobody."

"I can't help it, sir," I said. "Maybe my environment was wrong. Or maybe I haven't had the proper indoctrinization. I always put myself in the other guy's place. I even felt sorry for Mr. Knight. And he sure didn't need it."

"What happened with Mr. Knight was the proper action to take. It turned out badly, but he could have been a saboteur with a carload of TNT to blow the demolition."

"What will happen about Knight, sir?" I said.

"Mr. Knight is a big man in Hawaii. The Big Five run the whole territory. There may be some bad effects. I may even get an ass-eating. Nevertheless, Mazzioli acted correctly. In the long run, it will all turn out all right because we did what was right. The Army will take that into account."

"You believe that?" I said.

"Yes," he said. "I believe it. You don't realize how important that road-guard is to the whole war. What if the enemy had made a landing at Kaneohe tonight? They'd have a patrol on you before you knew it. The very thing you did out of kindness might be what lost the war for us. It's not far-fetched: if they took this road and cliff, they'd have this island in a month. From there it'd be the west coast. And we'd be fighting the war in the Rocky Mountains."

"All for the want of a horseshoe nail," I said.

"That's it," he said. "That's why every tiniest thing is so important. You're one of the smartest men in the Company, Slade. There's no reason for me to explain these things to you. There's no reason why you shouldn't make OCS, except for your attitude. I've told you that before. What would you have done? Alone there with the men on the hill?"

"I knew who he was," I said.

Lieutenant Allison turned on me. "Why in the name of Christ didn't you tell Mazzioli!" He was mad.

"I did," I said. "But he didn't listen. Orders is orders," I said.

Lieutenant Allison stopped. We were halfway up the hill. He looked out over the parapet and down at the sea, vaguely white where it broke on the rocks.

"What's the matter with you, Slade? You don't want to be cynical about this war."

"I'm not cynical about this war," I said. "I may die in this war. I'm cynical about the Army. It's a helluva lot easier to be an idealist if you're an officer. The higher the officer, the higher the ideals." To hell with it, I thought, to hell with all of it.

"Slade," he said, "I'd like for you to buckle down. I wasn't kidding when I said you could make OCS. I'd like to see you go to OCS because you're smart. You could do it if you'd only buckle down."

"I've been an EM too long," I said. "I'm too cynical."

"You know, you could be shot for talking like this in the German Army."

"I know it," I said. "That's why I don't like the German Army, or the Japanese Army, or the British Army, or the Russian Army. I could get ten years in the American Army if you wanted to turn me in."

Lieutenant Allison was leaning on the parapet. "If I didn't like you, by god I would."

"Trouble with me," I said, "I'm too honest. They didn't have indoctrination courses yet when I enlisted," I said.

"It's not a question of briefing," he said. "It's a question of belief."

"Yes," I said. "And also of who manufactures it."

"We have to be cruel now so we can be kind later, after the war."

"That's the theory of the Communist Internationale," I said. "I hear their indoctrinization courses are wonderful."

"They're our allies," he said. "When the enemy is defeated, why, it will all be set."

"I could never be an officer," I said. "I've not been indoctrinated well enough."

He laughed. "Okay, Slade. But you think over what I said, and if you want me to, I'll recommend you. You know, an intelligent man who refuses to use his intelligence to help win the war is a bottleneck. He's really a menace. In Germany he would be shot if he didn't use his intelligence to help win."

"Japan too," I said. "And in Italy and in Russia," I said. "Our country we only lock them up as conchies, as yet."

"Do you think I like being an officer?"

"Yes," I said. "I would like it. At least you get a bath and hot chow."

He laughed again. "Okay. But you think it over."

"I'll think about it," I said. "I'll think about all of it. But I never find an answer. Sometimes I wonder if there is an answer. The Greek is the man you ought to recommend."

"Are you kidding?" he grinned. "Mazzioli is a good sergeant."

"He believes the end justifies the means," I said. "He's been properly indoctrinated. I couldn't turn a man in if I had to."

Lieutenant Allison stood up from the parapet. "Think it over, Slade," he said.

"All right, sir," I said. "But I can tell you one thing. It's damn fine I can talk to you. But I always remember you're not all officers and I'm not all the EM," I said.

"Thanks, Slade," he said.

I walked on back down the road. I stopped every now and then to listen to the sea's attack against the cliff. It would be nice to be an officer. The sea and the wind were like two radio stations on the same dial mark. You could even have a bed-roll and a dog-robber. The old Revolutionists in Russia, I thought, they really had it all figured out; they really had the world saved this time. I kicked a pebble ahead of me down the road.

I must have gone very slow because the three men from the top were on my heels when I reached the bottom.

"Hey, Slade," one of them said. He came up. "I'm sorry we got you in trouble tonight. Nobody guessed this would happen."

"Forget it," I said. "All I got was a ass-eating."

Mazzioli was sitting on the culvert. "I'm going to roll up," he said belligerently

"Okay, Greek," I said. I sat on the culvert for a while, facing the wind. I liked to sit there at night alone, defying the wind. But a man could only do it so long. After a while a man got stupid from its eternal pummelling. A man got punch-drunk from it. Once before it made me so dizzy I fell down on my knees when I got up.

It was a wild place, the roaring sea, the ceaseless wind, the restless sand, the omniscient cliff.

I said good night to the man on post and rolled up myself. When I went under the wall it took my breath again. I lay in my blankets and listened to it howl just over my head.

It was three o'clock when the messenger from up on the hill woke me.

"What," I said. "What is it? What?"

"Where's the Greek?" he said.

"He's here."

"You gotta wake him up."

"What's up?"

"You're moving back up the hill. Lieutenant's orders."

"Whose orders?" I said. "What about the demolition? What about the road-guard?"

"Lieutenant's orders. The road-guard is being disbanded. Altogether."

"What's the story?" I asked.

"I dunno. We got a call from the Company CP; the cap'n was maddern hell. He just got a call from Department HQ; they was maddern hell. Told the cap'n to disband the road-guard immediately. The orders'll be down in a couple days."

I laughed. "Orders is orders," I said.

"What?"

"Nothing," I said. "Is the lieutenant still up?"

"Yeh. He's in hole number one, with the telephone. Why?"

"I got to see him about something," I said.

"I'm going back," he said. "This wind is freezin' me. You sure you're awake?"

"Yes," I said. "You take off." I got up and woke the rest of the detail. "Get your stuff together, you guys. We're moving out. One of you call Alcorn down."

The Greek sat up, rubbing his eyes. "What is it? what's up? what's wrong?"

"We're moving out," I said. "Back up the hill. The road-guard is disbanded." When I stood up the wind hit me hard. I got my pack and kicked my blankets up into a pile. I slung my ride and pack and picked up the blankets.

"You mean the *road-guard?*" Mazzioli's voice asked through the darkness and the wind. "For *good?*"

I climbed up around the wall and the wind caught at my blankets and I almost lost them.

"That's the way it is," I said.

TWO LEGS FOR THE TWO OF US

Esquire published this one in September 1951, when *Eternity* was famous, after having turned it down at least twice before that. The character of George was drawn from a good friend of mine out in Illinois who had lost a leg in the Pacific, and this character was one of the major characters in the early novel I wrote and re-wrote for Perkins and which was never published. In fact, the scene here, much less well written and with almost no dialogue, formed part of a chapter of that novel.

No," said the big man in the dark blue suit, and his voice was hoarse with drunkenness. "I can't stay. I've got some friends out in the car."

"Well, why didn't you bring them in with you, George?" the woman said in mock disgust. "Don't let them sit out in the cold."

George grinned fuzzily. "To hell with them. I just stopped by for a minute. You wouldn't like them anyway."

"Why, of course I'd like them, if they're your friends. Go on and call them."

"No. You wouldn't like them. Let the bastards sit. I just wanted to talk to you, Sandy." George looked vaguely around the gayness of the kitchen with its red and white checkered motif. "Jesus, I love this place. We done a good job on it, Sandy, you know it? I used to think about it a lot. I still do."

But the woman was already at the kitchen door and she did not hear. "Hey out there!" she called. "Come on in and have a drink."

There was a murmur of words from the car she could not understand and she opened the screen door and went outside to the car in the steaming cold winter night. A man and woman were in the front seat, the man behind the wheel. Another woman was in the back seat by herself. She was smoothing her skirt.

Sandy put her head up to the car window. "George is drunk," she said. "Why don't you go on home and leave him here and let me take care of him?"

"No," the man said.

"He's been here before."

"No," the man said sharply. "He's with us."

Sandy put her hand on the door handle. "He shouldn't be drinking," she said "In his condition."

The man laughed. "Liquor never bothers me," he said.

"Poor George. I feel so sorry for him I could cry."

"No, you couldn't," the man said contemptuously. "I know you. Besides, it ain't your sympathy he wants." He thumped the thigh of his left leg with his fist. It made a sound like a gloved fist striking a heavy-bag. "I pawned one myself," he said.

Sandy moved as if he had struck her. She stepped back, putting her hand to her mouth, then turned back toward the house.

George was standing in the door. "Tom's a old buddy of mine," he grinned. "He was in the hospital with me for ten months out in Utah." He opened the screen.

Sandy stepped inside with slumped shoulders. "Why didn't you tell me? I said something terrible. Please tell him to come in, George, he won't come now unless you tell him."

"No. Let them sit. We got a couple of pigs from Greencastle with us." He grinned down at her belligerently through the dark circles and loose lips of an extended bat.

"Ask them all in, for a drink. I'm no Carrie Nation, George. Tell them to come in. Please, George. Tell them."

"All right. By god I will. I wasn't going to, but I will. I just wanted to see you, Sandy."

"Why don't you stay here tonight, George?" Sandy said. "Let them go and I'll put you to bed."

George searched her face incredulously. "You really want me to stay?"

"Yes. You need to sober up, George."

"Oh." George laughed suddenly. "Liquor never bothers me. No sir by god. I ain't runnin out on Tom. Tom's my buddy." He stepped back to the door. "Hey, you bastardsl" he bellered. "You comin in here an have a drink? or I got to come out and drag you in?" Sandy stood behind him, watching him, the big bulk of shoulder, the hair growing softly on the back of his neck.

There was a laugh from the car and the door slammed. The tall curly-haired Tom came in, swinging his left side in a peculiar rhythm. After him came the two women, one tall and blonde, the other short and dark. They both smiled shyly as they entered. They both were young.

"Oh," said the short one. "This is pretty."

"Its awful pretty," the blonde one said, looking around.

"You goddam right its pretty," George said belligerently. "And its built for utility. Look at them cupboards."

George introduced the girls by their first names, like a barker in a sideshow naming the attractions.

"An this heres Tom Hornney," he said, "and when I say Hornney, I mean Hornney." George laughed and Tom grinned and the two girls tittered nervously.

"I want you all to meet Miss Sandy Thomas," George said, as if daring them.

"Sure," Tom said. "I know all about you. I use to read your letters out in Utah."

George looked at Sandy sheepishly. "A man gets so he can't believe it himself. He gets so he's got to show it to somebody. That's the way it is in the Army."

Sandy smiled at him stiffly, her eyes seeming not to see. "How do you want your drinks? Soda or Coke?"

"They want Coke with theirs," Tom pointed to the girls. "They don't know how to drink."

"This is really a beautiful place," the blonde one said.

"Oh my yes," the short one said. "I wish I ever had a place like this here."

Sandy looked up from the drinks and smiled, warmly. "Thank you."

"I really love your place," the blonde one said. "Where did you get those funny spotted glasses? I seen some like them in a Woolworth's once."

George, laughing over something with Tom, turned to the blonde one. "Shut up, for god sake. You talk too much. You're supposed to be seen."

"Or felt," Tom said.

"I was only being polite," the blonde one said.

"Well, don't," George said. "You don't know how."

"Well," said the blonde one. "I like that."

"Those are antiques, dear," Sandy said to her. "I bought them off an old woman down in the country. Woolworth has reproductions of them now."

"You mean them are *genuine* antiques?" the short one said.

Sandy nodded, handing around the drinks.

"For god sake, shut up," George said. "Them's genuine antiques and they cost ten bucks apiece, so shut up. Talk about something interesting."

The short one made a little face at George. She turned to Sandy and whispered delicately.

"Surely," Sandy said. "I'll show you."

"See what I mean?" Tom laughed. "I said they couldn't hold their liquor."

Sandy led the girls out of the kitchen. From the next room their voices came back, exclaiming delicately over the furnishings.

"How long were you in the Army?" Sandy asked when they came back.

"Five years," Tom said, grinning and shaking his curly head. "My first wife left me three months after I got drafted."

"Oh?" Sandy said.

"Yeah. I guess she couldn't take the idea of not getting any for so long. It looked like a long war."

"War is hard on the women too," Sandy said.

"Sure," Tom said. "I don't see how they stand it. I'm glad I was a man in this war."

"Take it easy," George growled.

Tom grinned at him and turned back to Sandy. "I been married four times in five years. My last wife left me day before yesterday. She told me she was leaving and I said, Okay, baby. That's fine. Only remember there won't be nobody here when you come back. If I wanted, I could call her up right now and tell her and she'd start back tonight."

"Why don't you?" Sandy said. "I've got a phone."

Tom laughed. "What the hell. I'm doin all right. Come here, baby," he said to the blonde one, and patted his right leg. She came over, smiling, on his left side and started to sit on his lap.

"No," Tom said. "Go around to the other side. You can't sit on that one."

The blonde one obeyed and walked around his chair. She sat down smiling on his right thigh and Tom put his arm clear around her waist. "I'm doin all right, baby, ain't I? Who wants to get married?"

George was watching him, and now he laughed. "I been married myself," he said, not looking at Sandy.

"Sure," Tom grinned. "Don't tell me. I was out in Utah when you got the rings back, remember? Ha!" he turned his liquor-bright eyes on Sandy. "It was just like Robert Taylor in the movies. He took them out in the snow and threw them away with a curse. Went right out the ward door and into the snowing night.

"One ring, engagement, platinum, two-carat diamond," Tom said, as if giving the nomenclature of a new weapon. "One ring, wedding, platinum, diamond circlet. —I told him he should of hocked them."

"No," Sandy said. "He should have kept them, then he could have used them over and over, every other night."

"I'll say," Tom said. "I'll never forget the first time me and George went on pass in Salt Lake City. He sure could of used them then."

"Aint you drinkin, Sandy?" George said.

"You know I don't drink."

"You used to. Some."

"That was only on special occasions," Sandy said, looking at him. "That was a long time ago. I've quit that now," she said.

George looked away, at Tom, who had his hand up under the blonde one's armpit, snuggled in. "Now this here's a very fine thing," Tom said, nodding at her. 'She's not persnickity like the broads in Salt Lake."

"I didn't really like it then," Sandy said.

"I know," George said.

"George picked him up a gal in a bar in Salt Lake that first night," Tom said. "She looked a lot like you, honey," he said to the blonde one. The blonde one tittered and put her hand beneath his ear.

"This gal," Tom continued, "she thought George was wonderful; he was wearing his ribbons. She asked him all about the limp and how he got wounded. She thought he was the nuts till she found out what it was made him limp." Tom paused to laugh.

"Then she got dressed and took off; we seen her later with a marine." He looked at George and they both laughed. George went around the table and sat down beside the short one.

"You ought to have a drink with us, Sandy," George said. "You're the host."

"I don't feel much like being formal," Sandy said.

Tom laughed. "Me neither."

"Do you want something to eat?" Sandy asked him. "I might eat something."

"Sure," Tom said. "I'll eat anything. I'm an old eater from way back. I really eat it. You got any cheese and crackers?"

Sandy went to one of the cupboards. "You fix another drink, George."

"Thats it," Tom said. "Eat and drink. There's only one thing can turn my stommick," he said to the blonde one. "You know what's the only thing can turn my stommick?'

"Yes," said the blonde one apprehensively, glancing at Sandy. "I know."

"I'll tell you the only thing can turn my stommick."

"Now, honey," the blonde one said.

George turned around from the bottles on the countertop, pausing dramatically like an orator.

"Same thing that can turn my stommick."

He and Tom laughed uproariously, and he passed the drinks and sat down. The blonde one and the short one tittered and glanced nervously at Sandy.

Tom thumped George's right leg with his fist and the sound it made was solid, heavy, the sound his own had made out in the car.

"You goddam old cripple, you."

"Thats all right," George said. "You can't run so goddam fast yourself."

"The hell I can't." Tom reached for his drink and misjudged it, spilling some on the tablecloth and on the blonde girl's skirt.

"Now see what you did?" she said. "Damn it."

Tom laughed. "Take it easy, baby. If you never get nothing worse than whisky spilled on your skirt, you'll be all right. Whisky'll wash out."

George watched dully as the spot spread on the red and white checked table-cloth, then he lurched to his feet toward the sink where the dishrag always was.

Sandy pushed him back into his chair. "Its all right, George. I'll change it to-morrow."

George breathed heavily. "Watch yourself, you," he said to Tom. "Goddam you, be careful."

"What the hell. I dint do it on purpose."

"That's all right, just watch yourself."

"Okay, Sergeant," Tom said. "Okay, halfchick."

George laughed suddenly, munching a slab of cheese between two crackers, spraying crumbs. "Don't call me none of your family names."

"We really use to have some times," he said to Sandy. "You know what this crazy bastard use to do? After we got our leather, we use to stand out in the cor-ridor and watch the guys with a leg off going down the hall on crutches. Tom would look at them and say to me, Pore feller. He's lost a leg. And I'd say, Why thats turrible, aint it?"

Sandy was looking at him, watching him, her sandwich untouched in her hand. Under her gaze George's eyebrows suddenly went up, bent in the middle.

"We use to go to town," he said, grinning at her. "We really had some times. You ought to seen their faces when we'd go up to the room from the bar. You ought to see them when we'd take our pants off." He laughed viciously. "One broad even fainted on me. They didn't like it." His gaze wavered, then fell to his drink. "I guess you can't blame them though."

"Why?" Sandy said. "Why did you do it, George?"

"Hell," he said, looking up. "*Why*? Don't you know *why*?"

Sandy shook her head slowly, her eyes unmoving on his face. "No," she said. "I don't know why. I guess I never will know why," she said.

Tom was pinching the blonde one's bottom. "That tickles mine," he said. "You know what tickles mine?"

"No," she said, "what?"

Tom whispered in her ear and she giggled and slapped him lightly.

"No," George said. "I guess you won't. You aint never been in the Army, have you?"

"No," Sandy said. "I haven't."

"You ought to try it," George said. "Fix us one more drink and we'll be goin."

"All right, George. But I wish you'd stay."

George spread his hands and looked down at himself. "Why?" he said. "Me?"

"Yes," Sandy said. "You really do need to sober up."

"Oh," George said. "Sober up. Liquor never bothers me. Listen, Sandy. I wanted to talk to you, Sandy."

Under the red and white checked tablecloth George put his hand on Sandy's bare knee below her skirt. His hand cupped it awkwardly, but softly, very softly.

"I'll get your drink," Sandy said, pushing back her chair. George watched her get up and go to the countertop where the bottles were.

"Come here, you," George said to the short dark one. He jerked her toward him so roughly her head snapped back. He kissed her heavily, his left hand behind her head holding her neck rigid, his right hand on her upper arm, stroking heavily, pinching slightly.

Sandy set the drink in front of him. "Here's your drink you wanted, George," she said, still holding the tabled glass. "George, here's your drink."

"Okay," George said. "Drink up, you all, and lets get out of this."

The short one was rubbing her neck with her hand, her face twisted breathlessly. She smiled apologetically at Sandy. "You got a wonderful home here, Miss Thomas," she said.

George lurched to his feet. "All right. All right. Outside." He shooed them out the door, Tom grinning, his hand hidden under the blonde one's arm. Then he stood in the doorway looking back.

"Well, so long. And thanks for the liquor."

"All right, George. Why don't you stop drinking, George?"

"Why?" George said. "You ask me why."

"I hate to see you ruin yourself."

George laughed. "Well now thanks. That sure is nice of you, Sandy girl. But liquor never bothers me." He looked around the gayness of the kitchen. "Listen. I'm sorry about the tablecloth. Sorry. I shouldn't of done it, I guess. I shouldn't of come here with them."

"No, George. You shouldn't."

"You know what I love about you, Sandy girl? You're always so goddam stinking right."

"I just do what I have to," Sandy said.

"Sandy," George said. "You don't know what it was like, Sandy."

"No," she said. "I guess I don't."

"You goddam right you don't. And you never will. You'll never be . . ."

"I can't help the way I'm made."

"Yes? Well I can't neither. The only thing for us to do is turn it over to the United Nations. Its their job, let them figure it out."

Tom Hornney came back to the door. "Come on, for Christ sake. Are you comin or aint you?"

"Yes goddam it I'm comin. I'm comin and I'm goin." George limped swingingly over to the countertop and grabbed a bottle.

Tom stepped inside the door. "Listen, lady," he said. "What the hells a leg? The thing a man wants you dames will never give him. We're just on a little vacation now. I got a trucking business in Terre Haute. Had it before the war. There's good money in long-distance hauling, and me and George is goin to get our share. We got six trucks and three more spotted, and I know this racket, see? I know how to get the contracks, all the ways. An I got the pull. And me and George is full-time partners. What the hells a leg?"

George set down the bottle and came back, his right leg hitting the floor heavy and without resilience. "Tom and me is buddies, and right or wrong what we do we do together."

"I think thats fine, George," she said.

"Yeah? Well then, its all all right then, aint it?"

"Listen, lady," Tom said. "Someday he'll build another house'll make this place look sick, see? To hell with the respectability if you got the money. So what the hells a leg?"

"Shut up," George said. "Lets go. Shut up. Shut up, or I'll mash you down."

"Yeah?" Tom grinned. "I'll take your leg off and beat you to death with it, mack."

George threw back his head, laughing. "Fall in, you bum. Lets go."

"George," Sandy said. She went to the countertop and came back with a nearly full bottle. "Take it with you."

"Not me. I got mine in the car. And I got the money to buy more. Whisky never bothers me. Fall in, Tom, goddam you."

Tom slapped him on the back. "Right," he said. And he started to sing.

They went out of the house into the steaming chill February night. They went arm in arm and limping. And they were singing.

> "Si-n-n-g glorious, glorious,
> One keg of beer for the four of us,
> Glory be to God there's no more of us,
> 'Cause . . ."

Their voices faded and died as the motor started. Tom honked the horn once, derisively.

Sandy Thomas stood in the door, watching the headlights move away, feeling the need inside, holding the bottle in her hand, moisture overflowing her eyes unnoticed, looking backward into a past the world had not seen fit to let alone.

Tomorrow she would change the tablecloth, the red and white checkered tablecloth. And it was not her fault.

SECONDHAND MAN

I spent the summer of 1945 in the Smokies, and it was there that I heard first of Hiroshima and the Japanese surrender. Originally it was about a cracked-up veteran trying to pull himself together by living by himself in the mountains (where he learns of the surrender), but somehow was always too sentimental and never worked. In 1948 I rewrote it as it is now, changing the character, adding the wife, and drawing on a couple I knew in Illinois. Reading it over I find I still like it but nobody ever wanted to publish it.

When the doctor told Larry and Mona Patterson he thought Larry should spend the summer in the mountains and suggested the Great Smokies, neither Larry nor Mona had even the vaguest idea of what it might be like there, and neither of them wanted to go. Also, they were both naturally pretty frightened too, by the pronouncement.

"Now for God's sake dont look so scared," the doctor said irritably. He was a big heavy floridfaced man they had had for years. "Its nothing permanent. And its nothing serious especially. I know youre both city dwellers. So'm I. But Larry's lungs are not in good shape."

"In other words, you mean Ive got spots on my lungs," Larry said. "TB."

"No, I dont mean any such a damn thing," the doctor said irascibly. "If you did, Id tell you." He hitched his chair up to his desk on the expensive carpet and looked off out the window over the rooftops of downtown Baltimore for a moment. Then he turned back to them. Patiently, explainingly, with the same awkward and irascible gentleness he had displayed all through Larry's illness and ever since they had known him, he spoke of the bad siege of double pneumonia Larry had been through, and of the run down condition in which it had left him. He did not say anything about the protracted bouts of hard drinking and exposure scattered over a period of some years which they all knew had occasioned the pneumonia. Slowly, and logically, he pointed out that the best thing Larry could do was to change his environment and normal practice for a while.

"You newspapermen," he said. "You dont lead any healthier lives than us doctors."

What Larry needed now was a complete change. He was past the convalescence, but he still wasnt built up enough to go right on back into working. "Just look how shaky you still are," he said. He shook his head. "Those lungs of yours have had a bad beating." A summer in the mountains should restore him. Larry—who had an invalid's gratitude to his doctor now that amounted almost to worship—had the feeling that while he talked patiently on, by far the larger part of his mind had gone on somewhere else. To contemplate some other patient's problem, probably.

"Then you mean I dont have any spots on my lungs?" he couldnt help saying anyway.

"Larry, spots on the lungs can come from just about any damned thing in the world; and they can mean just about any damned thing in the world," the doctor said with irascible patience. "No, you dont have any. But I will say this, Larry. You are not going to be able to go on living at the pace and in the manner you have been for the past ten years so lets face it. Your body wont stand it any more. Now, I dont know what your trouble is, with all this extended drinking and all, and everything," he said embarrassedly, with a look at Mona. "Im no psychiatrist. But I do know your body wont take it much longer."

Larry did not say anything to this. But Mona put out her hand on his and patted him and he turned to smile at her gratefully.

"He wont, doctor," she said embarrassedly.

"And right now your lungs are your weakest part," the doctor said. "It might be a good idea to start looking into the idea of whether your paper would transfer you somewhere out West. In the high country," he said. "They own papers out there, dont they? And after all youve been with them a long time."

"Well, I suppose they would," Larry said. "But if I dont have—"

"You havent," the doctor said. "Well, it doesnt matter. Thats just something for you to think about. Im not recom*mend*ing it. But you ought to think about gettin' out of here. And cities arent good for your type anyway. But right now, theres nothing wrong with you that a summer in the mountains wont fix. You need fresh air, and exercise, and sun, and rest. Chop wood. Breathe. Eat. Sleep." The doctor suddenly leaned back in his chair and looked out the expensive twentieth floor window of his office. "I use to hunt up there, myself," he said looking out. Then he turned back to them. "Still do. Whenever I get the time," he grinned, wistfully and almost unbelievingly, and then shook his head at his own lie. "Great country, anyway. Be the best thing in the world for you, Larry. I wouldnt suggest it if I didnt know you could afford it," he added.

"I couldnt afford it for more than a summer," Larry said.

The doctor nodded. "Your paper ought to be willin' to give you a leave of absence," he said. "With pay. After all, they dont like to invest money in sending a man to an executives' school and then lose him. No corporation does. You see about it. If you need any letter or reports or such like, call me up."

Larry looked dependently at his wife. His wife who for four months now had been nursing him back to health. Mona, who had looked as perturbed as he had at the idea of going to the mountains, smiled and nodded without hesitation. "Okay, doc," he said, "I always wanted to be a pioneer anyway."

"And remember, lay off the liquor," the doctor said as he shook hands with them.

"You mean I cant drink anything?" Larry said. He always felt like a chastened schoolboy whenever he was around doctors; at least, when on business. They were so positive. They were only men, but they had all this responsibility for telling people what to do, and he was glad he wasnt one. Of course if they were standing together at a bar having a drink it was a different thing.

"Larry, I dont intend to itemize how much you drink for you," the doctor said, and then grinned, with his heavy florid face which looked like the face of a man who drank his own full share, and in fact was, as they had known for years. "We both know a beer and a couple of highballs wont hurt you any. But youre going to have to cut out these protracted benders that wind up givin' you pneumonia. Thats for sure. Youre almost forty now."

Larry did not say anything to this either, and only nodded, dumbly, as if he superstitiously hoped perhaps in that way, by saying nothing, it would maybe not exist.

"And you see that he does, Mona," the doctor said cheerfully as he shook her hand. Mona smiled embarrassedly and nodded; "I will," she said, and he leaned back against his big expensive desk and folded his arms in the white coat.

"When you get to be our age, Larry—and Im older than *you*—" he grinned ruefully, "we become Second Hand Men. Thats what I like to call it. Second Hand to everything, we are. In this day and age. Second Hand to our jobs, to our country's military strategy, to the money we make or hope to make and then cant spend, to taxes and the cause of world peace; Second Hand to our children, if we have any. Three hundred years ago at our age wed be about ready to die, if we werent dead already. But now we can go on living for a long time yet, if we want to, in a Second Hand sort of way. Well," he said. He rubbed his hand over his face. "Tell Miss Pender to send the next person in in about three minutes, will you?" he said.

The sort of vague-eyed, reticent-faced embarrassment they had all been laboring under had apparently tired him out as much as it had them.

II

And so that was the way it ended, and a month later they were in the Smokies. The doctor had had friends up there and had written to help them get a secluded cabin. He had also handled all the papers and red tape necessary for Larry to get his three months' leave of absence with pay. The paper obviously knew that Larry was walking along a very thin ragged edge and as the doctor who apparently had handled many such cases, said, they had spent too much money grooming Larry into a potential future business manager not to want to protect their investment. Of course nobody said any such things to Larry down at the office, and there was a sort of great embarrassed constraint apparent whenever he was around and when he left everybody wished him luck. Heartily. As if they superstitiously hoped that in this way, by this sort of formal genuflection to human comradeship and hearty good feelings, they might make themselves immune to breakdowns. Needless to say Larry was glad to get away. He had kept on going down to work all during the month which was May although of course in reality he had done very little and had left early and was very shaky still.

Mona did not ask for leave of absence from her own job with Antoine's, but just quit altogether. As she herself said, she could get it back anytime she wanted it, or a better one. They kept their apartment in the city and only took a few little things with them and clothes they felt they would need for roughing it. They left the city, driving down, and took Route 1 toward Richmond, heading for Asheville, Larry driving until he tired which was soon and Mona relieving him, and as they drove they talked. They talked it all, everything, all of it, the illness, what had preceeded and caused it, what they would do now about it, and what they would do later. It was really the first time they really had talked about it openly together, without reservations, and it was not only nice but comforting. It was warm and close and intimate to them both in the car, alone together, as they drove south that evening, the headlights lighting up a short stretch of the perpetual highway that rolled slowly back toward them and then fled beneath them.

"It isnt the liquor," Larry said, "that isnt it. Or even the women, you know—" he added delicately and guiltily, but determined to be honest—"that I crave. I dont know what it is. I dont know what I crave. I dont know—" He floundered, caught up in his own ineptness. "I guess Im just weak," he concluded.

"We all are weak," Mona said, sparing him one warm glance from the road. She drove in such a characteristic way, hands high on the wheel, leaning forward on her arms against it. He knew it so well. "All of us. Everybody. There arent any strong people any more in America."

"You know, thats true," Larry said eagerly. "I can think back over every person I know, you know—and not a one of them is what you could call strong."

"Maybe its a good thing," Mona said; "but maybe its not. Either way, there arent any strong people any more. I mean—you read books about the frontier and the pioneers, and the wild west, and there seemed to be strong people then. But to be strong you have to be—dogmatic. Dogmatic and opinionated, and righteous. Self-righteous. And were not that any more."

"Wyatt Earp, Frontier Marshal," Larry said.

"Thats what I mean. Did you ever read a more horrible thing than when he made that poor shaking Mexican draw while he counted three, and then drew his own gun and shot him? And he thought he was being fair. He *believed* he was right. Maybe its a good thing we arent like that any more. Today we have to depend on each other more, because we all are weak."

"I think youre strong," Larry said.

"Oh, but Im not. Im very weak. My weakness just comes out in a different way from yours."

"Maybe so."

"I know so. But together well work it out," Mona said. "Wont we?" She released one hand from the wheel and reached over and patted his knee. "Well work it all out—for both of us."

"Yes," Larry said fervently, and took her hand and held it. "You know, I dont want all those things. I dont know what it is. You get started; somebody suggests something; one thing leads to another; you go ahead. You get wild. Must be some kind of frustration or other, I dont know."

"I understand," Mona said, "I understand. For the first time really I think, I understand. And I must help you more."

Larry released her hand to the driving and lay back and lit a cigarette feeling very safe. The thing that amazed him most about Mona was how she had changed when he was sick. It was almost unbelievable. From a very nearly silent, monosyllabic, cold withdrawn intractable woman who went her own way and rarely spoke to him, and whom he violently disliked and expected to leave him soon, she had changed into the most tender and thoughtful nurse a man could have, always cheerful and warm, always at hand to look after him, never tired. She had taken an indefinite leave from her own job to take care of him, and had not even gone back after he was up and around and able to go down to the paper. It had been Mona who, after the doctor had mentioned that idea about him moving to the far west, had urged him to write to Harold Beckett, head of the Department of Journalism at the University of New Mexico in Albuquerque, who two years before had offered him a job out there teaching which at the time he had declined. Beckett was a good friend of his and had once worked for the Sun-papers before he himself had removed to the west. Beckett had really had TB.

"I think it would be the perfect thing for us," Mona had said. "Both of us. Not only for your health but for everything. It would be a different type of life, teaching. A different environment. Calmer and quieter and less hectic, you know. Maybe we could sort of start everything over. Start from scratch. And youd be getting away from these influences which are bad for you."

Larry had agreed with her, and had written the letter. He had not always been in the business end of newspapering; he had started out as a cub and progressed to reporter and then on to article writing before they had put him into the business part and sent him to 'executives' school', and he could teach journalism from experience as well as Beckett. Of course it would not be near as good a job and it would not have near as good prospects for advancement. But as Mona had said, they would not need as much out there, either. What did they really need, actually? And anyway who the hell cared? What good was money if you were dead and couldnt spend it. Or half dead and laying it all out on doctor bills. Up to now they hadnt heard from Beckett yet.

Larry stubbed out his cigarette and through half closed eyes watched the road's moving treadmill and the canvas backdrops of scenery that rolled perpetually up along each side of them. They had passed Richmond now on the four lane and turned off toward Lynchburg and Roanoke and the Blue Ridge Parkway and were getting into the mountains. Lynchburg, he thought. Lynchburg, which was forty some odd miles from Lexington where old Lee had lived and labored in silence all his few years after the war. Larry had read all four volumes of *R. E. Lee* while he was laid up sick. Man, what a biographer that old Freeman was! Mona was right; there just didnt seem to be strong people like that in America any more. Every virtue seemed somehow to have turned back in on itself somehow—today—like an ingrown toenail, perverting its own purpose into an infected sore spot. Well, maybe she was also right about its being a good thing. In the way it made us all dependent on each other more, because we were weak. *God is Love!*

Larry looked over at her driving and smiled. Mona sensed the movement and turned her head slightly to smile back. As if in direct answer, and without taking her eyes again from the road, she said: "Its all going to be all right. Both of us. You wait and see. Its like weve both been living in some kind of a bad dream."

"I think it will," Larry said with strength. He still could not get over the change that had occurred in her and felt again his astonishment. And it had practically happened over night. He did not attempt to understand it.

As a matter of fact, he thought, it was as unbelievable as the change that had apparently taken place in him simultaneously. When he looked back at the him of then from now, at the drinking and the sorry straggly women—anything; anything he would take! and didnt know why—when he looked back at that he wanted to shudder. He felt it wasnt even him. It had been down in the sorry skidrow section of Baltimore that, in some vague liquor-numbed wandering about with one of them, that he had contracted the pneumonia. Why had he done it? It was absolutely unbelievable.

What had it all been about? What for? What could he have possibly hoped to gain? Love? Ha. He looked again at Mona. She didnt know how much he depended on her. She said she wasnt strong but she was. Even if he wasnt.

Through the half open car window, all at once, as if there were a definite dividing line in the air itself, a strong aromatic scent of pine began to pour in over him as, winding their way up slowly into the mountains, they passed through a big stand of them. Larry turned to look out at them. It was as if every breath he took of them was carrying health and strength back into him. They actually seemed to seep peace and drip it out into the air along with their fragrance. Larry slept.

III

That scent, those whiffs of pine, seemed to stay with Larry all the rest of the way, a promise. Through Roanoke, through Asheville where the doctor's friends lived. He loved the smell of the clean country and felt it would heal him. To get to the hunting cabin of the doctor's friends he had engaged for them, and which the friends themselves now guided them to, they had to drive on west on the highway west of Asheville, and then turned north on a blacktop road that wound straight up into the mountains along the edge of the National Park. The cabin itself was just off this road, and set at the foot of a whole mountainside of pines. Some of the other hills around them had been logged completely bare, but not this one. From the backdoor of the cabin it soared above them, incredibly, the arrowhead tips of the pines interspersed with hardwoods sharp against the sky. And that smell, that clean smell of pine and peace, permeated everything.

Inside, the hunting cabin was just that. Made of logs chinked with concrete, it had two rooms. In one was a big iron wood range and a table. In the other there were just beds. Outside was a well with a hand pump. For milk and green vegetables there was a farmhouse half a mile down the blacktop. Or they could drive to town. The farmer would also sell them cut wood for the stove. They set about unpacking their stuff from the car, mostly books, and then went out the back door together to bend their heads back and stare up at the mountain.

They found the place up in the woods the second day they were there. It was half a mile from their cabin, up the mountain of timber the loggers had for some reason never cut down. The place was on a side road, a steep gravelled road up and around the mountain, and from this road the land sloped down sharply through the great pine trees that made a shady canopy over the land as it fell to a rocky gurgling stream coursing down a hollow that ran diagonally down the side of the mountain. They were surprised to see how many hollows and level places their mountain had and how far back in they went. From the cabin it had looked like it went straight up.

They spent an hour that afternoon, planning how they could build a house without cutting down any of the giant trees, one room below the other down the hill on different levels and like stairsteps, with a high back porch that would hang out over the stream. And after that every afternoon they would take a walk up the mountain to the place and spend the hot hours loafing around in its secret coolness discussing the house they would build there if the place were theirs. They discussed it in great detail and drew sketches of it on the backs of old envelopes and became very elated with it.

The stream could be dug out to make a little lake below the house. The lake could be stocked with trout. Trout would stay in the same pool for years, Larry had read. The tiny falls at the upper end could be raised and fixed so they were two or three feet high. Then they would always have the music of falling water with them. Across the stream there was a little glade, where someone's cows pastured now, flat and grassy and rising to a bank that hid it from the open meadow beyond. It could be cleaned up for a barbeque pit and picnic table. It could even be made into a garden, with terraces of rocks and shrubs. The hillside where the house would be could also be terraced and fixed with walks and shrubs. The stream could be bridged in two or three places with those high arched Japanese style stone bridges. And all the time over it all the soaring pine trees and the wind soughing through them high up in the tops, and the sound of the water, and the sun dappled shade under the thick pine branches that dripped both peace and incense, and when they stood against the bank of the glade across the stream their heads just showing, they could look out from under into sunlight and across the meadow at the hazy mountains all around them. It was like a cave.

They were having a fine time. They were spending hours and hours together, almost the whole of every day, more time than they had spent together in years and years even including their annual vacations, and neither of them was ever bored. It was almost like a second honeymoon, Larry thought sometimes.

The house itself, they decided, would be made of mortared field stone, picked up right in the fields around. There would be a big stone living room, with a huge fireplace. One that would draw and that in winter they could heat with and that wasnt just for looks. There would be a studio with a big window for Larry where he could paint and write and a shop where he could do all kinds of work. There would be a sewing room for Mona which would really be a 'designing room', where she could design and make her own clothes and go on with the designing work she had done at Antoine's. And above all, there would be here right in this place right in this house among the pine trees, where the world could not come in, all the things each of them had ever wanted from the world or dreamed of.

And so in the cool peaceful afternoons away from the sun glare the place gradually became The Place, and grew and grew, until finally it became a game. There was no longer even any remote possibility of realizing it or any vain hope that whatever amount of money they might be able to amass together would ever be able to pay for it. But that did not matter. They didnt care about that. At all. What mattered was that they had it. They had the ideas—and their plans—for it and when they went west to Albuquerque to work for Beckett (whom they had not heard from yet) they could find a terrain just like it or almost like and began to work on it there, a cheaper version. What mattered was that The Place had become a symbol for both of them the opposite of which was Baltimore and the life they had lived in Baltimore.

In the midst of all this Larry progressed almost visibly. The weakness and shakiness disappeared. Each day he walked farther and farther. In two weeks he had gained seven pounds. He had some trouble making the farmer down the road understand that he did not want the wood delivered already cut for the stove and wanted to chop it himself. The farmer explained that it did not cost any more already cut, and that he did not mind doing it since he had a chain saw and it was only a matter of minutes to saw it to length. Larry finally had to explain that he just liked to cut wood. Once when he was there after the milk the farmer called him off to one side away from his wife and offered to sell him a pint of corn whiskey he got from a friend, a courtesy which Larry virtuously declined. Every day he took longer and longer walks through the woods by himself, and had Mona purchase a sheath knife for him in town.

Once a week every Saturday Mona drove in town in the afternoon to get the next week's supply of groceries, one afternoon in seven that they did not spend together up at The Place. Luckily, Mona's family had lived on a farm for a while when she was a girl, and she knew how to handle the wood range and cook on it. She fixed them cornbread in a skillet country-style, and they gorged themselves on green peas which were already in when they got there. A month later the farmer had green beans and new potatoes from his truck patch too, and shortly after that green corn. They gorged on all of them. Larry thought he had never eaten such delicious, or such healthfully nourishing food; he thought he could actually feel strength seeping back into him through the very membranes of his mouth as he chewed. And Mona, who thought she had long ago forgotten all about such things, loved it and enjoyed stumping around the cabin in levis and moccasins and was continually looking astonished at the things she remembered how to do. They both begrudged her having to go into town every week for groceries, and Larry never went with her. That afternoon he would spend chopping wood for the range or walking by himself in the woods with his sheath knife. He never went up to The Place when she was not there because in some obscure way he felt it would be unfair.

One Saturday after they had been there five weeks she came home from town bringing the letter from Beckett, which had been forwarded. It waxed enthusiastic about the West and was elated at the prospect of their coming to Albuquerque. He said he thought he could still fix it for Larry to start in the fall, even at this late date, if they would send him a note and give him the okay. They sent it.

IV

In this way they went about living out their summer, loving every minute of it, enjoying it more than anything either of them could remember. It was a full seven weeks before Larry himself went to town, and only then because he had to have his hair cut, and because Mona insisted on it. He would much have preferred to stay at home at the cabin. But by the time they were half way there he had to acknowledge he was beginning to feel excited at the prospect of seeing civilization again.

Strangely enough, he felt like an outlander hillbilly. The summer suit he wore felt strange and uncomfortable, and he could not get accustomed to the white shirt and tie and kept craning his neck and sticking his finger in the collar. He felt embarrassed as if he might do something wrong, for all the world like some mountaineer man who had only been in to this little jerkwater town twice in his life.

"Ill help you shop," he offered as they began to come in between the houses. "Then maybe we can get home soon enough to still go up to the place."

"You dont need to," Mona smiled. "I can manage it all right. Anyway, you have to get your hair cut."

"But I can still help," he said. "Youve got quite a list and therell be a lot of sacks to carry."

"Id really rather do it myself, Larry. I know just what I want and where to find it. And if you go get your hair cut, I ought to be finished almost by the time you are."

So while she shopped he went alone to get his hair cut. He walked along the streets slowly, feeling an almost irresistible desire to gawk at the buildings and neon signs. The barbershop was Saturday-crowded with men, but not all of them were waiting for haircuts, some were just loafing. So he did not have to wait as long as he had thought when he first went in. There were no children or women in the shop and three or four of the men were discussing the fully developed physical virtues of the blonde headed waitress who could be seen through the plate glass window of the restaurant directly across the street. Larry sat down, grinning to himself and feeling a little less uncomfortable. It might have been any barbershop in the world. Or at least in the US. When it came his turn he climbed into the chair feeling conspicuous and still very much the hillbilly.

"Hello there," the fat barber smiled.

"Hello," Larry said, and told him what he wanted. He was aware of some of the men watching him.

"Say," the barber said after a while, "seen you and your wife park your car down the street. Youre the folks took the Haines's cabin up on Salt Lick for the summer, aint you?"

"Yes," Larry said, surprised.

"You a newspaperman, aint you?"

"Thats right."

"From Baltimore?" one of the other men said.

"Thats right."

"Thought that was who you was," the barber said.

"But how did you know? Who I was," Larry said.

"See your wife come in every Saturday after groceries," the barber said. "Heard you took the cabin. This the first time you been in town, aint it?"

"Yes. Thats right."

"Heard youd been sick," one of the other men said.

"Thats right. I had pneumonia."

"Well, these mountainsll fix you right up all right," the same man said.

Larry grinned. "They just about already have."

"Well, if you want a good newspaper story to take back to Baltimore with you," said still another man, one who had not spoken to him yet, as if he were trying to drag his own topic back in and attach it to the rest of the conversation, "theres one right over there for you." He nodded his head across the street.

Larry was puzzled. "How do you mean?"

"Hes just kiddin' you," the barber grinned. "—And, also, tryin' to get back on the subject. Thats our doll over there, that blonde. Shes quite a gal. We kid with her all the time. Shes a great kidder—"

"—and that aint all," one of the men interposed—

"—that restaurant sells more beer than any other place in town," the barber finished up, "just because that gal works there."

"Here, watch this," one of the men said, and went to the plate glass window and leaning forward pressed his nose against it and hung his mouth open, eyes goggling, head on one side, for all the world like a kid panting at a candy store window.

Across the street the blonde girl looked up and appeared to be suppressing a grin, then took a salt shaker off the table she was clearing and very ostensibly and disdainfully poured salt from it into the palm of her hand. Behind the cash register the florid owner of the restaurant was grinning.

In the barbership all of the men laughed, including the ogler.

"Got you that time, Perc," one said. "She poured salt on your tail."

"She makes me think of a ripe peach," the barber said. "A big ripe juicy peach, ready to be plucked."

"My guess is she was plucked a long time ago," Larry said. It got a laugh all around.

"Oh, sure," the barber laughed. "That wasnt what I meant. What I meant was the way she looks. You know?"

Larry grinned at him. "Im a married man." That got another laugh.

"So'm I, pal," the barber said. "Believe me, so am I. So is all of us. Say," he grinned, lilting the hair up on his comb. "Shes gettin' pretty thin on you, Mr. Patterson."

"Yeah," Larry said. "Guess Im getting old."

Again they all laughed. "Well, once she starts to go on you there aint much you can do," the barber laughed. "Look at me. Why is it three-fourths all the barbers always bald as cue balls?" Apparently it was a sort of catechism.

"Because they use their own tools," one of the men chanted.

"Well, whatll it be, Mr Patterson," the barber said removing the apron. "Anything else?"

"No, thatll fix me," Larry said. Still feeling itchy but also feeling warmly friendly and having enjoyed himself immensely, he got up and paid. He wanted to remember to tell Mona about the whole thing.

Outside he looked up and down the street but Mona was not in sight, and she was not in the car either when he looked. After standing on the sidewalk a minute or two he walked back up to the restaurant across from the barbershop and then went in and sat down and ordered a bottle of beer. Across the street at the barbershop window the men were kidding him, making faces and shaking their heads and shaking their fingers at him. He couldnt help but grin.

"Those bums over there giving you a hard time, Mr. Patterson?" the blonde waitress grinned. She had a husky, wry, sardonic voice.

"No," he said. "So you know who I am, too, hunh?"

"Everybody knows everything in a little old town like this, Mr Patterson," she said wryly. "How you feeling?"

"Fine," Larry said. "This is the first time Ive been in town."

"I know," the waitress said. "I see your wife go by here every Saturday. Well, Im glad youre feeling better. Dont let those characters over there kid you now. Theyre always comin' over here devilin' me," she grinned. She started away and then came back.

"You know this ad for Carling's Beer on the TV? Where the men whistle and say Hey, Mabel, Black Label? My name's Myrtle. Well, they got it fixed up between them so when they come over here any of them they always holler Hey, Myrtle, Black Girdle." She laughed wryly. "So I tell them Im going to get the boss to raise the price of beer to them so they wont drive off all the decent customers. You know. You know how it is in a small town."

"Sure," Larry grinned. "I come from a small town myself, in Indiana."

"Oh, is that right? How come you ever to wind up in Baltimore then?"

Larry told her how he had worked in the Indianapolis paper after college and later got a better offer from the one in Baltimore.

"Ive always wanted to get away from this town myself," she said cheerfully, "and go north to some city like Washington or someplace. But I dont spose I ever will."

"If youre smart youll stay right here."

Myrtle laughed. "Youre probably right at that."

Across the street in the barbershop a couple of the men were trying frantically to attract her attention, and with a grin at Larry she turned her back on them.

"Theyre always kiddin' me about my figure," she grinned, and with a wink leaned forward and leaned on the heels of her palms on the edge of the table letting all her weight go on one leg. The movement called attention to her behind. "Kid them a little," she said confidentially.

From across the street someone stepped to the door of the barbershop and let out a long drawn out wolf whistle.

"They all like to think theyre don juans," she grinned. "But theyre really nice fellows. Wouldnt hurt a fly." She had been married, to a local boy in the Army, and lived in Texas for a while, she told him. But that didnt work out, "Guess we loved each other too much, you know? No more that kind of love for me", and she had come back home. She didnt like that Texas. But she still wanted to get out of this little town someday and go North. Even maybe to New York. She talked on for another minute or two and then walked off back to the counter.

Larry did not know if it was just then, as she walked off (she really did have a luscious figure), or if it had been with him longer than that, but it seemed he had been aware for some minutes now of a vague guilty sense of uneasiness. Maybe it had started when she leaned on the edge of the table, or maybe when one of the men in the barbershop had let out the long drawn out wolf whistle. Whatever it was he found that instead of feeling pleased as he had been he was now feeling very uncomfortable, and he realized he had not noticed if Mona had gone by the window.

Across the street the men in the barbershop were convulsed with laughter at their own wittiness while the grinning barber went on slowly cutting hair and one of them mock warningly shook his finger across at Larry.

God, Larry thought, it was almost like back in the Army, and with momentary warmth he thought suddenly of all the barbershops in the country, where men could go and laugh about sex away from women. The safety valves that leached off the pressure. Then he felt guilty.

A little hurriedly he got up and paid for his beer which he discovered he had finished some time ago. As an afterthought he bought a paper. Then he went outside. Mona was not in sight up and down the street, and he had not seen her go by the restaurant, but on the strength of a hunch and his increasingly strong feeling of uneasiness he went to look in the car.

There, he found Mona was sitting in it, staring straight ahead out through the windshield.

V

As he slid in under the wheel, Larry felt his chest begin to constrict on him. His vague uneasiness expanded and became a sharp knife of panic which sliced through him; and a mind-stunning feeling of guilt fell on him like a heavy weight dropped from a window. He had known it, he had known it all along. Even back there in the barbershop where, very faintly, the vague uneasiness had begun as soon as the men had started talking about the blonde waitress. It was less of a premonition than it was a memory. Mona's face was stiff.

"Where were you?" she asked, not unpleasantly. "Ive been waiting almost half an hour."

"I— I was— There were two or three ahead of me," he said. "And that took a while. You werent in the car so I stopped at the restaurant to buy a paper," he added. "And, while I was there, I drank a beer."

"Oh," Mona said, "if Id known you were going to do that Id of let you help me with the groceries."

"I offered to help you," Larry said desperately. "It was you that said no."

"I didnt know wed have to park so far from the store," Mona smiled pleasantly.

"I parked as near as I could get," Larry protested. He had the feeling they were arguing, and yet they obviously were not arguing. His sense of panic deepened.

"Hell," he said. "I was only there a few minutes. A single beer."

Mona did not say anything.

"Did you get everything?" he asked.

"Yes," she said.

He started up the car.

"Is that blonde waitress still working there?"

"Which blonde waitress?"

"The only blonde waitress."

"Oh, her. Sure, shes there. Shell probably always be there."

"Shes a good looking girl," Mona smiled. It was terrifying to him to hear such a pleasant easy voice coming out of such a stiffly frozen, wooden, smiling face.

"You think so?" he said. "I dont think so. Her face is ugly. Old already. Hard. Shes got a pretty good figure, but her face—"

"Thats true," Mona said, "her face isnt very pretty."

Larry was watching the road where it curved down steeply here in front of the courthouse, before it went on out and up the valley. "It sure isnt," he said. He waited till he was down the hill and then pulled over in front of some houses and stopped. "Well? Come on. Give it to me. Whatre you trying to say. You think I made a date with her? You think because I had one beer Im going back and get drunk tonight? Is that it?"

Mona turned her face toward him slowly, her violet eyes wide with incomprehension in the frozen face. But the myriad tiny muscles of her eyelids were crinkled slightly giving her a haunted look. Deeply haunted. "Lets go on home, Larry," she said, not at all pleasantly.

Larry's hands had begun to shake on the steering wheel. He put the car in gear and started off again. There it was. He knew now that he had been afraid of it ever since he first stepped into the barbershop and heard them talking. He should never have gone in the restaurant. He should have gone back and sat in the car. What was he going to do? Panic, sheer panic, completely engulfed him. If there was only some way to bring it out in the open and explain. Desperately he wanted to bring it out in the open. He *hadnt* been interested in her. He *hadnt*. But how? He couldnt even prove it.

"Its unbelievable!" he said forcefully; but it sounded weak. "Its unbelievable! This was the first time that I was ever there. I never saw that woman before in my life. I drank one bottle of beer, Mona, one bottle. How you can possibly think that I—"

"I bought us a chicken," Mona said pleasantly. "A nice broiler. I thought maybe we could cook it outdoors over an open fire in that iron pot."

With an effort commensurate to driving a cork in the spout of a steaming teakettle, and which left him feeling totally exhausted, Larry swallowed and brought his voice down from the high pitch it had reached.

"I think thats a fine idea," he said gravely. "Ill build us a place and fix it up for you. A regular outdoor fireplace. Ill dig a hole and floor it with stones."

"Ive wanted to cook something in that little three legged iron pot in the cabin ever since we came," Mona said. "Im sure its pre-Civil War. When we go home, I want to swipe it and take it with us."

"I think where the chopping block is would be a good place to put the fireplace," Larry said. "Its already got the grass and weeds worn off it from the wood cutting." Fright and adrenalin sang in his ears, and his hands trembled uncontrollably on the wheel unless he gripped it tight.

They drove the rest of the way in silence.

VI

At the cabin Mona took the green quart mason jar and walked down to the farm for the milk. Larry got the coal scoop out of the cabin and commenced to gouge a shallow hole in the ground where he had had the chopping block. When he had it finished he lined it with flat stones from the creekbed and then, wearing only trunks and light moccasins, got the doublebit cabin ax and slipped out into the woods to get some green poles. He hunted a while, stepping lightly in the light moccasins that made no sound, carrying the ax near the head and against his thigh. He felt very Indian as he moved his nearnaked body through the trees and brush: with nothing but his moccasins and breechclout he would carve his life and home and place out of these strong friendly woods that were his brother; he would build and provide the things with which his squaw would make their home. Finally he found what he wanted, two slender young saplings, perfectly forked up near the top. He exulted as the sharp ax bit into the young green wood. The tall saplings fell slowly, turning slightly and pulling themselves away from their neighbors. In a way he hated to do it and his heart jumped as they fell, and he imagined he felt the exquisite sorrow of the hunter who has killed. Then he measured and cut them, two green forks and a long pole for hanging, and took them back to the cabin. He sharpened the forks with the ax on the chopping block and drove them in the ground on each side of the fire hole and put the green pole across them and stood back and looked at them, feeling like a fool. Then, still feeling like a fool, he went into the cabin and very deliberately started putting on his clothes. He came out and started walking down the road toward the farm. Half way there he met Mona coming back.

"I thought Id take a little walk," he said cheerfully. "Your fireplace is all fixed."

Mona stood in the road holding the green jar of milk and looking at him with those almost mortally injured, haunted eyes out of that stiff frozen face.

"Well," she said not at all unpleasantly, "Ill go on back and get the chicken started. Itll be about two hours before its ready."

"Oh, Ill be back long before that," he said cheerfully.

"Ill go on back then," she said. Larry watched her go on off up the road, walking in the center of the narrow blacktop. He understood it was something she couldnt help, something she had absolutely no control over. Even so, the terrible tremendous guilt all larded over with panic that it made him feel, was almost unbearable. He knew it was nothing she had done, he knew it was something he had started. He wanted to stand and drive his fist into a tree until the bones broke.

"Ill be back in just a little bit," he called after her cheerfully. "Dont worry about me."

The farmer sold him two half pints of corn for a dollar and a half each. It looked like clear water and tasted sickeningly horrible. He walked back up the blacktop toward the cabin with one bottle in the hip pocket of his jeans and drinking from the other, but he did not turn off at the cabin and walked on past it. It was screened from the blacktop by a thick cover of young trees. He walked on up the blacktop uphill, carrying the bottle and drinking from it. Somebody had said this road went on up to the top of the mountain and deadended in the National Park, which was a game preserve. He must have walked a half to three quarters of a mile before he stopped and waded down through the weeds to the creekbank. There he squatted down on his haunches on a big rock and took another drink and listened to the never-ending whimper of the stream over the rocks.

Kee-rist, this stuff was terrible! He giggled. But it sure was potent though. The Indians used to squat like this, he reminded himself, poor goddam Indians. White man run 'em all off. Insurance company. Insurance company and meat packers. Second Hand Men, old doc had said. Larry began to whistle softly, a song. It had been one of his favorites when he was a kid.

Just a Japanese sandman
Dum de dum de dum dee

He couldnt even remember how the words went now. Yes, sir. Japanese sandman. Bogey man now. Or had been. When he was in the Army. Use it to scare kids with. Scare them into minding. Like his father used to tell him he would turn black. Then he remembered the words. That was it. Or part of them anyway.

Just a Japanese sandman
Dum de dum de dum dee
Just an old secondhand man
Trading new dreams for old

Yes sir, that was him all right. Secondhand man. Just an old secondhand man. Yes sure, thats what you are. And you might as well admit her. *God is Love!*

God is love, hell. God is not love; not any more. Maybe two hundred years ago God was love. Poor old God, if He had anything to say about it, He must get awful tired of bein' named. If He could get a word in edgeways, Hed probly change His name Himself. And it wouldnt be Love. Maybe God needed to be Love for old Wyatt Earp, Frontier Marshal or the Bastard of Orleans. But not for us today. No sir, God is not Love, he thought. *God is Will,* he thought, and took another drink.

"I cant stand it," Larry said out loud. "I cant. Its too painful. And I dont have no *Will.*" He killed the bottle and threw it viciously down into the creekbed and listened to it smash on a rock. Then he got up and waded through the weeds back up to the road and started back down to the cabin. The sun was out of sight now and the air diffused with the bronze light of the long mountain twilight. He had no idea of how long he had been gone. When he got to the cabin he very carefully hid the second half pint bottle under the corner of the plank bridge over the creek. Then he went on in the yard and around to the other side.

Mona was sitting on the little lean-to porch in the light of the fire she had built under the pot, her knees pulled up against her chest, staring off through the trees. Larry sat down on the edge of the porch beside her.

"Well, Um back," he said cheerfully.

Mona turned to look at him, startled then. Her face looked strong, absolutely expressionless. "You'd better eat something," she said quietly.

"Yeh, guess U had," Larry said.

She got up and went inside to get him a plate.

"Well, you'll always be able to get your job back at Antoine's, anyway, wont you?" he said thickly, when she came back.

"Ive been sitting here thinking it might be a good idea to open my *own* exclusive shop," Mona said. "There arent too many good ones in Baltimore."

"Yuh," Larry said. "Fine idea." The secret thought of the second bottle hidden under the bridge where he could sneak back out and get it later on tonight was a source of great comfort and satisfaction to him.

Mona went down off the porch with the plates, toward the pot over the fire.

"Yup, good idea," Larry said. Besides, who could tell, if that blonde waitress ever did decide to go up North to some city maybe she might go to Baltimore.

Well, he would have to write to Beckett.

NONE SING SO WILDLY

When translated into French for a French collection of my stories this story was given the title: *"Middle-West . . . Mon Middle-West!"* I guess that is as good a title as any for it, especially if you remark the supreme French irony in the punctuation. It was published in *New World Writing #2* November 1952. In introducing it I stated about it, and will still hold to, the following: "The very act of writing is at best a compromise—between what you want to say, and what you can say within the restrictions of the form. This is one time I didn't restrict. . . . It's probably as near to a real autobiographical story as I've ever come, though of course it's all twisted and changed. And things in it that would seem to be unimportant to the story are important to me, and I think important to it." Anyone interested may notice the Arky and Russ of this story are the direct ancestors of 'Bama and Dave Hirsh of *Some Came Running*.

Sylvanus Merrick took the cabin over at Fandalack that summer for two reasons. He had gone stale on his novel and he did not sell enough stories that year to go to the big woods up in Michigan. And, Fandalack was close enough to home that Norma Fry could come up from Vincennes nights and by getting up at 4 A.M. be back in time for work.

Sylvanus and Norma were getting married in the spring. She was getting her two-week vacation the first two in August and wanted to spend half of it with him. Michigan was too far to travel for just a week and she had to spend the other week of it at home with her folks. Norma was telling them that she was spending this week with a girl friend in Brazil she knew from college. Norma's mother was very careful of Norma, especially now since the Frys were planning on their daughter's marriage in the spring. Norma hated to lie to her parents, but it was the only way.

"You dont know how strait-laced my family has always been, Van," she told Sylvanus. "If you did, you'd understand. It would kill them if they knew, and they've done so much for me. I owe them that: they've taught me all I know."

"I understand them," Sylvanus told her. "And I know they mean well. But they don't realize you're a big girl now, capable of running your own life. And they don't like me."

"But they do like you, Van," she protested. "Its just that they don't understand you like I do. They cant see the possibilities in you that I can. They cant see the potential goodness in you."

"They sure cant," Sylvanus Merrick grinned. They did not like it because he had tended bar at the Moose Lodge over home in Illinois, before his stories started selling.

"They dont approve of you just up and taking off to all over the country for six months at a time," Norma said. "They think its time you settled down."

"So do I," Sylvanus said. "But I don't have to sell cars to do it, do I?" Mr Fry had the biggest car agency in Vincennes and he wanted Merrick to come in with him when they got married, and do his writing on the side. Mr Fry had a personal friend in Detroit who spent two hours at his typewriter every morning and still carried on his business.

"It isnt that," Norma said. "Its just that they cant see much future in writing."

"They're dubious of most of my ideas," Sylvanus said. Mr and Mrs Fry had read some of the stories when they first came out, but they could not see anything much to yell about. They certainly could not see an adequate recompense for having taken his mustering-out pay and the two thousand dollars gambling money into the North Carolina mountains, when he could have invested it as capital. Sometimes Sylvanus Merrick thought it was unbelievable that they could have had a daughter like Norma Fry. And then, of course, there was always the Army.

"It was the war," Norma explained, "and George Field being so close to Vincennes. You cant really blame the folks. No one in our income bracket bought more bonds and gave more to the USO than Dad did, but they cant understand your refusing to go to officers' school."

"I'm neurotic," Sylvanus said. "Tell them that."

"Van," Norma said. "I know you werent like most George Field soldiers, Van." Sylvanus did not say anything.

"I love you, Van," Norma said. "Do you think if I didnt feel in my heart that I was your wife already, that I'd be doing what I'm doing? To them?"

"I'm sorry honey," he said. "Its just that . . ."

"I live under quite a strain myself, Van," she said.

"I know you do, honey."

They were driving back from a dance at Zook's Nook and he stopped the car and put his arm around her.

"Lets not, Van," she said. "Not now."

"Okay."

"You're not mad?"

"Nope." He started the car.

She watched him drive a while "You know, Van, sometimes I think I cant stand it, the duplicity, living like this."

"If we take this cabin, it'll only be for a month."

"Its not just this vacation. I've been masquerading under false pretenses to my parents for over a year now." She gave a sharp little laugh. "It isnt easy, Van."

"'Cheer up," Sylvanus grinned. "I'll make an honest woman of you come spring." He looked around at her so they could share this joke. Her face looked as if she had been slapped. Tears came in her eyes as he watched. He was shocked. "Good Lord, whats the matter?"

"You think its funny," Norma said.

"But I was only kidding you," he protested.

"Kidding?" she said. "Or razzing. Or needling. There are lots of different ways to kid a person, Van."

"Now listen, honey," he said, to right it. "I didn't mean anything. If you'd rather, we can call this whole Fandalack deal off right now."

"Now why do you say that? Did I say anything about calling it off?"

"No. No, you didn't. But I don't want to make you unhappy."

"I'd be a lot unhappier if you went to Michigan," Norma said. "I cant bear the thought of you so far away."

"I dont have enough dough for that trip anyway," Sylvanus said. "I could borrow it from Russ or Arky though, I suppose. They've been winning lately. Poker's been going pretty good over home at the Moose lately."

"I dont want you to borrow money from gamblers," Norma said.

"They're all right. They're good guys. You just don't understand them. They're not gamblers; they've never murdered a soul, unless you want to count a few Germans."

"I still don't want you to borrow money from them," Norma said. "Please, Van."

"I don't need to borrow money from them, if I'm not going to Michigan," Sylvanus said.

"Promise me you wont borrow money from them," Norma said. "For anything. If you need money, I can get it from Dad."

"Okay," Sylvanus said grudgingly. "I promise."

"I never said I wanted to call it off about Fandalack," Norma said. "I dont want to call it off at all. It was the folks I was thinking of. You're an orphan, you dont know how they are."

"Oh yes I do," Sylvanus said, thinking how little wild cheering there had been when they announced to Mr and Mrs Fry that they were getting married. As it was, the only reason Norma would be able to get away nights was because she was not living at home. The school chum from Bloomington Norma shared the summer apartment with slipped her boy friend in at night all the time, so that Norma felt free to stay away at night.

But that was not what was worrying Norma. What worried Norma was her getting into the Park. It came out later on in the evening when they were in his place, over home in Illinois.

"Its all right coming in the evening, Van, because lots of people come to swim then. But what about driving out through the gate at four every morning? After the first couple of times the gate guards will suspect something."

"Let them suspect," he said. "What can they do?"

"They could do a lot. You know how strict the Park authorities are about that. You know what people think of a girl who does what I'm doing. And how do you think I'll feel, having them stare at me funny."

"They wont even notice you," Sylvanus said. "Listen, this Fandalack deal wasn't my idea in the first place. I'd just as soon we got married tonight, if it wasn't for all those big plans for a church wedding your mother is making."

"Its not the plans for a church wedding that are keeping us from getting married right now," Norma said meaningly.

"Okay," Sylvanus said. "I know it. But is it unreasonable to want to wait until that novel comes out in the spring so I'll at least have a little money? We couldnt live in a one-room apartment like this, without even cooking facilities."

"It wouldnt be unreasonable," Norma said, "except that you dont have to do it."

"I'm not going to go into your father's business!" Sylvanus said.

Norma was not looking at him, and her face looked to him to be sagging, like a dead sail without wind.

"Anyway," he said hastily, "at least not until this one book is done." Maybe they would pick it for the Book-of-the-Month Club.

Norma was looking at his mantel, at the Jap bayonet hanging crossed over its scabbard that he had cut off and made a fighting knife out of when the medic who brought him in had stolen his, and at the grandfather's old cap and ball rifle with its tiger-stripe maple stock his grandfather had hunted the stump for and carved out himself. She was not looking at him.

"All right, Van," she said resignedly. "You run it. And if we get into trouble over not being married, you run that too."

"Listen," he said. "We'd go right down and wake up a J P right now, if we could, and get married right now, if we could.

"I'll tell you what," he said desperately. "We'll tell them we're married. I'll tell the guy when I rent the cabin."

"But we arent, Van. Not by the law. What if they ask you to see the license?"

"They dont ask to see the marriage licenses, what they want is your money. They want it too bad to take a chance of offending you."

"All right," Norma said tiredly. "You run it however you want."

"It'll work out fine that way. And they wont look at you funny. Honest they wont."

"All right," Norma said tiredly.

"Okay then," Sylvanus said happily. "Then its settled. Come here to me. And lets see you smile with that pretty face," he grinned at her happily.

"All right, Van," she said. She smiled tiredly. "But, Van, women dont . . ."

"Stop that," he grinned. "Hear me? Or I'll stop it for you. In fact, I think I'll just stop it anyway."

He did not hear what she said then, against his mouth. It sounded something like, "Is that *all* you *ever* think about?" But he did not care.

II

So they left it at that. He wrote for the cabin. There was no trouble at all. Mr Lemmon, who had the contracts for the concessions, was very nice when Sylvanus drove the old Plymouth over to see him. He made out the gate passes for both Sylvanus' car and his wife's without noticing or commenting that her license was *Indiana* and his own *Illinois*. Sylvanus took the cabin for a full month, the last two weeks in July and the first two of August.

It was a nice cabin, set on a little hillock between two tiny brackish inlets on one of the long fingers of clean lake, in a patch of second- and third-growth timber. It cost him $30 a week, and he rented a boat for the four weeks at a dollar a day. They charged 50¢ an hour for a boat, otherwise. The whole thing came to about $170, after he stocked up some canned beans and bacon and bread.

Last year he had spent three weeks up on Sheepshead and Betsy Lakes back in from Tahquamenon Falls in Chippewa County Michigan for $95. But then he didnt have any cabin then, only the sleeping bag. And he hadnt had any Norma.

He had to borrow almost a hundred from Arky to make the hundred and seventy, but he did not tell Norma that.

Up there on Sheepshead, there hadn't been a sound in the silence for days except the sound of his breathing and the plop of the plug in the lake and the wind in the tops of the tall spruce on the lake. Here, cars of shrill tourists hummed by on the asphalt a stone's throw from the door and you could always hear babies crying faintly in the distance and the strident-voiced mothers' commands. Even out on the lake fishing you could not escape babies crying faintly and strident-voiced mothers trying to command a good time. They came and went in boats all around you. He preferred the big woods. In the big woods there never seemed to be garbage, and he felt safer out in the woods than he did in the towns. The bears and the deer and the cats seemed so placid and calm, after people, and who would ever want to drop an atom bomb on just woods?

This was a town camouflaged to resemble a woods, complete with all modern conveniences such as flush toilets and trash baskets and fountains. The tents of the traveling campers were as closely packed as the bungalows in a residence section of Vincennes or over at home, so that the campers had practically all of the discomforts of living outdoors, and almost none of the benefits, and all of them in the eyes looked soul-hungry. That look in the eyes bothered him, and he worried whether Norma would like it after all.

But Norma liked it a lot when she came up the first evening. She loved the little patch of woods hemmed in by the fields. He was glad because he knew then if she could only see the big woods she would like them too, and he described them to her—the island of high ground like a ship in the gray sea of buckbush and leatherleaf that stretched off to the wooden ridges, the great tall sweet-smelling spruces like a grove of ships' masts in the flesh that he camped under where there had once been a pole-shanty deer camp.

As he talked, she tinkered with the kerosene stove and made up the beds with sheets and hung up some curtains she'd bought and got him to take her fishing.

"Oh, it is wonderful, Van," she said in the boat. She looked off across at the trees that echoed themselves upside down in the water and her face seemed to bloom, open up. "And I wouldn't have come, if you hadnt insisted. Thanks, Van, for insisting," she bloomed lambently.

"Wait till you see the real woods," said Sylvanus.

"Lets make a pact," she smiled brimmingly, "to do something like this once every year after we're married. Just get out and go and get away from it all. Getting married doesnt mean people have to stop having adventures. What shall I cook you for supper? I feel like cooking. I brought something along to take the place of those old beans."

"You wait," he said. "You'll see. We'll live like this *all* the time after we're married, only better. And not just two weeks out of the year to be free. *We'll* be free *all* the time. Life should be *all* adventure. Not romance, but adventure."

Norma pulled her line up and flipped it back in and the bobber danced drunkenly, repeatedly shattering the mirror as it re-formed. "But it has to be serious too, Van," she smiled. "Dont forget that. Life cant be all play."

"Play!" he said. "Play?" He had started to say something. He couldnt remember it. "Say," he said. "Listen, you're not still planning on me going into your father's business, are you?"

She pulled her line in again and looked at the bait. The bait was all right. She threw it back out. "I want you to do what you want to do, Van," she smiled. "Thats all I want."

It was almost dark when they got in to shore and Sylvanus Merrick, adventurer, half-hitched the boat on the arm of the stump and helped his mate up the steep part of the path. She had green corn all ready to put on and the chicken she had brought up to fry and the salad, already made in the icebox. She was efficient, and an excellent cook, and it was fine food.

He had just lit them both cigarettes while she poured them both coffee when he saw the headlights turn off the asphalt and heard the car pull in grindingly and then the voices of Russ and Arky on the path in through the trees.

They appeared in the doorway suddenly, as if conjured there in mid-stride without warning, although they had both heard them coming. Everything seemed to stay that way a long time. Then they were at the table without having walked there and unloading the bottles whose necks seemed to stick out from all over them like spokes from the hub of a rimless wheel.

He never did see the two women come in. They were just there, standing grinning inside the door, once when he looked.

It was as if he and Norma were moving in one time and the four of them in another so that the two only got their gears meshed now and then. Then he recognized what was causing it. He had had that experience before, in combat. It was because he was scared, frightened stiff, so full of fear it was running out of his ears and gumming his reflexes. Men had been killed in combat, doing that.

Norma knew who they were. She had never met them, had not wanted to meet them, but he had talked about them enough so she could recognize them: Arky tall, sway-backed, hanging-bellied, wearing the pallor of a badly sick man who lives under too high a strain too long a time and the semi-western style hat that was to remind people he was no native of Illinois but had come here from Arkansas. Russ short, stocky, bullnecked and going to fat, but still with that natural coordination of incredible speed that was a family trait and had made him one of the best basketball forwards the U of Chicago had had in the '20s, up to the time he flunked out and disappeared without trace until he suddenly showed up at home after the war. Both of them fog-headed and indistinct-eyed from drunkenness and wearing the haphazard civilian clothes they always looked out of place in, just as they must have always looked out of place in any uniform but a six-weeks-unwashed field uniform, because whenever they did happen to stop long enough to think of clothes it was always too late, an afterthought.

"Where'd you get this stuff at, Syde?" Arky sneered to Sylvanus. As a gambler Arky always sneered, like the wife of a Methodist minister always smiles. "You been holdin out on us. This stuff aint from around home. Hey, hey," he sneered friendlily to Norma, "where's old Syde been hidin you at, pretty thing?"

"And to think," Russ said pontifically, "I ate Arky out all over Terre Haute because he wanted to bring some for you. I even called him perverted, because he knew you werent going out with anybody but Norma. And now look at the lie you given me. Hello, sweet thing," he said profoundly to Norma.

"This is Norma Fry," Sylvanus said. "Norma, Arky and Russ." But he already knew it was no good, that his fear and the time lag had cost him the split second he needed to give them the tip-off.

Arky looked like somebody had thrown a cod-lock into him on an extra big hand. Russ looked pontifical and profound, even though his eyes were two badly frayed irises burnt into red cloth. Looking pontifical and profound was a habit Russ had picked up living in Hollywood, where he had spirited himself to after disappearing into the air of Chicago, and no little case of mistaken identity was enough to cause him to lose it.

"Well, howdy, mam," Arky said, almost forgetting to sneer. "We dint know that you—we thought that he—what I mean is we dint mean t—"

"He means," Russ said profoundly, "we are both pleased to make your acquaintance, Miss Fry. We have heard a great deal about you, Miss Fry, from Syde here, and we have heard a great deal about you."

"All good, I hope?" Sylvanus said, trying a joke.

It did not come off. Arky was still stammering when Norma was on her feet and at the door and, looking distantly at the two women from Terre Haute still standing there grinning, turning and going out the other door through the kitchen alcove.

"We dint aim to mean—" Arky was still less than sneering.

"From what we have heard, Miss Fry; you are one of the best," Russ was still saying profoundly to the now empty chair.

"I'll be back in a minute," Sylvanus said, and followed her out.

She was standing with her hands on a tree and her forehead on her hands.

"Listen, honey," he said. "Please listen."

"I'm going home," she said to the tree.

"Ahh, dont do that."

"And I'm not coming back."

"You dont mean that."

"Unless you get them out of there, and get them out quick."

"But I cant do that to them, honey. They dont mean anything. Its just an act they put on. They didnt know who you were. They didnt mean to insult you."

"Then I'm going home."

"But they're my friends. I cant just run them off. They probably feel worse about it than you do."

"Friends," Norma said. "And what have they ever done for you? Except get you drunk and running with women. Women like those."

"Well," Sylvanus said, "they loaned me almost a hundred bucks so you and I could take this cabin."

"I told you not to take money from them. And you promised you wouldnt. I told you I could have gotten it from Dad, if we needed it."

"Sure," Sylvanus said, "from your dad."

"Doesnt your word of honor mean anything to you?"

"Listen, honey," he said.

"Leave me alone. Just get out of my sight. I dont even want to see you. Liar! Promise breaker! I've never had anything so degrading happen to me in my life."

She stood up and looked at Sylvanus and Sylvanus opened his mouth.

"No," she said, "dont talk to me. I'm going home. And you can have your dear friends. And see how you like it."

She went back to the cabin. Sylvanus stood in the dark by the tree with his arms feeling amputated, and hating himself because of the fear in him. He watched the lights of the cabin that made daylight spots on the ground, but not a sound came from it. Then she came back out, carrying her coat and her purse. She walked on the path past him. He turned and watched her. The car door slammed and the motor roared angrily and she pulled out, the headlights sweeping across like a machine gunner shooting him off at the ankles, and then she was gone, humming off down the Park asphalt into silence. In the next cabin over on the next little hillock he could hear people laughing and singing. He walked back to the house, his knees threatening him.

They were all four still standing just like he had left them as if he had not even gone out, except Arky was not stammering and Russ not talking profoundly, to the place where Norma was not any more. But they both looked like they might start in again any second.

"Sit down," he said. "Have a drink."

Russ was standing gravely, nursing some dead pride in himself, staring deadly ahead at the wall. "Why thank you," he said profoundly.

The still grinning women got themselves glasses. Sylvanus got one himself. It would be a great comfort in the coming prolonged silence of swallowing throats.

Arky moved then, and took it out of his hand and set it back on the table. Then he rubbed his hand haggardly over his red-rimmed thick pallor. "Well," he said, "I guess you had better go after her."

"Go after her?" Sylvanus said. "What will you guys do?"

"By the time you've caught her and brought her back we'll be long gone. If we known she was goin to be here, we never of come over anyways."

"Dont be a damned fool," Sylvanus said gallantly.

"Hell buddy, we dont aim to cause you no trouble with your woman, and you gettin married come spring. You cant expect no decent girl like her to approve of fellows like us."

Russ turned his head slowly and stared at Arky a moment and then went over and sat down with a glass by himself.

"I dont see why the hell not," Sylvanus said valiantly. "If you're my friends."

"Dont you be a damned fool," Arky said. "Decent women dont work that way. You may be a writer but even you're smart enough to see that."

"Maybe decent women got lots to learn yet."

"Now you are a damned fool," Arky sneered. "How can a decent women be any different than decent? Answer me that. If a man wants a decent woman he got to do what she says and be decent himself."

"Oh," Sylvanus said. "You mean like the decent guys you play poker with at the Moose and go on stags with to Sullivan."

"Thats differnt," Arky said. "They already married."

"Yeah? Then maybe a decent woman aint what I want."

"No? What kind you want then?" Arky sneered at him. "Something like these? Whats wrong with yore head, boy? You get ready and go after her, hear?"

"If she loves me," Sylvanus said, "she'll come back of herself. After she's cooled off. I can wait."

"If she loves me," Arky sneered. "And her thinkin': *If he loves me, he'll come fetch me and prove it.*"

"I'm talking about something else altogether. If she loves me, she'll come back herself and be willing to accept my friends."

"Sure. And her tellin herself: *If he loves me, he'll come fetch me and offer to give up his shady friends.*"

"Then it looks like a draw, dont it? Fifty-fifty, even-steven, kits all around."

"Yeah," Arky sneered. "Except that she's decent. Wise up, Syde. You aint like us, you're intelligent. You aint no bum, and you need a decent woman to settle down to and take care of you. Without a decent woman guys like you crack up."

"Why all this decency stuff? I'm pretty decent myself."

"Have you ever seen a man that was decent?"

"Sure I have. Hell yes. Lots of them."

"No you aint. And I aint neither. Because there aint a decent man ever been born. Its the decent women make the men decent. Smarten up, kid. You better go after her. The longer you wait the harder she'll make it on you. And I cant rightly say I blame her none."

"You dont mind if I have a drink first before I go, do you?" Sylvanus said.

"She'll smell it on your breath," Arky said.

"Jesus Christ!" Sylvanus protested.

"Okay, but its true."

"Arky the gambler," Sylvanus sneered. "Arky the cocksman. Hell, you're a worse of an old maid than any librarian I ever heard of."

"Listen," Arky sneered patiently. "One sniff and she'll imagine you out on a wild party with us and these pigs, cant you see that? Then she'll really make it tough on you, before she lets you back in."

Sylvanus looked at him and did not say anything. Quite suddenly he knew he was right. It had happened before. But somehow, he thought, I cant quite see myself living that kind of life for fifty years, just to get my picture in the *Daily News* for a golden anniversary write-up.

The picture of it made him go suddenly sick inside. And it was then he made up his mind he was not going after her, that if she came back on her own it would be a sign, an omen that this time it was different and would not end up like the others. Then the thought that maybe she would not come back hit him again and made his knees go unstable again.

"Another time, it would be differnt and she wount care for you having a drink," Arky sneered patiently. "You go after her now, and we'll haul ass, and she'll come back lookin so sweet sugar wouldnt melt in her mouth. We'll see you later, we understand how it is."

When he said haul ass, like that, then so sweet sugar wouldnt melt in her mouth, Sylvanus Merrick's ear automatically caught the inflection and recorded it. He liked that kind of talk, he liked being able to reproduce it on paper. Norma's parents, and her friends, never talked like that. They were always watching their words. Maybe he had been in the army too long. It seemed he wanted to write the wrong things.

"You going to go after her?" Arky sneered.

"No," he said. "I'm not."

"You got to understand the way women work," Russ said like a pope from the table. "Good women, that is."

One of the women from Terre Haute laughed. Russ shut his mouth like a clam and stiffened his neck and his face went into that deadness again.

"Shut up, you," Arky sneered. "What the hell do you know about decent women?"

"Well," she said. "I like that."

"Get out," Arky sneered at both of them. "Take off."

"Take off where?" the other one said. "I'd like to know. In this wilderness."

"Anywheres," Arky said. "Out. Go sit in the car. Go walk in the woods and lissen to the little birds. We got talkin to do."

"You dont have to go if you dont want to," Sylvanus said angrily. "To hell with him." Arky always made him mad when he acted like that.

"I guess we'd better," one of them said. "Come on, Clarisse."

"Good women are nervous," Russ said profoundly, starting right where he had stopped, in the same tone of voice, as soon as they were outside. "They're high-strung, like horses. Especially before they are married. You got to kind of nurse them along. Give them their head and they'll slow down of themselves. But you dont ever checkrein them. You go along with them."

"Thats it," Arky agreed. "Agree with her. Even go her one better, about how rotten we are. Lay it on thick. Make it good."

"I'm not going after her," Sylvanus told them.

"Hell Syde, you cant hurt us any. If you dont invite us down to your house after you're married, we aint going to be hurt. We'll see you around."

"What house?" Sylvanus said.

"Aw, be sensible," Arky said. "This is serious. We dont care what he tells her about us, do we, Russ? You tell him, Russ."

Russ didnt say anything. His face went back into that deadness again. "No," he said after a while, from inside the deadness. "Why should we care? We've got nothing to lose, have we?"

"There. You see?" Arky said. "We telling you this for your own god-damned good."

"I'm not going after her," he said.

"The fact is," Russ said heavily, "you cant tell her anything worse than the truth. When I think—"

"Oh for god sake," Sylvanus said. "Dont start telling me about your own lost great love and your subsequent failure in life."

"The kid's right," Arky said. "This is no time to get on no crying jag."

"I could tell you both many things," Russ said stiffly.

"Sure you could," Arky sneered. "Look at him," he sneered to Sylvanus. "He was a writer once, too, you know, out in Hollywood. He wrote on plenty scripts for the movies. And he had a great love, too. And now look at him. You want to end up like that?"

"She wants me to go into her father's business," Sylvanus said. "After we're married."

"Whats wrong with that?" Arky said. "Her old man makes plenty dough off them cars. You can live off the fat of the land and write on the side."

"It dont work that way," he said.

"Why dont it?" Arky said.

"No!" Russ hollered violently. He jerked up in his chair. "Dont never prostitute your art."

"Aw nuts," Sylvanus said.

"I mean it," Russ hollered.

"I dont see why it wont work," Arky said.

"Because," he said "They wont leave you alone. They act like they own you."

"I really mean it," Russ said to his glass. Big tears rolled down from his eyes and splashed into it.

"Take their money and live easy and write what you want," Arky said. "Thats no argument to offer."

"I'm not going after her," he said.

That was the way it finally ended. Arky was worse than one of his Arkansas mules when he got his teeth into a thing, but Sylvanus outlasted them both because he had in his mind the picture of the sign it would be and knew this was a test case of the whole entire deal. He tried one other time to explain it to them, but they were each looking at something entirely different. It was like the five blind men with the elephant, and they did not even hear what he said. He gave it up then and went back to his one single sentence.

Finally they let him have one drink. They were hoping it would loosen him up, he could see that in their eyes. It did not though, it only tightened him, so they all had another. In the end Arky called in the Terre Haute women from the car and they used the two sleeping alcoves that were without sheets, bringing in their own GI blankets from the car. Because of his tragedy, Sylvanus rated the porch.

He lay for a long time, thinking it over. He tried hard to understand it. Finally, he too was forced back to the one single sentence that had baffled the others and now baffled him because he had used it so long it had no meaning any more, only word sounds.

The very late-rising moon came up and he watched the light that you could not tell where it came from sifting down through the overcast and silhouetting the branches and leaves.

Finally he went to sleep. When he woke in the morning they were already gone, nothing but three empty bottles and the dirty glasses and the over-filled ashtrays to prove there had been a great party.

He straightened everything up and then fixed himself bacon and coffee for breakfast and washed up those dishes too, before he went out on the porch to the portable, so that everything would be ready and neat. Then he remembered she would be working all day. That put if off until evening. He did not feel much like working. In the middle of the morning he heated a can of beans and ate it and made some bacon and egg sandwiches and took the boat out for some plug casting. He did not get any strikes. In the afternoon he went over to the beach and went swimming. At dusk he took the boat out again, this time with the flyrod he was trying to learn how to use. He did not get any strikes. With the flyrod he did not expect any. For supper he had beans and bacon both. At ten-thirty he turned in.

She did not come the next evening either.

The novel was not getting any nearer to the Book-of-the-Month Club.

III

He was trying to learn to use a flyrod then. Every evening he would go out and fish the banks of the main lake at dusk. He would sit in the boat fifteen yards from the bank and keep casting and casting until his right arm gave out. Then he would shift the rod to his left hand and cast, working the boat along down the bank. The fish would be rising, feeding, making small circles. He would cast in and around all the circles. When his left arm gave out he would shift the rod back to the right.

He wanted to learn. But no one had ever offered to teach him. He could not just walk up and ask them, no more than he knew about it. It would embarrass him. He did not even know enough yet to be able to figure out what it was he was doing wrong. All he could do was keep casting.

It was like that with Norma.

When he got discouraged he would concentrate his ears on the dusk-stillness, when everything in Nature seemed to pause for a while and study the balloon-ing reddening sun and through their eyes replenish themselves in it. He had seen old fishermen stand like that in the dusk. His grandfather had used to stand like that in the dusk. And he wanted to learn. He would stay out till the mosquitoes would drive him in in the darkness.

Mr Lemmon, who had the contracts for the concessions, was over at the beach every afternoon when he went swimming. After swimming, with the towel scarfed around his neck, he would talk to Mr Lemmon and it helped some. Mr Lemmon seemed so stable, so rock-founded and secure. Every afternoon he would discuss things with Mr Lemmon.

Until the afternoon Mr Lemmon introduced him to Philips and Ohls.

Mr Philips was the Park Superintendent, and Mr Ohls was the one-armed guard who patrolled the beach and the Lodge. They ran the Park; Mr Lemmon only ran the concessions. Mr Philips was in the State Parks Service and wore suntans and Mr Ohls, who was of a higher status than the gate guards and al-ways wore side arms, was his right hand man—or rather his left hand man, since it was his right arm Mr Ohls had lost in France in the first war. Mr. Philips had been a Chief Machinist's Mate in the first war. Mr Lemmon had never been in a war, too young for the first one and too old for this one, and he kind of regretted it one way but he knew he was lucky. Mr Philips and Mr Ohls agreed with him that he was lucky and looked at Mr Merrick. Mr Merrick agreed too. Mr. Philips and Mr Ohls thought they were lucky too, in that their war had been easier than Mr Merrick's war. Mr Merrick guessed that was so. They discussed the third war, which would not be at all like the other two wars. They agreed that it would be more sensible in the long run if we would quit being squeamish and use the bomb now, before the Russians got it. If the man in the White House was a man, we would have done it before now. They agreed it would be more humane in the long run, would save more American lives and keep America secure.

Mr Merrick had heard Mr Fry's daughter Norma express somewhat these same sentiments, but Mr Lemmon agreed with this sentiment so heartily that he took them all down the basement for a can of beer. No alcoholic beverages of any kind were allowed in the Park; it was a considerable compliment to Mr Merrick. Mr Merrick was glad to get back to his cabin. He had a bottle of scotch there he had been saving. By sitting on his porch with his back to the door he could almost imagine he was out in the big woods. After drinking half of the bottle he could almost believe it. He sat on the porch and drank more scotch and went up to the big woods, to his brothers, the bears. It had been coming a long, long time. He had been putting and putting it off. He got very drunk. . . .

It was a fine Park, at Fandalack. It sated the prairie man's hunger for woods and for water, and you could see them all there, the stick-armed meatless-thighed young teen-aged girls, the pouchless-loined bone-hipped young teen-aged boys who followed them around with eternal optimism that was forever outsmarted, the fat old Jewish couples down from Terre Haute looking like the great fairy-story toads who eternally guard a mountain of gold for a goddess who never comes, the flat-eared thick-muscled miners in from Sullivan and Jasonville with their big-bottomed hungry-bellied wives keeping an eye on them while trying to manage four or five kids out of drowning, the tall dried-out farmers with sun-blackened faces and arms and chests white as milk, the picnicking young white-collar couples a little superior because they all owned new cars but embarrassed because even their faces werent tanned.

It was a fine Park. But there was a great misconception in it all, he thought bitterly, throwing the empty bottle away.

This land that was now Park was the same land that had been cut over, burned over, farmed out, strip-mined into a no man's land even the Boy Scouts found useless, before it was finally sold to the State for a Park by the baffled fifth- and sixth-generation heirs who could no longer find any other way to get profit out of it.

But you could not get away from a thing like that so easily, Norma Fry, by just shutting your eyes and not seeing it.

This land, he thought drunkenly, this same gelded land; that the grim Bible-toting fathers, who knew their rights God owed them and were prepared to take them, had trooped up the Wabash into it like sprinters from the gun and spread out in like a battalion being given open ranks march—so that they might bequeath us, their offspring, their heritage of mordant Protestantism; out of their lust for salvation, sometimes called security.

This land, this same spavined land; that their sons, and their sons, who already now loved God more than square dances, had scratched and re-scratched with the plough like surgeons innoculating the young against the pox of fertility—so that they, who were saved, might add to the Protestantism their own great faith in buying more land to grow more corn to buy more land; out of their lust for security, seldom called salvation.

This land, this same castrated land; that their own sons, having no soil left to farm, had stripped what was left of the surface off of and left it piled in raw mountains like a Jack the Ripper who is too tired to bother to put the clothes back over the emptied corpse, to get at the coal and oil that was the only virtue the land had left now, the last black memory of the once lush virgin forest—so that they, who were twice saved, might expend it in two wars for security, never called salvation now except in reference to other men.

This land, Norma Fry, this dead land; that we are now, out of our great spiritual inheritance that they left us, looking down from the walls of our donjon of security they have made us, could take now and refurbish with trees and log cabins like the best of interior decorators and dedicate to them, who made this fine Park possible, so that we might have a place to play at camping and woodcraft two weeks out of every year for the rest of our natural lives, while we continue to fight the world for security.

The misconception was in the security. It had all of it been done for security. Yet there never had been any security. Everybody fought and killed and gave up their young dream, for security. Just as we now were preparing to fight a third war, for security. But it was not security that was gained, security was not ever gained, only herding and mechanization, fear was gained, but never security.

In his mind he could see them all, trying to live by their great misconception, wandering vaguely frantic-eyed down the dim dust-haunted coal-mine corridors of their lives, trying to light their way along with the feeble kitchen match of their inheritance: the juiceless loveless Protestant-Catholicism with its attendant ritualistic sanctity of the vulva and the resulting great national fiction of romantic love and its products: the sixty-year-old mothers fat with the virtue of their multiple virgin births playing gin and bridge; and the sixty-two-year-old fathers fat with the vice of their guilty fear of cuckoldry talking business prospects and advice to their young they always feared werent theirs, and rightly, since how can any man ever father a virgin birth? All of them seeking the old druid god of woods and water that they all of them had helped somewhat to kill, with Sylvanus Merrick and Norma Fry right in there, leading the van.

"O my god," he hollered drunkenly, wishing now he had brought two bottles, "dont they make real women any where any more?"

IV

She came back Friday evening. He had taken the flyrod down to the South Lake, where they let him have a boat free since he had rented one on the big lake, and when he got back it was after dark and her car was sitting there in the clearing next to the road and the lights were on in the cabin in through the trees.

He did not go in for a while. She had left Thursday a week ago, so that he had eight whole days to begin to get used to it. Now he did not know what to expect. His legs were quivery, as if he had been walking up hill. It was too much to expect that in one week she had changed, just like that. He expected a big accusation scene. But there was none.

She had the stove lit and coffee made and there was a cup sitting on the table where she could reach it while she made up the beds fresh with the clean sheets she had brought. She had also brought a bag this time, because it was standing just inside the door and he almost fell over it.

She had her hair up in a green scarf wrapped tightly like a turban around the small fragile head on the long slender neck. It was almost as if she had never been gone. He did not know what to say, how to start talking, but she took care of that too. She did not mention Arky or Russ or the trouble.

"What would you ever do without me to take care of you?" she smiled frowning, and walked over to the door of the icebox. "Look what I brought you." She pulled out a center-cut T-bone at least an inch thick and held it up for him to admire.

"Stuff like that comes pretty scarce." It sounded hollow. He could feel himself still waiting for her to begin the big scene, and he could not stop waiting.

Norma shrugged and laughed merrily at him. "Well, I got paid today, didnt I? I would have had it already fixed for you to sit right down to when you came in, but I didnt know what time you'd be back."

"I didnt know you were coming," Sylvanus said.

She offered no explanations. "Did you get any fish?"

"I didnt go after fish," he said, and held up the flyrod that he had forgotten to uncouple and put in the corner.

Norma laughed, merrily. "I dont think you were cut out for a fisherman, Van."

He began to stop waiting a little. "I guess not," he said. "How were your folks?"

"Just fine. They sent their regards."

When he heard that, he stopped waiting entirely. It seemed almost too good to be true. He had had himself all wound up to refusing to apologize, and now he felt ungrateful and guilty, thinking how it had been Norma who swallowed her pride and not him. Arky had been right all along about women.

She went into the little kitchen alcove, smiling back out at him, to put the steak on. He stood in the doorway and watched the lithe pert way she moved. You had to admire courage like that. She cut off a piece of the fat and rubbed it lightly over the skillet and laid the steak down tenderly into its cradle. After she had both sides properly seared to her satisfaction she came over to where he was standing and kissed him lightly. Then he kissed her back, but not lightly. She had to squirm loose.

"Van," she said breathlessly. "Now you stop it. You want me to burn up this steak?"

"Not that steak," he said.

"Then you just better watch out."

"I'm not in much of a condition to exercise much control," he grinned.

Norma looked at him. Then she smiled. "My poor darling," she said. She patted his shoulder on the muscle up near his neck. "I was hoping you'd get back in time so we could go swimming after we ate." She smiled. "I wanted us to go swimming tonight."

"We can still go, if you want."

"Not now." She went to the window and looked out through the trees and across the lake to the high arc lights on the beach. She looked at her watch. "Its too late. They'll be closed by the time the steak gets itself cooked and eaten."

"Let the steak go then," he said. "Cook it later."

"You cant, after its already on. It would ruin it. And I want you to enjoy it. We'll go tomorrow. Oh, didn't you see? I brought a bag, so I could stay till Monday morning. We'll have plenty of time yet to swim."

"Sure we will," he said. "After next week we'll have nine whole days of it, all to ourselves. Just the two of us."

"We *will* have, wont we?" she said. "Oh, and Van. I brought my new swim suit you bought me. You havent even seen me in it yet, have you? I'll wear it tomorrow."

"Why not give me a preview?" he said. "Try it on for me now?"

Norma laughed sideways at him. "All right, I will. But not now. Later on. We've got to eat first. The steak ought to be done soon."

"Okay," he said. "But dont forget, thats a promise."

The steak was the best steak Sylvanus Merrick ever had eaten. The swim suit was fine, too. It was one of those terrycloth Stunners, by Cole. She had seen it advertised in *Life* Magazine. He had ordered it from Marshall Field's by mail. It was the first one around here, and when she wore it next day on the beach it made a little sensation over there too.

"Look how everyone envies me my new swim suit," Norma whispered happily as he spread out the blanket. "They're all of them watching it."

He looked around. Guys all around them were giving her the camera eye, even some of the high school boys were putting their minds on it.

"Well, dont look, silly," Norma said, flushing.

"The suit may be what the women are watching," he grinned. "Thats not what the men are looking at."

Her face changed as he looked at it. "Oh now, Van," she smiled icily. "Dont start that again." She lay down on the blanket on her belly with her feet carefully toward the sun.

He lay down beside her. For a minute he thought she was making him pay for last night. Women did that, sometimes. She had done it before. But she was changed now, wasnt she?

"Dont start what?" he said.

"You know what," she said, her face still turned the other way, into the sun. "I dont need to tell you."

"No," he said. "No, I dont know. Start what? Tell me."

She turned her head then and looked at him. "Every man isnt as oversexed as you are, Van," she smiled gently. "I'm willing to accept you as you are, you dont have to excuse yourself to me by trying to prove all men are like you are. I wont stop loving you. I came back, didnt I? But you know all men dont look at women the way you do."

"They dont, hunh?" he said.

"No, of course not, they dont."

"Name one," he said.

"Well, I could name plenty."

"All right," he grinned, "name one."

"All right," she smiled thinly. "My father. There."

She looked at him, her face condensed into this smile that was more like an exasperated frown. But already a light of triumph was beginning to shine through. It was in her eyes that she had taken an unfair advantage, and that she had him.

He made his eyes look away. He did not want to say anything about her father. Her father had the best car agency in Vincennes. He was a good solid Rotarian. He belonged to the Chamber of Commerce. Well, that was all right, if he wanted that, Sylvanus would not hold that against him, he still liked him. He liked him because in all the times he had run into Mr Fry down along the river- front in Terre Haute and in some of the joints in Evansville Mr Fry had never asked him not to say he saw him. Mr Fry did not complain to anybody because he had to go away from home to get his sheep dipped properly, he did it with dig- nity, even when he was drunk. And for that he liked Mr Fry, even though he was sure at least half of the reason the Frys had tried to break up the marriage was because Mr Fry had run into him down on the riverfront.

But he could not explain all this to Mr Fry's 21-year-old daughter. And Mr Fry's 21-year-old daughter knew it.

"And I could name others," Norma said. Her smile was all triumph now. "Plenty of them, boys I used to go with in Vincennes, boys who respect women, only you wouldnt know them."

"No," he said. "I wouldnt know them."

"I'm sorry, Van," she said softly. "I didnt mean that."

"Its all right," he said. "Lets forget it. Lets swim."

"Now sulk," Norma said. "I didnt mean it like that, and you know I didnt. But it makes me so mad, the way you're always trying to convert me, when every in- stinct in me cries out against what you say."

"Me convert you!" he said.

"Hush," she frowned. "Do you want someone to hear us? Yes, convert me. How do you think I feel, your future wife who has given you all of me, to see you eyeing up every girl that walks in front of your nose?"

"Dont you like to have men admire you?" said Sylvanus.

"Thats different. Why do you always twist things so? Its natural for girls to like to have men admire them."

"Well, its natural for men to admire girls. And I admire all of them," he said. "And if I said anything else I'd be lying. Listen," he said, "lets go swim, shall we?"

"I dont feel much like swimming just now," Norma said. "Admiring them and mentally undressing them are two different things," she said.

"Oh they are?" said Sylvanus. "Okay. And I suppose buying your clothes to show off what you've got to the best advantage, and wanting to be admired, are two different things too?"

"Absolutely different," Norma said. "I dont— Say," she said, "are you listening to me?"

"Yes," said Sylvanus. There was another loving young couple spread out on their blanket next to him, except that this loving young couple really looked loving. He was watching them. They did not know there was anything in the world but themselves. He wondered if they ever had theoretical arguments, too.

"I dont believe you've been listening to me at all," Norma said, looking at them.

"I have though," said Sylvanus.

"Girls dont think about 'showing off what they've got,' as you so meticulously put it," Norma said. "Its only girls like the two your *friends* brought to the cabin who are cheap enough to do that. With most girls it is only an interest in fashions. They want to look nice and they want to be fashionable. They arent even thinking what men think about them."

"You really believe that, dont you?" said Sylvanus.

"Why, of course I believe it," she said.

"Then all I can say is somebody better explain that to the men, but quick," he said, watching this couple. It made you feel hopeful, watching them, and then suddenly sad with a self-pity because you were too old for that any more apparently, because somewhere in the last two years you had outgrown it. Hell, he thought, even you cant get away from the great national fiction of romantic love you are decrying.

The boy lay on his belly propped up on his elbows and the girl leaned down over him. They talked and laughed softly. The boy favored his right arm and it was whiter than the rest of him, as if it had just come out of a cast. There was a thumbstall on that thumb and the girl was playing with it tenderly. She leaned down once more, still whispering, and kissed him on the shoulder.

"It isnt all men," Norma said, "that ought to be told. Its only a few men. They need it explained to them. Like you looking at the girl over there, making over that boy."

"I was looking at both of them," said Sylvanus.

"Of course you were," Norma smiled. "You probably didnt even see the girl, did you?"

"Yes, I saw her," he said. She was really making him pay for last night all right. It was as if they were either ashamed of it afterwards or else afraid you would leave them. He could never tell which. Maybe it was both. For a second he thought of asking her why she always did that. Instead, he sat up and lighted a cigarette.

You paid for everything in this world. If you wanted the merchandise, you had to pay the full market price. Well, he was willing to pay, and he might as well pay it to Norma as any of the rest of them. It seemed a cold-blooded way to look at it when you looked at the loving young couple there. But then where would they be five years from now?

He tossed the match away and looked around at the rest of the people, trying to see them as clearly, while the honesty of the insight lasted, because it never lasted long any more.

That was when he saw Mr Ohls, the one-armed Lodge guard, coming down the hill fast in that lumbering gallop old men acquire when their coordination has started to go.

Mr Ohls was in uniform and wearing his gun. He was very much on duty. And he looked very mad. Sylvanus' heart swelled up and jumped once with that old fear of the Law, even after two years he had not gotten over that part of the army, but then it was gone. He remembered he was a civilian. He looked around, but he could not see anything that seemed to call for the Law.

Mr Ohls saw it though. Mr Ohls came straight down through the crowded Saturday people to the loving young couple next to Sylvanus. Mr Ohls' eyes were blazing with that kind of impersonal triumph a towerman has when he discovers a fire in the big woods.

"This is no lovers' lane, you two," Mr Ohls said to them.

They both looked up, startled.

Shades of the Protestant forefathers, thought Sylvanus, *Calvin and Wesley and Cromwell.*

"What?" the boy said.

"You heard me, son. I said this aint no lovers' lane," Mr Ohls said outragedly. He looked around at the people who were all sitting up now watching him, the people Mr Ohls was protecting. "This is a public bathing beach," Mr Ohls said, "and we dont like stuff like that to go on around here."

"Stuff like what?" the boy said.

The girl did not say anything. The red was mounting into her face like the line in a thermometer, even under her tan.

Mr Ohls leaned over and shook the finger of his good hand at the boy. "Listen, son," Mr Ohls said. "Dont talk back to me. I know what I saw. If you and your girl friend havent got the decency to keep from making a display of yourselves on a public beach, why we will see to it for you that you dont, thats all. Thats why we're here."

"Yeah?" the boy said. It was beginning to dawn on him. "I thought maybe you were here to prevent anybody robbing the till of all that money this concession takes in here for those lousy hamburgers." He turned back to his girl. "Dont pay any attention to him, honey," he said.

"I'm still talking to you, boy," Mr Ohls said.

"I wasnt talking to you," the boy said, without looking around. The backs of his ears were very red.

"I think you and your friend just better pick up your stuff and come with me," Mr Ohls decided. "This is a State Park, boy. Run by the laws of the State of Indiana. We're paid to see it stays a respectable place. I dont think we want your kind of trash around here."

"Oh, go peddle your papers," the boy said. "We werent doing anything," He had his hand on his girl's arm trying to soothe her.

"This is the *Law* you're talkin to, boy!" Mr Ohls said. He reached down with his good hand and grabbed the boy by the hair and stepped back, jerking the boy's head back on his neck first, then bowing his back, then bringing him up. The boy came to his feet without a struggle.

"Hey!" the boy said, surprised hurt in his voice. "Whats the idea anyway, mister?"

Mr Ohls did not answer this purely rhetorical question. He got the boy by his right arm, the thin one, with his one hand that looked as strong as both might have been once, and started him up the hill toward the watchful figure of Mr Philips who was already coming down at a dogtrot. Mr Philips got him by his other arm.

"Hey, take it easy," the boy said. He hung back and tried to disengage his bad arm. "I'll go with you. You dont have to hold me. You're hurting my arm."

Mr Ohls did not bother to inquire after this request either. Instead, Mr Ohls swung his false arm, putting his body that was in mid-stride behind it, and without letting go of the arm hit the boy in the mouth with his gloved wooden fist.

Maybe Mr Ohls had not heard him. Sylvanus had heard him. Sylvanus heard also the very hard unflexible sound the wooden fist made on the boy's face, like a club with no give in it.

The boy's head bounced back against the pull of their arms like a man on the ropes in the ring and his knees went slack for a couple of steps so they dragged him. Then his head came back up some. Sylvanus was interested to see that he had not gone clear out. The boy tried to look back at his girl, but he did not offer any other suggestions. As an old soldier, Sylvanus was forced to admire their efficiency.

The girl was still sitting looking stupidly after them, her hands still cupped and just beginning to come away from her face. The people all around on the beach were still staring. They were yackety-yacking now in flushed holiday phrases, excitedly, and a woman's voice broke up out of the rest saying, "They ought to of known better than act like that here." The girl dropped down and lay flat on the blanket as if she would have liked to crawl under it.

Sylvanus got to his feet then, feeling his heart kicking down in his belly and his body trying to shrink back and sit back down out of it, away from conspicuousness. Maybe it was the happy holiday sound in the voices. Maybe it was the righteousness of the woman's high voice. Maybe it was the girl dropping down on the blanket. He had to get up.

"Van," Norma said in an agonized voice. "What are you doing? Sit back down here. Its none of our business."

"I'm going up there," he said, loud, and waited. He was hoping somebody else would get up, too. Nobody got up. Most of them looked at him and then looked away, their eyes curiously flat.

Okay, he thought, okay. Then to hell with all of you.

"You're not going to do any such thing," Norma said. "You sit down."

Sylvanus did not say anything. Maybe it was because he had felt the old Law-fear and was ashamed of it. Or maybe it was because he had been beaten up once by two big Second Army MPs in Memphis and had his nose broken. After they wore their bars, or their pistols, so long a time they got to believing it. You had to say something once in a while, if you wanted to go on with the pretense of being a man.

He pulled a couple deep breaths down into the fluttering and waited for the big rage, the red rebel rage, to come. He could always depend on the big rage, could Sylvanus. He had learned how to utilize it in combat, when you were more scared than this, when there was nothing nowhere to depend on but the big rage that was the only thing that could burn the fear and the cowardice out of you for a little while. Maybe the boy did not know about the big rage yet, well he would learn soon enough when his war came along. When you had the big rage, not even the screaming wild men of Japs could scare you. And certainly not the Strong Arm of The Law that had, ironically, taught it to you.

He had walked down the main street of Memphis where he was in the hospital carrying a fifth of whisky at right shoulder arms and rifle-saluting every officer he met. For that theyd beaten him up and broken his nose. Yet it hadnt hurt him a bit. He hadnt felt it at all.

It was not that he hated or blamed them, they were only doing what they had been taught and got paid for, it was the ones down here on the beach that made you sick to your stomach, that forced you to be different from them. He could feel it rising all through him in a red ecstasy of no-consequences.

He started up the hill after them. "Van!" Norma said. "Van, come back here. Dont make a fool out of yourself."

V

He headed for the path around the corner of the Lodge back to the maintenance parking lot, where they were taking him.

Mr Lemmon was already there ahead of him. Mr Lemmon was standing wide-legged arms-akimbo in the middle of the narrow path. Mr Lemmon had his back to Sylvanus, and was watching them with the boy, like a hotel manager watching his houseman move some nasty-drunks out of his lobby before going back to soothe his ruffled guests. Sylvanus could not get past him, not without some hard elbowing, or else crashing through the thick eight-foot shrubbery.

From the parking lot the Park pickup roared and then faded off down the double dirt path to the asphalt.

Mr Lemmon turned around then.

"Oh, hello there, Mr Merrick," he said easily. He shook his head. "I always hate to see things like this happen, you know? Dont you?"

Mr Lemmon had got the drop on Sylvanus, but he was not going to rub it in. All over now, his face said, lets forget it.

"Where they taking him?" Sylvanus said.

"Over to Sullivan. He'll be tried probably, and fined."

"If he pays them any fine, he's crazy. What he ought to do is prefer counter-charges against both of them."

Mr Lemmon looked surprised. He shook his head. "That wouldnt do any good. That kind of thing always does more harm than good. The best thing that boy can do is write it off to experience and learn from it."

"Yes," Sylvanus said. "It should teach him a lot. If he thinks about it," he said. "Its a great credit to your Park, Mr Lemmon. Its even a fine comment on the whole of our great Middle West culture. For a minute there I thought I was in Georgia."

Mr Lemmon smiled. He moved his shoulders tolerantly. "It isnt my Park," he said. "I only run the concession. It isnt going to help my business any. If I ran this Park—or this world—I'd probably instigate a change of policy in both. But I dont run either, Mr Merrick."

He was right of course, and Sylvanus had to admit to himself grudgingly he was glad now he stopped him, and then their eyes met with some kind of tacit agreement that made Sylvanus Merrick feel warm, and at the same time shocked him with dislike for himself as a hypocrite. It was the first time he could ever remember having been on the other side of the fence.

"I'm going over there," he blurted out suddenly.

"Over where?" Mr Lemmon said friendlily.

"To Sullivan," he said.

"Well, thats up to you," Mr Lemmon smiled. "I suppose in your business things like that help make material."

"Something like that," said Sylvanus.

Norma was waiting for him at the corner.

"Well, I hope you're satisfied now," she said. "You've played the hero—"

She stopped long enough to smile at Mr Lemmon whom she had not seen. Mr Lemmon nodded smiling and discreetly passed by. Sylvanus had no doubt that Mr Lemmon believed they were married. Norma waited till he was clear out of earshot.

"—and made a laughingstock out of both of us," she said. "Everybody on the beach is laughing."

"Let them laugh," he said.

"I couldnt very well stop them," Norma said sadly.

"I'm going to drive over to Sullivan," he said. "Do you want to go along?"

"To Sullivan? What on earth for?"

Norma looked at him incredulously. Then, behind her, he saw the girl come up from the beach carrying their things and go up to Mr Lemmon guiltily. Mr Lemmon was very polite to her, he told where they had taken the boy and advised her to drive their car over there and pick him up there. Mr Lemmon hoped he could be of some service, and just to call on him. The girl thanked Mr Lemmon.

"Havent you had enough heroism for one day?" Norma was saying. "Do you have to go over there and make fools of us again? Do you—"

"All right!" he said violently. "All right! To hell with it! Lets go home, shall we?" The violence in his voice startled him even. It was obvious it startled Norma.

"I think thats just what we'd better do," Norma said stiffly.

They walked along side by side. She did not say anything else. Neither did he. All during the walk down around the lake and back over across the dam with the wild cherries growing tall on both slopes and almost making a tunnel out of the road. All the way back to the cabin.

By the time they got home she was no longer angry. She went into the little kitchen quietly and started getting the lunch. He went out on the porch to get dressed, still thinking what he had been thinking all the silent trip home, how fine it had been yesterday evening when he came home and found her there.

It was too much to expect of a man. You had no right even to demand so much of yourself, if nobody else saw it but you. Life was all compromise anyway. It always had been. It always would be. There would never be any more justice than there was now. Conquer the plague and smallpox arises, conquer smallpox and typhoid arises, conquer typhoid and polio arises. It was not that he expected what he did to make any difference. And he knew how much she loved him. It was a decision that came at some time in every man's life, he knew that too. Maybe you could call it the last death rattle of youth. Twenty-six was a good age for it. And after the spasm was over it wasnt so bad, you could have a good life.

Nature had made it that way, hadnt she? and it was silly to fight Nature, wasnt it? He used to be contemptuous of the men like her father, like his father. Not any more. They were the men who kept the world going, and if they had to be liars to do it, well, the world was based on a lie, wasnt it? There were worse ways of living than lying. And a man could not just renounce the whole heritage, he could not escape it that way, he had to have some place to stand if he wanted to rupture himself moving the world.

He must have known all the time he was dressing what he was going to do. Maybe that was why it took him so long. He went out to the kitchen. Norma was smiling and humming a little as she worked on the lunch.

"Norma," he said.

"Yes, dear?" she said.

"I'm going over to Sullivan."

She put down the bowl and laid the spoon carefully beside it. He guessed she must have known too, then. "Now what?" she said. "I thought we decided that, didnt we?"

You had to admire courage like that.

"You decided it. I didn't. I wanted to go. I wanted you to go too. If you dont want to go, you dont have to. But dont try to keep me from going. You have no right to keep me from going."

"I'm not trying to keep you from going. If you want to go, go. But you'll only be making a fool out of yourself. Out of both of us. If thats what you want to do, go ahead."

"It isnt really my going," he said. "That has nothing to do with it. This is something else, between you and me."

She looked at him a couple of seconds and started to smile, then changed it into a laugh. "I dont see how whether some lovesick boy pays a fine for spooning has something to do with you and me."

"Yes you do," he said. "I'm not saying its sensible. Maybe its crazy. Maybe it wont do any good at all. But its not the boy—I got used to seeing that in the army. Ohls's fist wasnt aimed at that boy, Ohls's first was aimed at you and me, Norma."

"Oh now," Norma laughed. "Back onto Fascism."

"Look," he said. "Lets you and me face it for once. Lets tell the truth to each other for once. We've both lied to each other since we first met, even. You've always intended for me to go into your father's business: all the time we've been talking about other plans, you've intended that, havent you?"

"No," Norma said. "I've wanted you to do what you wanted to do. Always."

"Come on," he said, "come on. Lets both quit being proud, quit being respectable, quit being loving, quit being ashamed of what we honestly think. Lets be honest. For just once."

She looked at him a long time. "I think it would be just as easy for you to do your writing and make some money too," she said finally. "I think that. I dont see why you have to play a part and live in a garret and starve, to be a writer. Do you?"

"I've never starved," he said. "I live pretty good, one thing and another."

"You mean like tending bar at the Moose?"

"Sure," he said. "At least they never try to influence my thinking."

"Maybe that was all right for you by yourself," Norma said. "But as your wife, Van, you owe me something too. I dont want to live like a gypsy. I dont want to be looked down on as cheap. And low class. I want security, for myself and my children."

"You think your mother has security?" Sylvanus said.

"But of course," Norma said. "She never wants for a thing, that my father doesnt buy it for her. If its within reason."

"Then you dont think she ever lays awake nights scheming and worrying and scared to death she'll lose that security, lose your father, every time he goes on one of his bats to Terre Haute or Evansville. Scared that maybe, some day, he might find one he'll keep going back to? That there might not just happen, some place, to be some woman good enough to outsmart her and take him away from her? Do you call that security?"

Norma moved her head and looked down at the bowl. She picked up the spoon and began to stir the salad again. "No woman ever has that kind of security," she said.

"But they could have," said Sylvanus. "If they would only stop living their lives like your mother lives hers."

Norma moved her head on her neck again, looking down at the salad. "I'd rather we didnt discuss my parents," she said. "I think we can leave them out of this. If you want to go over to Sullivan and make a fool out of yourself, you just go right ahead." She looked up at him. "Only remember this, I wont be here when you come back."

He nodded. That was what he had dreaded. He had tried to avoid it every way he knew how.

"You're still using yourself as a carrot under my nose to threaten me, arent you?" he said.

"If you want to put it like that, yes," Norma said.

"You ought to know it wouldnt work any better than it did last time. You ought to know it would only force me into it more."

"But this isnt the last time," Norma smiled cheerfully. "This is now. Go to Sullivan, if you want. There wont be any coming back and giving in dutifully. This time I mean it," she smiled.

"Okay," he said. "I hear you." She still believed it would work.

"We cant go on like this forever," Norma said. "We might as well settle it, once and for all."

"You mean settle who's boss," he said. "Settle who wears the pants."

"Is that whats bothering you?" Norma smiled. "No," she said. "Not at all. But if you cant do one simple thing like this that I ask you— You do owe me something, Van," she said meaningly.

"Yes," he said, "and you always make damned sure I never forget you gave it to me, dont you?"

"Thats a rotten thing to say to me," she said contortedly.

"You asked for it," he said. "You ought to know. You've always said I was a regular blackguard without ethics. Well, you decent women put too high a price on that thing for its actual worth. Some day the bottom will drop out of the market. Some day," he said, "in spite of the decent women, this country will have to start advertising something besides sex. If it just lasts that long."

"But theres no need to get angry, Van," Norma smiled at him. "I'm only doing what you've been wanting, what you've been hoping I'd do."

"I'm not angry," he said. "What in hell gave you that big idea?" She still believed the old carrot would work.

"You really ought to be grateful," Norma said sweetly. "I'm really doing you a big favor. I'm giving you the chance to get free. All you have to do is go to Sullivan. Then you can lie to yourself and say I left you and get out from under without having your conscience bother you. But then," she smiled, "you always have known just how to handle me, havent you, Van?"

"You're quitting me," he said. "I'm not quitting you. Your loving old daddy cant very well get me out and horsehide me for betraying his daughter when its you quitting me. Now can he?"

"Ha," Norma said. "Is that whats scaring you?"

"But cheer up," he grinned. "Cheer up, kid. Theres plenty of other men around you can work on. It wont take you a week to find one, and you can use what you've learned on this one to help you sink the old hook into the next one. Most women need a couple failures to get their technique down letter perfect, anyway, dont they?"

"You son of a bitch," Norma said.

"Kind of hit home, didnt it?" he grinned.

"Get out," she said. "Go back to Arky and Russ and their Terre Haute pigs they keep in stock. Thats where you belong. Go on, get out. Get out. You dont leave a thing, do you? When the warrior dies they not only burn the wives and the weapons and horses but even the dogs and the cats and the utility bills. Dont they? Get out."

"I was just leaving," he grinned, and went out the front door and down the homemade brick steps, thinking it was the first time he had ever really been actually glad they were not married, because there was nothing to make him come back now, thinking he should have mentioned that too.

But outside, where she could not see him, the grin faded out. He could not hold it. He was not mad any more. He felt sick at his stomach. Human beings could be so rottenly disgustingly stinkingly honest, when they got mad enough, and let themselves go.

As he walked out through the trees to the car the house was stiffly silent behind him as if she was listening. He walked very slow, hoping she'd call him. If she called he would go back. But he could not go back on his own hook. Because it would only be the same thing all over again. As soon as she realized she had won she would start right in making him pay. And nothing he could say would be able to reach her.

When he opened the car door he paused to give her a last chance to call. Instead, she started to sob. The sobbing came out clearly through the summer stillness under the trees. She was using the sobbing to make him feel guilty enough to come back without being called. She *still* believed the old carrot would work.

The old familiar sound of the sobbing hanging on the quiet peace of the air made him so furious with outrage he wanted to smash his fist into something. Into the Middle West maybe. The sobbing rode like an old-fashioned ketch, outmoded by steam, on the waves of blue air, affronting him with its absolute female confidence, so that in the midst of the fury he was suddenly bored, tired of the whole thing, the same going over and over, that never made any decision except the same old weary resorting to ruses that in the end they both always employed. He did not want that any more.

He got in the car and slammed the door hard. The sobbing stopped suddenly, as if shocked. But the echo seemed to hang on in the air over him, as he backed out to the asphalt.

He felt as if somebody had just taken handcuffs and a big rope off of him—so that he could reach in his hip pocket and find his wallet was gone.

VI

He drove straight in to the courthouse in Sullivan. There was nobody there except one deputy in the sheriff's office and the usual handful of loiterers out on the steps. The boy had already paid his fine and left with his girl. Mr Philips and Mr Ohls, they told him, had gone right back to Fandalack. He had not passed Philips and Ohls driving in, so he figured they must have stopped off somewhere to have a couple of beers before going back. It was hot work there, at the Park.

He drove very fast going back to the cabin. She was already gone. The sheets were gone off the beds and the curtains she had put up had been taken down. The place already had that fusty vacated smell in it. It was the same smell that had been there when he moved in. The salad bowl was still sitting on the sideboard with the spoon in the uneaten salad. He started packing his own stuff. She had not taken the extra food she had brought up for him. He packed it too. There would not be enough money left to go to Michigan now, but he could take a cabin at Lake Lawler for a month on the refund from the Park. His beans and bacon and bread and the two cans of coffee were still there. He packed it all.

Mr Lemmon was very nice about the refunds for the boat and the cabin. He did not ask Sylvanus down to the basement for a parting beer. Maybe he thought Sylvanus was leaving because of the boy. Sylvanus did not enlighten him. He was keeping his mind on Lake Lawler.

For a man who had made a fool out of himself twice in the same morning Sylvanus felt pretty sharp-edged yet. Lake Lawler was no Fandalack, but it served a purpose. Norma would have considered it more his kind of a place anyway, because while it might have been high class in the '20s, it had all been down hill for Lake Lawler since then so that they had started catering to a less finicky clientele, and Norma's parents would not let her go there any more, so it would be a good place not to run into Norma, and he felt he was not quite up to running into her yet for a while, and it had a dance pavilion with a jukebox on the lip of the lake and a beer concession behind it and there were plenty of dark places to park cars, he might even run into Russ and Arky down there, and if there were no bass in the lake there were at least bluegill and crappie, and it was privately owned so there would be no uniformed hoods running around wearing themselves out protecting its purity, a month at Lake Lawler looked pretty good, he did not feel so bad about leaving Fandalack.

VII

There was a red-headed widow from Mount Carmel, Illinois, staying at Lake Lawler, leasing one of the bungalows—as distinguished from cabins—around on the other side of the lake, who was interested in artists and writers and did not like the Middle West either. She was afraid of a new husband taking her for what the first one had left her. She felt she had earned it and she meant to enjoy it. But she did not let this hurt her appreciation of art. She had chanced to read two of

Sylvanus Merrick's stories, and when she found out he was him, in the flesh, she was anxious to see what his novel was like. So he started in to read the whole thing to her. She bought wonderful scotch, and he thought perhaps he might get new ideas by watching her reactions. But when he read what he wrote to the widow she giggled at all the wrong places, the same places Norma Fry had always used to look shocked at. He even found after a while that he would take to defending the Middle West against her attacks.

It was as if in moving from Fandalack to Lake Lawler Sylvanus had moved from one end of a teetertotter to the other, a teetertotter whose bar and fulcrum was the great Middle West heritage and culture he had almost been ready to believe he had escaped. But he was willing to overlook this because he felt the widow would be a good antidote. Sylvanus had discovered he needed an antidote.

The cabin he had got at Lake Lawler was only one room and there were no trees around it. It was very hot, now that the rainy spell had finally broken, and at night the jukebox music from the pavilion pervaded the cabin and helped the heat keep Sylvanus awake. The sound of the cars that kept driving down toward the swimmers' outhouses to park at the foot of the hill where his cabin was did not help either. A lot of giggling and laughter came from the cars. The people in the cars sounded very happy, they did not seem to mind losing sleep. Sylvanus Merrick, on the other hand, felt he needed a lot of sleep very badly. This was because the heat and the music and the cars kept him awake. And because he was determined to work.

Then, quite suddenly, the novel began to come again. Out of a clear sky. For no apparent reason. Coming all at once, the way the last dozen pieces of a jigsaw suddenly fall into place. He could even see the end of it. That was the fine thing about writing. Sylvanus even quit worrying about the Book-of-the-Month Club. Maybe that was what helped him to sleep. But then writing was the only religious ritual Sylvanus Merrick had ever found that did not require a third party and he worked at it very seriously in the same way a good Catholic has to go to Mass every morning, so that by evening he was always very tired now. Tired enough to sleep.

He gave up going over to see the widow. It embarrassed him to find himself suddenly defending the Middle West which he did not like, and he did not want to upset the balance now, or stop it, now that it had started coming again. He fly-fished for bluegill and drank beer at the concession and slept. Every now and then a great pressure would wake him up in the middle of the night and he would get up and get dressed and tramp hard four or five miles out on the highway under the burnished gunmetal sky that sparkled pulsatingly now that the hot corn-growing weather was here.

VIII

It was on one of these walks that it suddenly came to Sylvanus that maybe he should try living in the Far West, when this novel was done. He had never lived in the West. But he had read that it was the Western women who had first forked a horse, when the side saddle was still a God-given law of propriety. Surely, with mountains and deep woods all around them, they ought to be different out there, Sylvanus Merrick decided. All you had to do was get out of the great Middle West.

GREATER LOVE

I've already given most of the interesting bits on this one in the Introduction. I remember it was the summer when they were filming *Intruder in the Dust* down in Oxford. A friend of mine studying to be a photographer on the GI bill wanted me to go down there with him and introduce ourselves to Faulkner, but I didn't want to. Almost anybody can recognize Sgts Warden and Welsh in "The First." I once served on a Graves Registration Corps detail where a man helped to dig up his own brother. That memory set me to thinking. Published in *Collier's*, Summer, 1951.

ere's that detail roster," Corporal Quentin Thatcher said.

"Thanks," the first sergeant said. He did not look up, or stop working.

"Would you do me a favor?"

"Probably not," the First said. He went on working.

"I wish you wouldn't send Shelb down to the beach on this unloading detail. They've been bombing the Slot three or four times every day since the new convoy got in."

"Pfc Shelby Thatcher," the First said distinctly, without stopping working, "just because he's the kid brother of the company clerk, does not rate no special privileges in my outfit. The 2nd Platoon is due for detail by the roster; you typed it out. Pfc Shelby Thatcher is in the 2nd Platoon."

"So is Houghlan in the 2nd Platoon. But I notice he never pulls any these details."

"Houghlan is the Compny Commander's dog robber."

"I know it."

"See the chaplain, kid," the First said, looking up for the first time. His wild eyes burned the skin of Quentin Thatcher's face. "That ain't my department."

"I thought maybe you would do it as a favor."

"What are you going to do when we really get into *com*bat, kid? up there on the *line?*"

"I'm going to be in the 2nd Platoon," Quentin said. "Where I can look out for my brother Shelb."

"Not unless I say so, you ain't." The First grinned at him evilly. "And I ain't saying so." He stared at Quentin a moment with those wild old soldier's eyes. Then he jerked his head toward the typing table across the mud floor of the tent. "Now get the hell back to work and don't bother me. I'm busy."

"Damn you," Quentin said deliberately. "Damn you to hell. You don't even know what it is, to love somebody."

"For two cents I'd send you back to straight duty today," the First said calmly, "and see how you like it. Only I'm afraid it would kill you."

"That suits me fine," Quentin said. He reached in his pocket and tossed two pennies onto the field desk. "I quit."

"You can't quit," the First grinned malevolently. "I won't let you. You're an ass, Thatcher, but you can type and I need a clerk."

"Find another one."

"After I spent all this time training you? Anyway, there aint a platoon sergeant in the compny would have you. And I still got hopes maybe someday you'll make a soldier. Though I wouldn't know the hell why. Now get the hell out of here and take them papers over to the supply room like I told you, before I throw you over there with them bodily."

"I'm going. But you don't scare me a bit. And the last thing on this earth I'd ever want to be is a soldier."

The First laughed. Quentin took his own sweet time collecting the papers. The two pennies, lying on the field desk, he ignored.

The pennies were still there the next morning when Quentin came out of the orderly tent for a break. He watched the First legging it off down the road toward Regiment, then he walked across to where the four men were sitting on water cans in the tracky mud in front of the supply tent like four sad crows on a fence. They had only got back from the detail an hour before.

"Any news yet?" his brother Shelb asked him.

"Not a bit," Quentin said. "Nothing."

The waiting was beginning to get into all of them. The division had been here a month now, and both the 35th and 161st had gone up to relieve Marine outfits on the hills two weeks ago.

"Where was the first sergeant going, Quentin?" Al Zwermann asked hopefully. "He looked like he was in a hurry." Al Zwermann's brother Vic was in C Company of the 35th.

"Just to Regiment," Quentin said. "See about some kind of a detail."

"Not another detail!" Gorman growled.

"Sure. Ain't you heard?" Joe Martuscelli said sourly. "They done transferred the whole Regiment into the Quartermaster."

"You don't think it might be the order to move, then?" Zwermann asked.

"Not from what I heard over the phone. From what he said over the phone it was just another detail of some kind."

"A fine clerk," Gorman growled. "Why the hell dint you ask him what kind of a detail, you jerk?"

"Go to hell," Quentin said. "Why the hell didn't you ask him? You don't ask that man things."

"How'd the unloading go?'

"The unloading went fine," Shelb grinned. "They only bombed twice, and I stole a full fifth of bourbon off an officer's orderly on one of the transports."

"Yeah," Martuscelli said sourly. "A full fifth. And he has to save it all for his precious big brother."

"You think you'll have time to help drink it, Quent?" Shelb said, getting up, "before the First gets back?"

"Sometimes I don't think we'll any of us ever get to see any action," Gorman growled.

"To hell with the First," Quentin said.

"I'll go get it then," Shelb grinned.

"A hell of a fine way to treat your own squad," Martuscelli said sourly, watching him leave.

"I took a bust from corpul to transfer into this outfit," Gorman growled. "Because it was shipping out. They put me in Cannon Compny and I took another bust from pfc to get in a rifle compny. All because I wanted to see action."

"We all enlisted," Martuscelli said sourly.

"All I ask is they give me a rifle," Gorman growled. "None of your 155s for this soldier. Just a rifle, a bayonet and a knife. That's all. Gimme that and I'm ready." He thought a second, then added inconclusively, "Maybe couple grenades."

"You talk like my brother Vic," Zwermann said.

Somebody grunted. On the road that had not been a road a month ago a couple of jeeps hammered by, fighting the mud that came clear up to their belly plates. From where the men sat, the rows of coconut trees wheeled away in every direction like spokes from a hub. The sun was bright and clear in the sea air under the tall trees of the grove. It was a fine summery morning. Whenever the wind veered you could hear the sound of the firing from back in the hills.

"Vic's up there now," Zwermann said wonderingly.

"Well, when we do go up," Quentin said suddenly, committing himself, "I'm putting in for straight duty. With the 2nd Platoon. Soon's we got our orders to move."

"What the hell for?" Gorman asked, startled.

"Because I want to," Quentin said.

"If you do, you're nuts," Martuscelli said sourly.

"Ha," Gorman growled. "He won't. You know where he'll be when we go in, don't you? He'll be sitting under a hill on the first sarnt's lap punching his typewriter. That's where."

"You think so?" Quentin said.

"I know so. You don't think the First is going to let his protégé get where it's dangerous, do you?"

"I'm putting in to the Company Commander," Quentin said. "Not to the first sergeant."

"So what, clerk? you think that'll make any difference?"

"Don't worry about the clerks," Quentin said. "There's a lot of things you don't know about soldiering, too."

"What do you want to do it for, Quentin?" Zwermann said.

"Oh, a lot of things," Quentin said vaguely, "but mainly so I'll be able to look after Shelb."

"I'm glad my brother's in Africa," Martuscelli said sourly.

"I'm gladder yet," Gorman growled, "I ain't got one."

"Vic can take care of himself," Zwermann said. "Better than me." He was looking away from them.

"In a war," Gorman growled, "*every* man's got to take care of himself. That's my philosophy."

"That's a hell of a thing to say!" Quentin said. Then he began to laugh, feeling a wild need to do something—he didn't know what—and there was nothing to do.

"What're you laughing at, clerk?" Gorman said stiffly.

"Because," Quentin said, stopping himself. "I'm laughing because here comes Shelb with the bottle, and here comes the First back from Regiment just in time to spoil everything."

"What'll I do with it?" Shelb said.

"Well, don't just stand there," Martuscelli said savagely. "Hide the damn thing." He grabbed the bottle desperately and stuck it down between two of the stacked water cans.

"If he finds it," Gorman said bitterly, "I know where it'll go."

"Thatcher!" the First bellowed. He was raging.

"Yes, sir," Shelb said resignedly.

"Not you," the First raged, "damn it."

"What do you want?" Quentin said.

"Go down and get Sergeant Merdith. Tell him to get his men together and report to me. The 2nd Platoon is going out on a detail."

There was a dull pause of adjustment.

"But hell, First," Martuscelli protested, "we just now got back from one."

The First said, "And you're just now going out on another one. Ain't you heard? There's a war on. The 1st and 3rd Platoons and the Weapons Platoon already out. Who you think I'm going to send? the cook force?"

"What kind of a detail is it, Sergeant?" Zwermann asked.

"How the hell do I know! You think they tell me anything? All they tell me is how many men. And how soon." He ran his fingernails through his hair a moment. "You're going up in the hills," he said, "with a shavetail from the Graves Registration Corps. You're going up to dig up casualties and carry them down to the graveyard so the Quartermaster Salvage can come in and clean up."

"That's great," Martuscelli said.

"Well," the First raged, "what the hell're you waiting for, Thatcher? Get a move on. The truck's on its way."

"Sergeant," Quentin said, "I'd like to have permission to go along on this detail."

"What do you think this is, Thatcher? A vacation resort? There's work to be done."

"I've done everything you had laid out for me."

The First looked at him shrewdly. "Okay," he said. "Go. *Now get the hell down there and get Sergeant Merdith.*"

"Right," Quentin said, and took off.

Behind him, he heard the First say, "The rest of you men can wait here. But first Martuscelli, I want that bottle. Maybe it'll teach you not to be so slow the next time. You men know better than to have whisky in camp. It's against Army Regulations."

There were four trucks with the GRC second lieutenant. The detail rode in the first two. They wound away down through the endless coconut grove, breasting the mud like swimmers, the two empty trucks lumbering along behind.

"I always wondered how they got them down to the cemetery," Martuscelli said.

"Well, now you know," Gorman growled.

It took them an hour to get through the belt of jungle in low gear. Then they came up out of it into the hills like submarines surfacing and ground on for another hour up the hills before they stopped at one that had a crumbling line of slit trenches along the rearward slope.

"Okay, everybody out," the GRC lieutenant said briskly, climbing out of the cab of the first truck. "Each man get a shovel."

The drivers dropped the tail gates and the detail clambered down and went immediately to the lip of the hill. Beyond the crest was a wide saddle that led up to the next hill. The saddle was littered with all kinds of equipment—packs, entrenching tools, helmets, rifles, bayonets, abandoned stretchers, even stray shoes and empty C ration cans. It gave the impression that everyone had suddenly dropped everything in a mad rush to cover ground.

"If any of you are interested in tactics," the GRC lieutenant said, pointing to a faint haze of smoke three miles to the east, "that's the present line of the 35th Infantry over there. Three days ago the 35th was here, and jumped off across this saddle."

The men looked at the distant hills, then at the far-off line of smoke from which sporadic sounds of firing came faintly, then at the saddle below them. There were a few half-muttered comments.

"Okay, fellows," the GRC lieutenant said briskly. "First, I want to warn you about duds and unexploded grenades. Don't touch them. There's nothing to worry about as long as nobody gets wise, but the Ordnance hasn't been in here yet.

"Now," he said, "I want you to spread out. We're only covering the saddle today. Make a line and whenever you see a grave, stop. Some of them, as you see, are marked with bayoneted rifles stuck in the ground. Others are marked with just helmets on sticks. Still others aren't marked at all, so be watchful. We don't want to miss any.

"If there are dog tags on them, make sure one is fastened securely to them and give the other to me. If there's only one, leave it on them, and come get me and I'll note the information. If there's no dog tags, just forget it.

"It's best to work in threes or fours. Two men can't handle one very well, as advanced as the decomposition is by now. And there's no rush, men. We've got all day to cover the area and we want to do a good job. Someday after the war they'll be shipped home to their families.

"There are shelter-halfs to roll them in in the last two trucks. The best way is to work shovels in under the head, the knees and the buttocks; that's why it's best for three to work together on one; and then roll them up out of the hole with one concerted movement onto the shelter-half which you have already placed alongside. That way you don't get any on you, and you also keep them from coming apart as much as possible.

"Now. Any questions?" the GRC lieutenant said briskly. "No? Okay then, let's go to work," he said, and sat down on the running board of the first truck and lit a cigarette.

The line spread out and moved forward down the crest out onto the saddle and began breaking up into little huddles of moving shovels from which there began to come strained exclamations followed by weak laughter and curses.

As each mound was opened, the smell, strange and alien as the smell of the jungle, burst up out of it like a miniature explosion and then fell heavily back to spread like mercury until it met and joined the explosions from other mounds to form a thick carpet over the whole saddle that finally overflowed and began to drip down into the jungled valleys.

"Just like a treasure hunt back home in the Y.M.C.A.," Martuscelli muttered sourly, sweating heavily.

"You don't reckon I'll ever look like that, do you?" Gorman growled, grinning.

"If you do," Shelb said, "I won't speak to you."

"What his best friends wouldn't tell him," Quentin laughed wildly.

"Well, I hope you're happy now, clerk," Gorman growled. "You finally got to come along and find out what straight duty in a rifle company's like. You still putting in for it?"

"Sure," Quentin said. "Wouldn't miss it."

Al Zwermann, of them all, was the only one who did not say anything, but nobody noticed. They were all too busy trying to carry off the collective fantasy that they were unmoved.

It was Quentin's turn to feel for the tags at the sixth mound, and when he brought them out and cut one off and read it he was somehow not surprised at all. The tag read:

ZWERMANN VICTOR L

12120653 T43 B

and Quentin put it in the handkerchief with the other five and straightened up and wiped his hand off and heard his voice saying toughly, "Well, let's get him out."

"Let me see that tag, will you, Quentin?" Zwermann said.

"What tag?" he heard his voice say. "This one?"

"I've seen all the others. Let me see that one."

"I don't even know which one it was, now, Al."

"Quentin, let me see that tag!"

Shelb, Martuscelli and Gorman were still standing at the head, knees and buttocks with their shovels. They had all known Vic back at Schofield, and Vic's battalion of the 35th had come over on the same transport with them. Quentin noticed that there was an odd, distant look on all their faces except Zwermann's and it made him think of those slugs in the garden with their eyes on the ends of two horns and when they got scared or worried they pulled in the horns.

"Well," Martuscelli said with a voice that had been pulled in along with the horns, "we might as well get him out of there."

"Don't touch him," Zwermann said, still holding the tag.

"But, Al," Quentin said, "We got to get him out of there, Al. We can't leave him there," he said reasonably. "That's against orders."

"I said don't touch him, damn you!" Zwermann yelled. He picked up one of the shovels and started for Martuscelli and Gorman and Shelb, who were still holding theirs and standing all together like three hens in the rain. "You're not going to put any shovels on *him*, damn you!"

They let go of their shovels and stepped back guiltily, still all together like three hens in the rain. Zwermann stopped and brandished the shovel at them and then flung it over the edge of the saddle into the jungle.

"Nobody's going to touch *him* with shovels!" he yelled.

The four of them backed off slowly, back up the saddle toward the hill where the GRC lieutenant and Sergeant Merdith were watching. The men working at the other mounds near them began to back off, placatingly in the same way, still holding their shovels, collecting the men at the further mounds as they moved, until the whole line that had descended into the saddle was slowly backing up out of the saddle.

"Nobody's going to touch *him!* I'll shoot the first man that touches *him!* Nobody's going to see *him!*"

The line went on backing placatingly out of the saddle, and Zwermann stood holding them off as if at gun point and cursing, his bald head shining in the afternoon sun.

"My Lord," the GRC lieutenant said dismally, when they were hidden behind the number one truck. "I wouldn't've had this happen for anything. What do you suppose he's going to do?"

They stood, milling a little like nervous sheep, listening to Zwermann moving around down on the saddle. Then they heard him staggering up the slope to the number two truck, where he dropped something heavily onto the iron floor and then clambered in. Then there was silence. It was Sergeant Merdith who finally peered over the hood.

Zwermann was sitting on the bench of the truck, glaring out at them. He had gotten his brother out of the hole by himself and wrapped him up in the shelter-half and carried him up and put him instinctively, without thinking, in the same truck he himself had ridden out in.

"Let's just leave him alone," the GRC lieutenant said. "He'll be all right now."

Sheepishly they straggled back down onto the saddle and went back to work. When they had the rest of the corpses wrapped and stacked in the two empty trucks, as many men as could squeezed into the first truck. Only an unlucky handful rode home in the second truck. Zwermann sat on the bench, holding a shovel, and glared at them forbiddingly all the way down.

At the cemetery on the Point there was a moment of unpleasant suspense when the handful of GRC men, who had taken over with the swift efficiency of long practice, prepared to unload the number two truck. But Zwermann only glared at them with a kind of inarticulate fury and seemed to feel he had relieved himself of some obscure obligation and did not protest. He climbed down and started off to walk the mile and a half back to the bivouac.

"Somebody better go with him," the GRC lieutenant said apprehensively. "He's liable to wander off in the jungle or something. I'm still responsible for you men till I deliver you back to your outfit."

"We'll go," Quentin said, "the four of us. We're sort of his buddies."

"Then you're responsible for him, Corporal," the GRC lieutenant said after them. "You and these other men."

When they caught up to him, Zwermann glared at them with the ferocious suspicion of a man who has learned not to trust strangers. But he did not protest their walking behind him.

That night, instead of waiting till they got marching orders, Quentin Thatcher put in to the Company Commander personally to go back to straight duty with the 2nd Platoon immediately. His request was immediately rejected, emphatically and with finality.

Five days later the Regiment moved out, and Quentin marched with the Company Headquarters at the head of the company column beside the First, who carried a Listerine bottle full of whisky and took frequent gargles for his sore throat without offering Quentin any for his. The 2nd Platoon was somewhere in the rear.

Their battalion hiked seven miles the first day and bivouacked that night in the jungle, dead beat. The next day they crossed an Engineers' bridge and started up a steep hill that rose abruptly up out of the jungle from the riverbank. The noise of the firing did not sound any closer than it had back down on the beach.

Then they came up over the crest of the hill and found themselves in combat. The noise that had sounded faint in the jungle beat about their ears and fell upon them with both drumming fists. It seemed a little unfair for no one to have warned them.

The hilltop was alive with men, but none of them noticed the new arrivals except to curse them for being in the way. The men cursed one another ferociously and ran back and forth, with boxes of ammo and C rations. Over on the next hill the men in Quentin's battalion could see the little black figures of the 3rd Battalion toiling doggedly up the slope toward other little black figures at the top.

Their first reaction was to tiptoe back down the hill and get the hell out of the way before they disturbed somebody or were run over; or at least to go back down and come up properly this time, in squad column with scouts out. They stood around awkwardly, trying to see, waiting for someone to tell them what they were supposed to do, feeling like poor relations at the family reunion.

Quentin found himself standing beside Fred Beeson, the supply sergeant, who had insisted on coming to see the fun.

"I thought they'd have a better system of supply than this in combat," Beeson said excitedly. "Didn't you?"

"Yeah," Quentin said, wondering what had become of the First. He looked around to see if he could see Shelb. His eyes found the First, over on the right. The big man was kneeling over some cases of grenades and hacking at them with his bayonet as if he were using a machete, deftly splitting box after box open around the middle.

"Hey, hey! let's go!" the First, who still had his Listerine bottle, whooped, drunkenly happy. "Let's go, let's go. Here's grenades. Who wants grenades?" he hollered, pulling the black containers out of the racked boxes and forward-passing them like footballs at arms raised out of the crowd.

"Let's go, you men!" he roared at them. "What the hell you guys waiting for?"

"Yeah," somebody said indecisively, "what we waiting for?"

They started fixing bayonets, as if each man had thought of it first, individually by himself, and then they were walking down the hill with the Company Commander in the lead, as if that were the most nearly normal thing to do, under the circumstances.

"Get your eggs here!" the First howled at them happily as they passed. "Nice fresh yard eggs!"

Quentin found himself in motion between the mess sergeant and two of the cooks. They had also come along to see the fun. Wondering again where Shelb was, he looked around and discovered he was surrounded by fun-seeking members of the cook force.

"This is better'n slingin' hash any day," one of them grinned at him excitedly.

"Yeah," Quentin said. *We're in combat,* he thought; and then repeated it: *we're in combat.* Was this all there was to it?

Ahead of them the hill sloped down, long and gradual and quite bare, to a brushy creek at the bottom. Ahead was the steep hill where the black figures of the 3rd Battalion were still toiling doggedly, but closer to the top now.

As Quentin watched them, he saw one marionette at the top throw something down at another marionette below him. The second marionette turned without hesitation and jumped out from the side of the hill as a man jumps out from a ladder. He fell maybe seven yards before he hit again and began to roll. From where he had jumped something burst black like a cannon cracker. The second marionette stopped rolling and got up and began to toil doggedly back up toward the top again. The first marionette had disappeared over the crest.

Then Quentin's company was at the bottom, fighting through the brush and starting up the slope, and Quentin could not see the men at the top any more.

Mortar shells were beginning to drop down here and there around Quentin's company, and that was when Quentin noticed that the explosions did not make any noise. Men around him were beginning to shuck out of their combat packs and leave them where they fell.

Quentin shucked out of his own pack, wishing momentarily that he knew where Shelb was. He looked around.

He could not see Shelb, but way off to the left he saw Gorman a second, climbing doggedly. Then somebody came between. Gorman had no pack. Gorman's face looked peculiar, as if somebody had poulticed it with plastic wood. The heel.

The silent mortar shell explosions were getting thicker, and the 3rd Battalion was puffing hard and digging holes along the military crest, in the shelter of the real crest of the hill. As the uneven line passed through between the holes on toward the real crest, the diggers glared up at them furiously without stopping digging. Then Quentin's company was over the crest and going down the second hill toward the jungle that came halfway up, only this time there was nobody in front of them and everything changed weirdly and seemed to shift its gears. Quentin felt as if a light bulb had been turned off in his mind. He was all alone in the silence of the dark locked closet.

He was also getting very tired.

Two strangers who were walking beside him on his left suddenly quit and lay down to rest. Quentin closed over automatically, wishing he had guts enough to quit and lay down to rest. That Gorman. Quentin's legs ached, and a dull rage began to grow in him at this obvious laziness that would only leave more dirty work for him and Shelb to do.

A mortar shell burst silently in front of him and he saw three more strange men he did not know lie down to rest. Quentin felt like kicking them, but he closed over further left and went around. Smoke burned his eyes. One of the strangers yelled something at him. The other two strangers were asleep already. Quentin went on. There sure were a lot of strangers with the company today.

It was when he closed over that he saw Shelb for the first time since at breakfast. Shelb was walking with Joe Martuscelli and Al Zwermann and Gorman, off to Quentin's left. Quentin had difficulty telling them apart; they all four seemed to be wearing the same poulticed face. As he opened his mouth to yell at them through the silence, a mortar shell geysered silently in front of them and three of them jerked, and lay down to rest. Only Shelb went on walking.

Quentin was outraged. *Who do they think they are? They're no better than I am. Or Shelb is. Is everybody going to quit but me and Shelb?*

Joe Martuscelli sat back up and looked at Quentin dully. Shakily, he got to his feet with his rifle, holding his left arm close in to his side, and started on.

Sure, Quentin thought furiously, *that damn Martuscelli, he always was a goldbrick. Looks like me and Shelb will have to do it all.*

Then Shelby, who had moved perhaps ten yards, dropped his rifle and put his hands to his face and fell down.

Why, damn him! Quentin thought outragedly. *I thought at least he would stick with me. What do they want me to do? win this war all by myself?*

Shelb did not move and Martuscelli stumbled past him and went on. Shelb lay as he had fallen, face down and shoulders limp, his lax hands still up by his face.

Well, I'm damned, Quentin thought disgustedly, *if he hasn't fainted dead away.* Embarrassment for his brother made him suddenly hate him for failing in the clutch. *Gone yellow. Can't take it. Ought to go and kick him up.*

"Hey!" the man on his right said. "There's one. I see one."

"Where?" Quentin said.

"There," the man said. "Right there. See him?"

"No," Quentin said. The man was a big man and right beside him but his voice came from a long way off.

"Well, I see him," the big man said. He raised his ride and fired the whole clip into the jungle. "Must of missed him," he said. "Come on."

"Okay," Quentin said. Then he stopped. Fifteen yards away on the edge of the jungle was a dark blob of wood on the side of a tree. Somehow his eyes had fastened themselves upon it and recognized it for a helmet. He was astounded.

"What is it?" the man beside him said.

"Shh," Quentin said craftily. He dropped down to a kneeling position. No shooting from the offhand this time; he was taking no chances. The big man beside him stopped, trying to see what it was, and Quentin chuckled to himself.

As he took up the slack and started the squeeze, the helmet moved. Slowly and carefully it raised itself and a face appeared over the sights. Quentin was astonished. He touched her off and in firing was even more astonished to see the same plastic-wood poultice on this face, too.

Ha, he's afraid, he thought savagely; and all the hate and fear of the past two hours compressed itself into his forefinger vindictively.

The recoil slammed his shoulder and he kept both eyes open like he had been taught and saw the face open redly like a thrown tomato. A piece of bridgework popped out of the mouth.

"I got him!" Quentin yelled. "I got him!"

"Good work," the big man said. "Congratulations."

"Come on!" Quentin said. He jumped up to run to the tree. A mortar shell, a ninety, burst close by and slammed him right back down. He lay there stunned by the concussion, reminded that there were other Japanese. He had forgotten the war.

"Come on," the big man beside him said "Get up. You ain't hurt. Get up!" A big hand grabbed Quentin by the shoulder and hoisted him back up.

His chin was bleeding from a cut where it had hit a rock but it did not seem important. He wiped it off and started to walk on toward the jungle. The big man stayed close beside him. All around them groups of men were entering the jungle.

The dead Japanese lay sprawled out on his back. The bullet had gone in just below his nose and smashed the teeth. Thick glue-like blood had filled the mouth and run out at both corners to hang in strips down to the ground.

"He looks awful dead," Quentin said, looking at the other man. Slowly, he recognized him; it was the First. But his face looked different.

"Your face looks different," Quentin said.

"So does yours," the First said.

"It does?" Quentin said. He felt of his face. "I need a shave," he said. He picked up the piece of bridgework that had popped out of the Jap's mouth and stuck it between his helmet and the liner strap and struck a pose for the First.

"The immortal infantryman," the First said. "How about his wallet?"

"I forgot!"

Quentin fished it out of the grimy shirt pocket. There was a picture. It showed a Japanese woman holding a baby and smiling toothily. There was Japanese writing in up-and-down lines on the back. There was no money.

"Tough luck," the First grinned.

"Mine by right of conquest," Quentin said. "I guess you won't be so damn wise about clerks now, will you?"

"Nope," the First said. "I guess not."

"You and Gorman."

"Want a little drink?" the First said.

"Sure," Quentin said. The rifle fire was getting heavier down below in the jungle. He wiped his mouth. "Hear that? Come on." He turned down toward the firing, then turned back. "Did you see that damn Shelb poop out back there on the hill?"

"No," the First said. "I didn't see him."

"He was right beside us."

"I didn't see him," the First said, impassively.

"You don't have to kid me," Quentin said. "I know you saw him. Wait'll I get my hands on him! I'll beat his damned head in!" He moved away between the trees down the hill toward the firing, looking for more Japs to kill.

"He'll never make a soldier. Come on, First, let's go," he said earerly to the man moving slowly behind him. "Come on, damn it, let's go."

"I'm coming," the First said, watching up in the trees. "Go ahead. I'm right beside you. Go ahead, you're doing fine."

"He ought to be shot," Quentin said.

"Watch the trees," the First said. "You're doing fine."

THE KING

Playboy bought and published this one in October 1955 right after I wrote it, largely because I was famous then and they were jazz specialists. *Playboy* thought of it as "a sort of Profile, not a story" but didn't know what to do about this and printed it anyway. I myself think of it as a good example of the 'Double Plot' story, in which two stories, almost unrelated but spiritually connected, are taking place. For me the real story is the story of the college band, and what happens to them, like has happened to so many hundreds and thousands of others.

Whon we met Willy Jefferson, "King" Jefferson, our band had already been following his progress for over five years. His records used to cause more argument in our band than Stephen Grappelly's Hot Four and the question of whether the violin ought not to be morally disqualified as a jazz instrument. All we had to do was to put on some of King's records and listen to that trumpet and we would end up by bringing in everybody from Panassié and Rudi Blesh to Dave Dexter, Jr.

Our whole band were juniors in high school when they were combing the backwoods of Louisiana looking for King. The next summer, when Bob Rhynolds of US Records finally found him, our band was playing its first booking away from home ground as a truly professional outfit. We manufactured schmaltz for ten weeks in the pavilion at Seraphan Lake upstate for the dancers. Our high school music director led the outfit. We had to put up with him because he got the job for us. He was friends with the owner and also had the soft-drinks concession. We came home from there sick of Guy Lombardo, but with our minds made up to all go together in a body to the same university so we could continue to develop our band as a unit, in spite of the parents.

Bob Rhynolds was already making plans then to record Mister King. He started collections, via *Down Beat* and some others, to buy King a new horn and some teeth. And he wrote a couple of articles about him for *Down Beat*, telling how at sixteen the old man had played second cornet with Buddy (King) Bolden's Band; how, when they finally carted poor Buddy off to the nut ward, he had apprenticed himself to Freddy (King) Keppard, Buddy's successor; how later, while slow-developing Joe (King) Oliver was still earning his feed as a butler, he had organized the Triple Eagle Band and with it won himself the title of third King in that dynasty which would die with Joe Oliver in a Savannah poolroom cleaning spittoons. And how finally, when they closed down Storyville in the First War to protect the virtue of the soldiers and sailors, he had disappeared off with a circus band and not been heard from since, mainly because after his horn got busted up in a fight at a dance and the rest of his teeth started to go he was forced to retire to the New Arcadia rice fields where he had started, without the money for a new horn, or for new teeth. And there he stayed for twenty years, until this letter from Rhynolds addressed in care of the New Arcadia postmaster found him, still working in the rice fields.

The story caught the public's imagination, and the response was terrific. A lot of people who were not even jazz fans sent in money for him. Our band would have sent in ten bucks on that horn and them teeth ourself if we had not been so short of cash.

Bob was writing King regularly, because King was giving him the dope about the early days for his book *Jazzbabies,* which was why he contacted King in the first place, but now this offer of recording him had taken hold of him, and he published King's thank-you letter in *Down Beat.* King wrote he was very pleased and proud over the response, and that he was excited over the prospect of being able to play again for the audiences of the world, whom, King admitted, he had not even expected would even remember him. He said maybe his hair was gray but the only thing old about him was his clothes. And he was waiting eagerly for the chance to play for all the good people who were helping to get him his teeth and his horn.

By the time the Rhynolds records, which were to create such a stir, finally reached the market, our band had graduated and were playing our second big summer job, at Edmond's Point in Ohio. Our drummer's uncle owned the amusement park there. He talked to the pavilion owner. Edmond's Point was a summer resort on Lake Erie but not of the class of Russell's Point or Cedar Point and they only had the name bands in on the weekends. We did the playing the other four nights of the week.

It was our drummer's mother, together with two of the mothers of our reed section, who had hatched the idea to write the drummer's uncle and appeal to him. They did that after the band had declared itself about to embark for Chicago to seek a summer playing job somewhere down around the vicinity of South State Street.

Actually, it was not nearly as bad as it sounds. Our drummer's uncle hardly ever bothered to check up on us. We could buy all the bottles we wanted. And our two cabins were off by themselves on a spit, so that after we knocked off from work at midnight we could go home and play our own kind of music and jam to our hearts' content without waking up anyone. And of course, we had our records and player.

We bought the Rhynolds records as soon as they were out.

You have to remember we were all serious about the future of jazz music in general, and our own in particular. Coupled to this was the fact that they were important historically. They were the first cuttings ever to be made of King Jefferson's legendary trumpet, and they would provide a lasting link between the lost music of Buddy Bolden and King Oliver's old acoustical recordings from the days of Dreamland and Royal Gardens. We held great expectations for them.

Well, what we heard, sitting there on that screen porch looking out over Lake Erie, was a style of trumpet that was rawer and coarser than any we had known existed, including our own grade school efforts when we first got our horns. Gutty wasn't the right word for it at all. Armstrong played gutty trumpet, with a high polish and technical refinement of guttiness. This trumpet had no polish. It was as unpolished as our bass man's fingernails he had never learned to stop biting. King Oliver's cornet might occasionally sound antiquated to modern jazz ears—mainly because of the old acoustical-type recordings—but always it had a sensitivity of tone and precise originality of phrase that nobody, not even Armstrong, could beat, though he might tie it. This trumpet didn't have that either. This trumpet sounded as if a man whose reflexes had forsaken him was fumbling and choking to get half-remembered things in his head out through the mouth of his horn. And to complete it, there was not a single original phrase in the whole collection of sides. The numbers were all traditional old New Orleans numbers, and the trumpet's treatments of them were the same old trite treatments, solos so ancient they had beards, so hackneyed we all knew every note before it came out the horn. And yet, with all the faults and blunderings, you couldn't deny that there was power in the trumpet, a strong emotional power, that hit you hard.

All this was a pretty big lump for our musical natures to swallow and digest. We were disciples of men like the early Hawk, and Jimmy Archey, and Pops Foster, and Art Hodes, and old Sidney Bechet, mostly men whose music had grown and smoothed out and changed since they left New Orleans. And here we were being asked to appreciate a man whose music had not changed since around 1910. But we made it. Not all in one day, naturally. But by the end of the summer we were ready to admit he was almost as good as Bob Rhynolds maintained he was. Maybe the opinion of the public in general had something to do with it.

Even our reed section who disliked him (led by the saxes, naturally, but also reinforced by the bass and piano) argued against him theoretically, rather than personally. By that I mean, they too had accepted him as a permanence, as a big man in the field who would have to be reckoned with. They would have only sneered at a third-rater, not argued.

The critical opinion didn't agree any better than our band did. Some of the critics, who had previously lauded Bob Rhynolds' rediscovery of King, were frankly shocked and disillusioned, they said. The Opinions ran all the way from the prophecy that King Jefferson would immediately sink back into the obscurity he deserved, to the prophecy that King Jefferson would immediately rise to the top and remain there for good, above Armstrong. Several writers feared King would give jazz the *coup de grâce* of cacophony. Others maintained jazz had at last reached the long-awaited fulfillment of its golden promise.

Whatever effect the argumentative reviews had on King himself when he read them, they certainly didn't hurt his popularity any. The general non-jazz public went wild over him. King and his band began to get more engagements in New Orleans than they could handle. A couple of record store owners in L.A. made a trip clear from California to record him under their own label. Another guy, from Pennsy, drove all the way down to New Orleans to record him himself. Before long King was recording right and left, for just about everybody but the big companies.

Our band enrolled en masse in James Millikin at Decatur that fall, majoring in Business Administration, a concession made to our various parents in return for the right to enroll in a body, and continued to follow the Cinderella Story from up there.

For that was what it was. We could see it in the change in our own band. The college kids, instead of asking for swing a la Goodman or Dorsey, at the dances we played, wanted to hear New Orleans a la King Jefferson. It was hard on our saxes, and the bass and piano, but the rest of our people thought it was great.

In the spring King appeared in Frisco with a series of Rudi Blesh jazz lectures, as a sort of living example. He played to an overflow crowd and told them the story of jazz in his own words, and of his happiness at finding so many good people who still liked his music. The critics' Greek chorus immediately swelled in volume, some pointing out that the story of jazz King told wasn't anywhere near the truth, while others pointed out that the music in King's soul made him use words like a poet.

Then a small group of rebels, led by Bob Rhynolds naturally, voted him into third place in the *Esquire* Jazz Poll, and he was in.

In January of our sophomore year he played the Jazz Poll Concert from New Orleans. That spring Sidney Bechet brought him up to play with his band at the Savoy in Boston. That didn't last long, but King had stopped off in New York for a sensational jam session at Jimmy Ryan's that made all the trade papers, and appeared on Condon's coast-to-coast program. That fall he and his old band opened at the Standish Casino on the lower East Side. They were an immediate sensation. *Time, The New Yorker, Mademoiselle, Vogue, Esquire,* and the New York papers ran pics and stories on them. *Collier's* ran a full length feature on King and he was interviewed over the local radio stations. At the Standish he was pulling them in, not only the jazz fans but the general public.

Actually, it didn't happen all that quickly. There was a time lag of over a year of hard luck in there, but looking back you tend to forget that. When King went out to Frisco our band were still freshmen at Millikin; when he opened at the Standish we were juniors. But looking back on it it still seems it all happened in one long breathless rush.

Maybe that is because the popularity, when it did come back, came so hard and so strong that it was as if it were not fickle and had never faded, but had instead kept right on growing.

New York had taken him into its arms with all its enthusiasm for what is new, and the out-of-towners asked to go to the Standish the first place, when they got in. And in the newspapers he was The King.

Our band was having its own troubles all through that time. It was all right for us during the school year, what with the dance jobs, but during both of those summers the only jobs we could get were dances at the local Moose, Elks and Country Club, and some weekends at Lake Lawler right next to home.

It was the same thing the next year, too, the summer after our junior year at Millikin. The home-rule was, if we couldn't get a regular-paying job playing, we had to work. And when the band wanted to try Chicago on its own again, the parents set their collective foot down on that.

When we went back to school our senior year, we had what amounted to a signed ultimatum. If we could not get the band established as a self-paying proposition during the summer after we graduated, then we would all come home and go into the various businesses. Our bass man had an uncle who owned a couple of newspapers in Connecticut, and he promised to use his pull to get the band a job there for the summer, but after that we were on our own. Our parents were financing us for that one summer. We all knew how that would end.

It wasn't much of a deal, but it was all we could get.

The first thing we did when we got our bags unpacked in Stamford, where the job was, was to take in New York. There were only five of us, the others were coming to Stamford in another car and hadn't got in yet. In New York we headed straight for 52nd Street. Bechet was playing at Jimmy Ryan's, and we went straight there, without even stopping to look at the strippers' pictures down along The Street, and we did not come out till they closed at four in the morning.

We had hit town on a Saturday night and Ryan's was crammed. There was a fog of beery breath and tobacco smoke that burned your eyes, and so much screaming you could not hear yourself think and had to concentrate hard to even hear Bechet any at all. It was wonderful. We stood at the bar to save money. We were dressed right, cardigans and drapes, double-Windsors and spread collars, and pretty soon some of the cats there had swept us in and we were arguing Mezz Mezzrow, musician versus writer.

We had the best time we'd ever had in our lives. The first time of anything only happens to you once, in your life, I guess.

Maybe there was something significant in the fact that we went straight to Ryan's, to hear Bechet. We did not even consider going to the Standish Casino. King Jefferson was still playing there.

When we left, one of those cats yelled to be sure and come down for the jam session tomorrow.

We knew all about the Jimmy Ryan's Sunday afternoon jam sessions, of course. I mean, we knew they paid the players. And we knew they charged a buck and a half. We knew sidemen didn't just bring their horns down and sit in. In other words, we knew they were commercialized. But we also knew—how well—musicians had to earn a living, too. And hick strangers from the Middle West don't get into the apartments of featured strippers. Or of unfeatured strippers.

We got there early Sunday. The instruments weren't set up yet. A couple of the featured artists were floating around accepting drinks from the cats. The rest weren't there. We bought our tickets, and went across the street to Johnny's Tavern to do our drinking. We had already learned that trick last night. The rest of the featured artists were over there where rye is thirty-five a shot. Ryan's was having Pet Brown on alto, Ed Hall on clarinet, Jerry "Wild Bill" Bailey trumpet, Baby Dodds drums, Pops Foster bass, and somebody else on piano and guitar. By the time we had our drinking done, they had all sifted out and gone back across the street to work and you could hear them clear outside as we crossed the street to Ryan's.

It was during the second break of the afternoon that we saw King Jefferson standing at the bar. We were on our way out to Johnny's to have a drink. King was talking to Baby Dodds about Punch Miller, and we stopped to listen. It was a minute before we noticed Baby was embarrassed and trying real hard not to be constrained, King had his trumpet case under his arm.

"Is Punch Miller in town?" one of us asked.

The King swung around so hard he almost fell over. He was real drunk. "You know old Punch?" he asked eagerly.

"Naw," one of us said. "Just his music. We got some of his records."

"Yeah, he in town. I just telling Baby."

That was when we noticed Baby was gone. He had moved down the vacant bar and was talking to some cats at the other end.

"So you boys know old Punch," King said. "Whyn't you go look old Punch up."

"We don't know him," one of us said. "We just—"

"Here. I give you his address," King said. "He be real glad to see you boys. Old Punch is down and out. He on his uppers, and he sick. That's nowhere to be, not in this New York town." He wrote the address on one of Ryan's cards and handed it to the nearest one of us. "I just telling Baby about old Punch. You go see him."

"We don't know him," one of us said. "We just—"

"Why don't you put your name on it, too, King?" the one who had the card said. "I'd like to have it."

The King's eyes kindled. "You boys know me? Sure, I sign it. Here. Gimme that card."

"Hell yes, we know you," one of us said.

"You ever hear me play?"

"Just on records."

He nodded. "You boys stick around. I going to play here, pretty soon. They din't ask me, but I going to anyway." He shook the trumpet case at us. "They don't ask ol King no more to these jam sessions. But I just come down anyways. I see you boys." He went off down the bar toward Baby Dodds and the talking cats.

"I'm going to keep this card," our bass man said, shaking it at us, as we crossed the street to Johnny's. "I'm going to keep it forever." He put it in his pocket carefully.

"It don't belong to you," our trumpet man said. "Belongs to the whole band."

"Like hell," the bass man said.

We argued about the card over our series of rye-highs in Johnny's Tavern, without reaching a decision, until we heard them start up again across the street, and then went back over there.

There wasn't any minimum at the Sunday sessions and we got bottles of beer and moved down to a table as close to the band as we could get. They were already gone and going strong on *Nobody's Sweetheart*, with Wild-Bill-Bailey punching out the drive in that surcharged style of his.

King Jefferson was standing in the passageway around the left of the stand to the men's room with his trumpet in his hand. He would play a few bars, low, along with them, and then he'd stop and reach up and pluck at Baby Dodds' shirt sleeve. Baby would look down at his drums embarrassedly until he couldn't any longer, and then he'd look down at King and frown and shake his head and say something, and then smile, with that constrained look of trying not to look constrained on his face embarrassedly. It was bothering his playing. King didn't even leave him alone when he was on his solo choruses. He kept it up all through the set, but Baby never got mad.

Once we saw Wild-Bill-Bailey lean over and say something to the colored guitarman and they both shook their heads and laughed disgustedly. When the set was over, Wild-Bill climbed down and cut out quick. So did Baby and Pops Foster. King Jefferson lingered around the stand, after they were all down, and blew little bleats on that exquisite trumpet as if he were warming up his lip. He would blow a bleat and look around and grin and nod his head and then blow another bleat.

When we came back from Johnny's Tavern and refreshments, they had already started the fourth set and King was standing in the passageway at Baby's elbow again. Finally, about the sixth or seventh set, we came back from Johnny's and he wasn't there any more.

When the jam session was over and Ryan's deserted, we crossed the street to Johnny's Tavern through that almost unbearably melancholy, lonely twilight New York has, to do some drinking and decide where to go for the evening, and to argue some more about the card. We were still sitting at the bar there when King Jefferson came in with his trumpet case under his arm.

He didn't seem to be any drunker. But he wasn't any soberer. He remembered us.

"You boys come on and have a drink with old King."

"Sure," one of us said. "It'll be a privilege."

"We'll be proud to," another of us said.

We seemed to kind of fall into it, the way all the rest of them did, except Wild-Bill-Bailey, humoring him. You couldn't help it.

"Let me show you boys my horn," he said, after we had been served the drink. He got the case down on the floor and squatted by it and lifted the horn out lovingly. It was a beautiful trumpet, inscribed to him. He showed us the inscription.

"They gimme that horn in France," he said. "Las year. They know real music over there. That Mr. Panassié, he a fine man.

"You boys heard my band?"

"Just on records, King," one of us said.

"No, that's my old band. I mean my new band. I got me almost all new boys."

"We've been meaning to hit the Standish, King," one of us said. "But we only got in town last night."

"You don't want to hear it," King said. "Don't come down there. They all good boys, you understand. I like my boys. But they just don't play old King's kind of music. And all the people come they want to dance, not hear old King's kind of music. Have to play dance music. Most all my old boys lef me. They getting better jobs, see? That's all right. That's fine. You know I the man brought Buddy Ferrill back? He working in a lime kiln in that great old city of New Leans. You know Buddy Ferrill?"

"Sure. On records," one of us said. "Bob Rhynolds says he's the greatest jazz drummer ever lived."

"No he aint. Baby Dodds is." The King's eyes kindled. "You boys know Bob Rhynolds?"

"We just read about him," one of us said. "We never met him."

"He my good friend," King smiled at us proudly. "Bob Rhynolds my old buddy." He put the horn back into its case lovingly and looked at it and then rubbed the bell with a piece of flannel and closed the case. "I got to go, boys. Got to go to work pretty soon."

We all stood up. "We'll be down and see your band later on tonight, King," one of us said.

"You don't want to see my band. It a good band. They all good boys. But they aint like the old band, and they never going to be. Old King wouldn't lie to you. I can tell you boys know good jazz. Don't you boys come down.

"Boys," he said, "I'd like to pay for this drink. But thas all the money I got." He turned his pants pocket out; there was seventy cents in change in it. "I made a lot of money in this town, but I spending it just as fast."

"That's okay, King," one of us said. "We'll get it."

"I surely thank you boys," he said. "You boys write Bob Rhynolds, you tell him old King asking after him. I be seeing you boys sometime."

We watched him leave, the trumpet case tight under his arm. Then we paid for his drink.

Bechet was off that night and Ryan's had some other band so we ended up at Bop City. Louis Armstrong's All-Stars were playing at Bop City, and we had heard a lot about their young bassman, Arvel Shaw. He was as good as they said, too.

I guess it was about a year or so later—anyway, we were all back home, in business—that there was a little piece in *Down Beat* that said King Jefferson was anxious to hear from any of his old friends across the country or people who had seen him play and he would answer any letters faithfully. The address was New Arcadia, Louisiana.

That was the first we'd heard about his not being renewed at the Standish, and it shocked us. We'd always thought of him as a perennial. The five of us who'd met him agreed to write him a long newsy letter, but something else came up before we got a chance to do it, and we figured a lot of other people, people he knew really well, would write him.

It was probably a year after that, maybe two, before *Down Beat* mentioned him again. They gave him a double column spread and used his picture, his best one, the one that was on his first Victor album. It was good writeup. I had read the obits for both Fats Waller and Johnny Dodds, and it was as good as them.

A lot of us musicians felt his death, personally. I remember I was sitting in the Rec Hall poolroom on the Square, when I first read it. It was Tuesday and the new issue had just come in up at the newsstand. I had taken my morning-break-for-coffee at the store and used it to beat it over and get my copy. Tom Myers, our old band's bassman, and I always took our morning breaks to get our copies when they came out and read them in the Rec Hall with a bottle of coke, where it was quiet. Other mornings, we would go to Adams's Drugstore and have coffee at the fountain like the other peasants.

Tom came in from his father's insurance office just as I finished reading it. Tom had already seen it, on his way down from the newsstand. Both of us felt pretty somber, and we sat and talked about him so long we were both late getting back to work. We both felt the world had lost something pretty important, a piece of jazz history. No matter what the critics said, he had been important, a big man, a landmark. He was a great jazzman. Tom said he still had the signed card the King had given him that time at Ryan's, had it with his music stuff somewhere.

"It ought to be worth something some day, don't you think?"

"Sure," I said, "I don't see why not."

"You going to be to City Band practice tonight?"

"I don't know. Marcia's been having trouble with the baby. She's been sick. But I'll try and make it."

"How's the other one?"

"The boy? Oh, he's over it already."

"You ought to make it if you can."

"I'll try," I said.

" — You know, we met a great jazzman, when we met King Jefferson," Tom said, as we left.

"We sure did," I said. "There won't be no more like him."

THE VALENTINE

So now we come to the last batch of four, all done in 1957. This one, the first of these, is probably the least unconventional in its approach and its material. I like the Woolworth scene, the Newsstand scene, and the delivering of the papers at dawn, but particularly I like that last scene with that poor little youngun standing out there with his head hid in the coats, totally destroyed, and nobody in the whole damned world knows about it, or gives a good goddamn. And, in the end, isn't that the state that we all of us are in, too? give or take a handful?

H e had not meant, when he started the whole thing, for it to become such a big operation, such a production. But from the moment he had first stepped inside Woolworth's with his mind made up and had gone up to the candy counter and silently picked out the box, that was what it seemed to become nevertheless. And now, with it the last day before Valentine's Day, and Woolworth's ready to close up in just a few minutes, everything couldn't have been worse.

In the first place, there were two of the other paperboys from the Newsstand standing there at the candy counter. And the man behind the counter was a man he knew. He was the sort of assistant manager. And he had squinchy eyes and liked to needle the kids. And the other two paperboys from the Newsstand, where he himself John Slade worked too, were both freshmen while he was still only an eighth grader. It couldn't have been a much worse of a situation to try and buy it in.

And this time he couldn't go away and come back another time, as he had in fact already done at least three other times during the past week when he had come up and found other people standing at the candy counter. Woolworth's would be closing in a few minutes, and tomorrow was the day; he either had to do it now, or not do it. Unless he went somewhere else like the drugstore and he didn't want to do that. He had a distinct uncomfortable hollow feeling that that would be cheating, like. And anyway he knew the box he wanted, had in fact picked it out as long as two weeks ago, and it was, for the money, which was eight-ninetyfive, the best box in town he believed—all hearts that all interlocked with each other within the big heart that was the box shape itself, and with the two small paper cupids in the center of the white paper lace in the middle of that striking, eye-stopping deep deep red. A really beautiful box. And if he didn't take it now, after having promised himself faithfully that he would, he felt quite distinctly, although he did not word it quite that way, did not word it at all in fact, but nevertheless felt quite strongly, there would be no really moral or justifiable way out of having to face the fact that he was, after all, afraid and a liar to himself, and morally a coward.

It was the first time in his life that John Slade had ever really bought anything for a girl, and he wanted so bad for it to be right, to be really grownup, to be professional as if he was used to doing it a thousand times. Especially since the girl herself, whose lovely beautiful name was Margaret Simpson, didn't know anything about it at all yet, and wouldn't, until he handed it to her tomorrow. He wanted it to be a surprise. And he wanted it to be a secret. As far as that went, he was forced to admit, he didn't have nerve enough to do it any other way. Because he couldn't just go up to her and mention it to her. She might refuse. And now—

Some secret this would be! he thought desperately. And in the low-key, late-afternoon, February winter light, against which the lights had been turned on in the store without in the least changing its effect or cheerfulizing it, he stood irresolute just inside the door in his corduroy sheepskin-collared mackinaw, full of despair.

What did those guys have to be there for? And why did that sort of assistant manager have to be behind the counter? Any clerk in the store would have been better than him. Hell, he John would have been better off if he'd gone ahead and bought it one of those other times before when he'd chickened out. He didn't want it to be a big operation. But everybody made it that.

There wasn't any possibility of waiting those two guys out until they left, they obviously weren't leaving, and there was less than five minutes left till closing. And he knew Woolworth's well enough to know they weren't going to stay open one minute after five for any twelve year old kid. Unless he could succeed in covering it up from them some way, and how could he do that with that loudmouth needler behind the counter, it would mean he would take an awful lot of razzing at the Newsstand for the next month or so. The Newsstand was a good place to work, the elite in fact of all the several possible papercarrying jobs in town, much better than carrying for either of the local dailies or the Saturday Evening Post and magazine routes, and was not, in their town at any rate, the kind of poor-people-low-class sort of idea like people thought of paperboys like say in a city for instance. The boys who worked at the Newsstand were a cross section of the whole town, from the very poorest like Otis Cole to the most well off, just as of the two boys at the counter one was a doctor's son and the other a lawyer's, even as he himself was the son of a dentist. But that, just the same, did not mean they were not capable of inflicting the most roasting kind of humiliating razzing, especially when it came to anything like girls. Sex was one thing, and everybody talked about that and about screwing girls even though none of them ever really had as yet, except maybe Otis Cole, and they all collected and traded dirty books, but when it came to girlfriends and being in love — ! That was something else again and you were liable to get yourself laughed and razzed right out of the back room of the Newsstand in the pre-dawn early mornings where everybody folded their papers before taking off. And if they found out about anybody buying a girl a great big heart-shaped box of candy for Valentine's Day!

In his case it would be even worse, since Margaret Simpson (Gee, what a lovely, beautiful name, that was.) was not his girlfriend and never had been; and had never had any dates with him, (He had never had any dates at all, in fact, yet; although Margaret was known to have dated freshmen in high school and even a few sophomores this past year; but he was going to ask her for a date as soon as he gave her the box tomorrow.) and so nobody knew he had the hots for her and had fallen in love with her. That would make terrific news at the Newsstand, after tomorrow, and it wouldn't do him any good to deny it, although he would. It wouldn't even matter if the whole thing wasn't even true, for that matter; once the guys got the idea in their heads from someplace.

For a moment, as the seconds ticked agonizingly on toward five o'clock and the hanging moment of ultimate decision, John seriously considered the phantom luxury of just abandoning the whole project, of just turning around and going off and forgetting the whole thing and just buying her a cheap little box someplace else. Nobody would even notice a small cheap box. Just the idea of it was an enormous relief. But he knew he could never do it. Not after having exacted of himself a solemn faithful promise that he would go through with it. He would never be able to trust his promises again. That was the very reason he had done it, had made himself promise. So he couldn't back out.

Miserable, and with an acute feeling of desolation, he took hold of himself mentally and as it were placed both hands in the center of his own thin back, and shoved himself slowly over to the counter as if he were shoving a friend on roller-skates, and mumbled.

"What is it, boy? What is it? Speak up."

Louder, John said: "I said I want that eight-ninetyfive one there. How much is it?" His hand in his pocket nervously fingering his money, he knew immediately his mistake and cursed himself for it. Old squinch-eye was staring down at him from across the counter with the beginning of his evil grin all the guys knew so well amongst themselves and talked about, did he think he was fooling them?

"How much is it!" the assistant manager said loudly, laughing. "You just told me yourself. It's eight-ninetyfive. What do you mean how much is it?"

"I'll take it," John said nervously, fighting to keep his eyes looking straight at the squinchy ones. "Wrap it up." Down the counter in the corner of his eye he could see the two guys from the Newsstand nudging at each other.

"Yes, *Sir*, Mr Slade!" the Woolworth man grinned, his squinch-eyes squinching up even further. "Right *away*, Sir!" He grinned down the counter at the other two guys. "Will there be anything else, Sir?"

John tried to make it sound offhand but he could tell his voice was shaky: "Nope. I guess that'll be all."

"Got yourself a new girlfriend, hunh?" the assistant manager said loudly, as he began to wrap the box. "Man, you really must be stuck on her. Eight-ninetyfive for a box of candy." He lowered his voice in a make-believe confidence. "Want to tell me who she is?" he said slyly. The other two guys from the Newsstand were sidling down the counter, grinning in that way John knew so well, since he himself had done it so many times too with other guys, when they knew they had some guy in a corner and by the short hair. The Woolworth man winked at them, grinning.

Inspired by embarrassment, John came up with an idea: "It's not for a girl," he lied, "it's for my mother." He managed to look at old squinch-eye steadily, but his voice gave him away and he knew it. Just the same, he knew instinctively not even the guys would dare make fun about anything as sacred as a fellow's mother, so it was a good lie.

The Woolworth man appeared to be a little nonplussed. There was a short pause as everybody stopped the game and thought solemnly of their own sacred mothers. It made John think suddenly of how he had seen Catholics look when they came out of a church and stopped and crossed themselves. Then old squinch-eye, having paused respectfully, winked at the two guys, including them, and grinned: "Aw, come on, Johnny. You can tell us. Who is she. Really."

"Yeah, come on and tell us," one of the guys, Ted Wright it was, said.

"Yeah. We'll find out anyway, Slade." the other one, Hank Lewis, grinned.

"I told you," John said, as stoutly as he could muster. "I aint got a girl. This is for my mom." The box was wrapped now, but old squinch-eye was reluctant to let go of it and spoil the fun. John took the once-folded bills, nine dollars in all, that he had been saving back out of his route, (He had even made a special trip around, when he wasn't carrying, to collect up some of the back bills, so his percentage would be higher, so he would have enough.) out of his pocket and extended them, and at the same time held out his other hand.

The Woolworth man passed over the package with his right hand and took the money with his left, but then he would not quite let go. His hand clung to the box of candy teasingly.

"Is she in your room?" he asked. "Is she in 8A? Come on, you can tell *us*."

"Maybe she's in 8B," one of the guys grinned. "Maybe she's from down in Sacktown."

"Yeah. Maybe it's one of the Linder girls," the other one grinned. "Is it one of the Linder girls, Johnny?"

"I told you," John said. "Can I have my change, please?"

Finally, reluctantly, old squinch-eye let go of the box. "Your change? A whole nickel? I'm not sure I've got that much on hand," he grinned, his eyes squinching; but he turned around to the register, and then finally the ordeal was over. How could any guy get so mean, in only just thirty years or so?

Trying hard not to walk too fast, aware of his chest breathing fast and his arms and legs both trembling and hoping none of it showed, John went to the door with as much dignity as he could muster up.

"We'll find out anyway, Slade," one of the guys called after him teasingly. "We'll find out anyway; tomorrow."

And they would, too. It was a threatening promise of what he could expect to be coming his way. Outside he lay the wrapped package carefully in the basket of his bike, kicked up the kickstand and pushed off throwing his leg over. Well, to hell with them. Let them find out. Let them find out he had the hots for and was in love with (Oh, sweet lovely name.) Margaret Simpson. He didn't care. He was proud of it. So let them find out. They would anyway.

At home he went in and straight upstairs to his own room and put the wrapped box carefully away in a drawer of his dresser, and he did not tell anybody, neither his parents nor his kid sister, about it. But that night, after supper and the radio and homework and some reading, when he went to bed, he lay with his arms behind his head and thought about it. Finally he got up and took it out and unwrapped it (He could put it in a paper sack tomorrow to take to school to keep it clean—and hidden.) and looked at it. He was both excited and scared about tomorrow. He wished there *was* somebody he could talk to about it. He hoped it would be all right, and he *thought* it would. Certainly it would be the best, the most expensive valentine any girl in the class would get. That was for sure. But you couldn't be sure with Margaret. She was a pretty sophisticated girl, Margaret. Love and desire for her welled up in him at the silent pronunciation of her name, and he put the box carefully away and climbed back into bed.

Actually, he had never spoken to Margaret about his feeling for her. Maybe he should have. His *love* for her, he corrected himself, (And of course he *couldn't* speak to her about his having the hots for her. The very idea of that made his face feel flushed and made him feel guilty. He shouldn't even feel that about her. But then, the two things were entirely different, weren't they. They didn't really have anything to do with each other at all, did they.) his *love*, he said again. Actually, she was easily the most popular girl in the class, and had been elected most popular girl last year in seventh grade, and undoubtedly would be again this year in eighth grade, as well as being the best looking. She wore lots of skirts and sweaters, with the sleeves pushed up, and she had the best developed chest in 8A. Actually, she came from a very poor family, and lived in a very poor tacky little house on the far side of town. Her mother was dead and she kept house for her father and those of her five big brothers who still lived at home, which was two. Actually, she was really much better off than that sounded though, because old Mrs Carter, who was rich and has a sort of estate like right next door to Margaret's, had taken her under her wing as a motherless girl and paid for all her clothes and things and was going to send her to college. Also, all her five brothers were musical, as she was herself, and played instruments and had played in bands around town, and so Margaret herself had been singing with a band that one of her brothers ran, at places like the Elks Club and the Country Club, ever since she had been in sixth grade. That, right there, probably accounted for a lot of her sophistication. Everybody said she was really very talented as a singer and might have a chance to go a long way someday. Also she made excellent grades; always.

Well, he bet she had never had as expensive, or as big, a valentine as this before, even from a sophomore; and thinking about her in the warmth of the bed under the warm covers, John rolled over and curled himself up and went to sleep. But he was still worried.

Once, two years ago it was, almost, during the summer after sixth grade, he had tried to make love to another little girl. This little girl was two years younger than him, the same age as his kid sister, and she lived across the street and they all used to play together a lot, with all the other kids from the block, in the summer. But one night, after dark, just the three of them, his sister, this girl, and himself, were sitting on this girl's porch across the street. The porch light was out so it was dark and he and the little girl were in the swing, his sister in a chair not far from them. All afternoon and all evening, when they'd been playing, this little girl had been poking him and pinching him and grabbing him and tickling him and accidentally falling against him, and then giggling. He had assumed from this that she liked him and was giving him a sort of invitation, so in the swing in the dark, strangely excited, he had put his arm around her and whispered to her to let him kiss her. Actually, he didn't even completely get his arm around her because she had moved away from him immediately in the swing before he could; and where before she had been warm and practically rubbing herself against him she now was suddenly cold and untouchable. Still excited, in a wholly new way he had never felt before, he had slid over after her in the swing and tried again, tried several times, whispered for her to please let him kiss her, with the same result. So, knowing vaguely that this was the way adults did it in similar circumstances and feeling dimly there must be some magic open-sesame in the words themselves, he had whispered: "I love you." It was the first time he had ever said the words, except possibly to his mother, but they now had a completely different meaning. They did not, however, open any doors for him. The little girl's reaction was forceful and immediate. "You're lovesick," she said accusingly in an almost angry voice full of contempt. "That's what you are. You're lovesick." It was a word he had never thought much about or paid any attention to, although when he heard her say it he knew it was a word he had heard before somewhere, and it was clear to him in some subtle way that it was a word this little girl had only learned recently and was using for the first time with the same sense of surprised discovery her use of it was also giving him. Lovesick. He had got up out of the swing and left the porch immediately and gone home, leaving the two girls, his sister and the other one, there giggling. But instead of going in the house, where he would have to face his parents, he had gone around behind to the vacant lot next door in the center of the block, where the kids of the block all played, and sat down by himself on the terraced hillside of it, filled with a strange admixture of emotions the like of which he had never felt before, but the sum total of which was bad. Very bad, and very sad, and very unhappy. And whenever he thought of the two girls giggling, he felt sick-mad all over. It was a beautiful warm summer night, and the stars shimmered and shown overhead with a marvelous clarity and even the milky way looked bright. Lovesick. It was like some strange and terrible new disease he had discovered in himself without any preparation for it at all, and he kept saying it sickly over and over to himself: "I'm lovesick. I'm lovesick. I'm lovesick." and he was afflicted with a sense of terrible doom that brought horror and terror and fright and helplessness into him through some opened gate, together with a vague, but sure, knowledge of forces at work in people that would inevitably, someday, destroy him. Finally he got up and went in the house to bed, and after that he did not think about the incident often but whenever he did it brought a sense of shame, and a flush to his face, and the terror, diluted now, would creep back into him, and when he awoke on the morning of Valentine's Day he did not know whether he had dreamed about it during the night or whether he had thought about it just as he was dropping off to sleep, or whether it had just popped into his head for no reason as he was waking. But he was still worried.

The alarm clock was still ringing, its luminous hands showing at exactly four-thirty in the dark, and he shut it off and switched on the light. It was always exciting. Nowhere in the silent, dark house did anything move or stir, nor were there any lights, nor movement, in any of the houses he could see through his windows as he dressed. Savoring the daily excitement, he dressed himself warmly; flannel shirt, two sweaters under his mackinaw, warm socks inside his boots, knit cap down over his ears, heavy scarf; then he took up his heavy fleecelined leather mittens and tiptoed down the stairs to the front door. Outside it was steely cold and the handlebars and sprocket of his bike creaked with frost when he moved them. The air burned his nose like dry ice, and as he tucked the scarf up over it and put on his goggles, his eyes were already watering. The freezing cold air flushing the last threads of sleepiness and of reluctance out of his mind, he took off on his bike, giving himself joyously up to, and embracing happily, the discomfort which always made him feel important and as though he were accomplishing something, riding the bike downtown along deserted streets of darkened houses where nothing moved or shone and people slept except for a few boys like himself, scattered across town, converging on the Newsstand where the city papers would already have been picked up by the owner off the train.

Actually, nothing much happened at the Newsstand that morning. He was razzed unmercifully by the two who had seen him buy the box last night, and of course it was immediately taken up by all the others as they stood at the benches folding their papers and stuffing their paperbags under the bare bulbs in the back room—but he kept his mouth shut and said nothing and did not get mad. It was easy to do because he kept the mental picture of Margaret Simpson happily opening his box in the forefront of his mind, as a shield. Nobody could touch him when he thought of that. Anyway, the folding of the papers and the stacking of them in their proper sections only took ten or fifteen minutes, and then they were outside and separated, spreading out across the town, and he was by himself again, able to enjoy ecstatically again the physical discomfort that he suffered not only because of the money it made him but because it made him feel he was strong and had will power, and to dwell also upon, and to worry over in his nervous excitement, the valentine and his happy picture of Margaret, as he made his route. Then it was back home for breakfast and to change for school.

Twice as he was dressing, and as his nervous excitement mounted to almost unbearably unpleasant heights as the time left slid away, he almost decided once again to drop the whole thing. He could leave the box right here in his drawer and gradually eat the candy up himself, and no one would ever know where the box had disappeared to. But once again his ironbound promise to himself, which it was against his private rules to break, would not let him, and sustained him;

that, and his happy picture of Margaret Simpson's face, warm and loving as she opened up his box, and its natural sequence which automatically followed: of him telling her how much he adored her, and always had, from a distance, and her warm understanding of it, and then his hands and face moving against her lovely chest. When he took the paper-sacked box downstairs and his mother asked him curiously what it was, he told her it was a couple of books he was taking back.

On the way to school, as the other kids converged, it was harder to say that. He knew of course that the moment would come (It appeared to be rushing down on him swiftly, in fact, like a freight train.) when it would have to be made public. When there would be no avoiding saying what it was, or who it was for. So gradually he was forced back to saying simply, "Aw, nothing." or "Nothing that would interest *you*." Everybody of course knew by now though that it was a valentine.

There were several valentines on his own desk in the 8A room when he got there, from different kids, two of them from girls in the back of the room who thought they were stuck on him but whom he didn't like because they both of them came from Sacktown and were poor, and not very smart, and often not even very clean. All these he opened and looked at, in a kind of daze of nervous excitement, hardly even seeing them, and then put them down. Then, painfully aware that he was being watched, he carefully pulled the big box out of its paper sack and laid it on his desk. Big; it was huge! It looked monstrous to him. He had attached a little card in a little white envelope to the ribbon which said: "To Margaret, with love, John Slade." He stared at that a while. It had cost him deeply in pride and fear, to even dare to write it. That word. But he couldn't stare at the envelope forever. Margaret Simpson had not yet come in the room, and it was still three and a half minutes till the bell rang. Abruptly, suddenly, he knew he couldn't stand it, just could not wait any longer; he hadn't made a promise to himself he would hand it to her, had he? And besides, if he waited to give it to her himself like he had planned, the way he was now he wouldn't be able to say a word, not a single solitary goddamned word. Panic had enveloped him. He wanted only to be out of sight of everyone. The valentines on his own desk had given him an idea. Jerkily, cursing himself for looking so foolish, he picked up the box and walked across the room with it and laid it on Margaret Simpson's desk, and then came back to his own desk and went out into the cloakroom pretending he had forgotten something in his overcoat.

There was a little buzz, sort of, that he could hear from the cloakroom, and when he peeked around the door there were several kids standing around her desk looking at it, admiring it maybe. He stayed in the cloakroom. How he could manage to while away three whole minutes in the cloakroom he didn't know, and once, as a subterfuge, he went back in to his desk and got some handkerchieves and things out of it, pretending he wanted to put them in his coat to take home.

Then, finally, one minute before the bell would ring, Margaret Simpson came in, with two boys who were on the gradeschool varsity basketball team, and they hung up their coats and went inside. John busied himself with his own coat and did not look at them. Completely degenerated now, no longer able even to control, he could not resist and sneaked to the door and stuck the top half of his head around it, grinning foolishly. Margaret Simpson was just showing the card, his card, to the two boys. She said something he could not hear, and then laughed and gestured with her head toward the cloakroom where he was hiding, and the two boys laughed. Then Margaret looked down at the big red box with amusement.

John, who had already seen enough, jerked his head back and crept back to his own coat, pretending to himself he had to get something out of the pocket. But then, when he got there, he leaned his face against his coat sickly and shut his eyes, trying to shut out with the light existence also. He put his hand in the pocket of the coat so he could make it look like he was hunting something in case anybody else should come in. How could he ever go back in there, when the bell rang? How could he possibly? Sickness ran all through him, all over him, in long waves, at the thought. And everybody had seen him standing peeking around the doorjamb like a silly idiot. He had ruined it. He'd messed it all up. He should have made himself stay and hand it to her. Then it would have been all right. He stood that way, clenching and unclenching his fists, until the bell rang, knowing it would ring, listening for it.

When the bell rang, he forced himself to walk to the door and to his desk and sat down, trying hard not to look at anybody.

A BOTTLE
OF CREAM

This one was written right after "The Valentine," and is probably my favorite in the whole book. I like the mood and tone of it. *I love* the character of the bar-owner. I like everything about it. Particularly I like its form. I have tried since several times to reutilize the character of the bar-owner who exists in this story, but have never been able to recreate him. Apparently he belongs only in this story. An interested reader will note the reference to the tennis game against the garage which reappears as the main theme later in "The Tennis Game."

Even when I was very young, I had learned that telling the truth did not necessarily mean that you would be believed. Not that I was less prone to lie than any other child. But even on those occasions (and they were not what one could actually call rare) when I did tell the truth to grownups, and consequently expected to be patted proudly on the head, I more often than not found myself in hot water instead, was challenged and told I was lying anyway. Naturally, since I was not stupid, after a good big number of such painful experiences I began to realize that it did not really matter what you told people as long as it was something they wanted to believe—something that you knew by some sure sly instinct of childhood they *would* believe, because they thought that way—and that the actual fact of whether you were really telling the truth or not had nothing to do with it.

Not long ago I went with a friend to pay a reckless driving fine, and I quite by accident heard mentioned the name of a man who was intimately involved in these deep philosophic problems of my childhood and whom I had not thought about for years. Chet Poore was his name. And, in my home city, I never heard him referred to any other way. I assume his first name was Chester. He was what you might call a criminal, sort of.

Now, this thing of going to pay a reckless driving fine is always a slightly embarrassing business, if not downright cowing. It was especially so in my friend's case, since while the charge was reckless driving, the sin itself was actually drunken driving. In our State, as in most others I guess, though I don't actually know, so awful has the crime of drunken driving become that the first time you are caught at it you are not even charged with it. You are charged with only reckless driving, but given a very stiff fine. But of course, as in my friend's case, everyone involved knows that your sin is really drunken driving.

In case anyone is interested in the rest of the progression, the second time you are caught at it you are actually charged with it, and given a stiffer fine; and you lose your driving license for a year. Automatically. The third time you are caught at it you will probably spend a year in prison. And you will lose your driving license forever. This of course, in our day and age, is comparable to having your feet lopped off back in François Villon's time, if not as bloody. If anyone should be so foolhardy as to be caught a *fourth* time, after all this and with no license to drive, I have no idea what the penalty is, and don't want to. I shudder to think of it.

But this is how serious the crime of drunken driving has become today. This, of course, is due to two things. One is that perforce we are a nation of drivers in the U.S., and the other is that we are a nation of drunkards. Really compulsive drunkards. Everyone knows this, but it is considered impolite to say so. I myself attribute this peculiarly American type of drunkenness to the fact that as a nation we are so repressed in our social and sexual lives. But of course I cannot prove it. And even if I could, what? But I am forced to grin whenever, in my tavern that I run, I hear TV newscasters or read newspaper editorials that chide the Russian leaders for downing so many double shots of vodka.

At any rate, because our government is worried (and rightly so), our propaganda about drunken driving has reached really astronomical proportions. Everyone now knows what a horrifying crime it is. Did you ever notice the sequence of thoughts in your own mind which follows the mention of it? It runs something like this: What? Drunken driving! Why, he might have hit a poor little innocent child. He might have struck down a poor old lady wending her tired way home with her laundry bundle upon her back. The by-now-ingrained thought sequence, you see. It appears in everybody's mind automatically at those two heinous words: drunken driving. Your mind and my mind and, I'm quite sure, the minds of all drunken drivers when they are sober. And the moral stigma is of course tremendous. It does not matter that the child might have run out in front of him deliberately to scare him and show off to its friends, not knowing he was drunk. It does not matter that the old lady may have stepped in front of him purposely to commit suicide, being tired of being forced to carry her laundry bundle on her back all her life in everybody's imagination whenever she steps out of the house. It does not, in fact, matter that there was in actual fact no child at all, and no tired old lady. They appear. They appear, and they exist, at the mention of those awful words, and remain to plague the hapless driver who really injured nobody and did nothing actually except get himself a load on and then attempt to drive himself home to safety.

Thus, for perhaps the first time in human history, due to circumstances involving high-powered means of transportation, an honest upright law-abiding ordinary citizen of a politically stable nation can suddenly find himself in the eyes of his peers placed in the company of thieves, second-story men and murderers. All because of high-powered machinery which he could not handle. The drunken driving situation is somewhat analogous to the atom bomb, I sometimes think.

On the other hand, I myself (I cannot speak for my friend and others, though I'm sure they would disagree with me) would not mind so much being placed in the company of criminals if they were all like Chet Poore who was a house-breaker and a car-thief, as well as being an excellent pool- and poker-player.

At any rate, my friend and I appeared at court. My friend, looking shamefacedly criminal, pleaded guilty to reckless driving. The judge (a very nice young man, with whom my friend and I had been drunk many times) looked embarrassed too and pronounced his sentence of a stiff fine. Then the sheriff (with whom we both had been drunk too), also looking embarrassed, escorted us to the County Clerk's office to pay the stiff fine, accompanied by the deputy sheriff who had made the arrest and therefore did not look embarrassed but proud. The sheriff, of course, would never have arrested my friend; he would have taken him home instead, his deputy still had this to learn. The County Clerk, who accepted my friend's money, did not look embarrassed because he was not a drinking man. My friend's lawyer, who had accompanied us but had nothing at all to do, stood and chatted cheerfully with the proud deputy sheriff without looking embarrassed at all since to him this was only business, and he did not believe being drunk was a sin, or even being caught at it driving a car, and all of this to him was only a matter of legality and legal wordings, not morality at all. He was that kind of a lawyer. As well as being an excellent thief in all of the estates he handled. A healthy type to be around, sometimes.

It was then, standing with my friend while he wrote out his check for his stiff fine, and looking shamefaced and embarrassed too myself, I'm sure, that I heard the lawyer mention Chet Poore's name to the deputy sheriff.

"Chet Poore. Yes," the lawyer grinned. "They just picked him up again in Detroit in a stolen car. It was in the city paper."

"That'll make him a three time loser, won't it?" the deputy asked.

Chet Poore. Chet Poore. The name echoed resoundingly back and forth from side to side of my suddenly empty head and left me feeling startled. Not actually living in my home city but in an adjoining county, not only had I not heard the name, I had not thought of the man in years and years. Whenever I did though, like now, I had a very definite mental picture: a huge tall man stood over me and stared grinning down at me. And always a feeling of intense smiling pleasure came over me.

"No-o; I don't think so." The lawyer shook his head. "They've only had that habitual criminal law fifteen or twenty years. And anyway he's beat several raps, I think."

Both of them were grinning in a curious way now, at each other. As if the thought of Chet Poore just automatically made them grin. It was not a hateful grin, but was really affectionate. With perhaps just a hint of superiority in the affection. But the superiority was much more noticeable in the tall deputy's face than in the short fat lawyer's.

"Well, he's a helluva lot more than a three time loser if you count all those jobs he pulled on his old man," the deputy grinned. "I'm just glad he's not around here any more."

"Oh, he comes back," the lawyer grinned. "He always comes back, Chet does. Couldn't stay away from here. He was back about a year ago for a few days and stopped up the office to see me."

"Yeah, but I didn't have this job then."

"Well, you won't have it when he gets out this time, either. If he gets out. I'll have to look up and see. If he's a three time loser and gets life or not. I'm not just for sure."

"I'll bet he is," the deputy said.

"He might be. Christ, remember the time he stole his old man's car and robbed the till of the store and wound up in Kansas City before they picked him up? The old man let them send him up that time. Got two years. But that was years ago. God, the old man was mad."

The deputy, whom I did not like, and still don't, though I'm always polite to him, laughed a little, softly, almost shyly. "I never knew him very well. He was older than me. What makes a guy be like that, anyway?"

"I don't know. Chet was always wild. And he just didn't give a damn," the lawyer grinned, as if this in some way pleased him immensely.

It was then that I interrupted. My friend, still looking shamefacedly criminal, was still signing and receiving whatever it was he had to sign and receive. I began to question the lawyer about Chet Poore. Actually, I found out little more than the preceding conversation had already told me by implication. But I wanted to know everything about him that I could learn so I continued to question, but not eagerly. Long ago I had learned that uneager people always look at you oddly whenever you show eagerness about something they think does not deserve it. And I do not like to be looked at oddly. But, as I have said, I learned almost nothing. Chet came and went; sometimes he stayed a while; sometimes he even worked; sometimes he worked in Detroit too, or Flint; or Chicago or Hammond. All this apart from his criminal activities of car-thievery or cashbox-lifting. The last time he had been home for any length of time, which had been six years ago, he had stayed for two years I learned and had worked for his uncle a house-painter, until finally getting bored with that, the lawyer said and grinned, he had happened to make a big win at poker and then stole his uncle's car and just took off. They never did find the car. The uncle did not turn him in. It was an old car.

But I learned nothing more. Nothing, certainly, of all the things I hungered to know about Chet Poore. But then, what did I hunger to know? My friend finished all his paying and signing and receiving, and, leaving the law enforcement officers, the three of us—my friend, his lawyer and myself—left the hollow high-ceilinged courthouse and stood on the steps outside in the sun a while chatting and speaking to everyone who came by, to show that we really did not feel we were criminals after all. I did not take much part in this performance, because I was still thinking of Chet Poore.

I am thirty-one, and I make a good living, in my business, which is operating a tavern. A bar, if you will. In the town where I live it is too small for anything like cocktail lounges. So I operate a bar. People will always drink, my father who was an insurance man used to say. And he was right. I am married, to a fine woman—naturally, since if she were not a fine woman I would not have married her; and I have two small sons. I try to be a companion and a counsellor to my children, but they will not let me inside their lives any more than I would let my parents inside my own. I am, in short, a solid man, fast approaching middle age. I see it coming at me, and it appears to move faster and faster the closer it gets.

But if I am this, at thirty-one (and this is the point I was leading to in describing myself to you), look at Chet Poore. What about him? He must be at least fifteen years older than me, perhaps more. And yet he is still doing the half-prankish criminal things he used to do when he was young, as almost all of us did. But now, because he is no longer young, they have become serious for him. Then why does he not stop them? He has not, so far as I have been able to find out, ever married. He is not a father. He has never congealed himself a solid place out of the welter of protoplasm we call life and are forced to flounder in. And now he was in prison again, perhaps as a three time loser which would mean for life.

Standing with my friend and his lawyer on the steps of the courthouse in the warm spring sun, with the blindfolded concrete statue of Justice above the lintel behind us, I went back inside my childhood to the one time that I ever had anything at all to do with Chet Poore personally. It is hard to go back inside your childhood, I mean really back inside, after you are twenty-five; and it becomes increasingly harder as you, and in that order: 1) go into a business, 2) marry, and 3) have children of your own. Increasingly you forget what you really used to feel, because after all it is no longer really very important. But such was my emotional state standing in the spring sunlight on the steps of the courthouse, that I was able to do it. That, and the fact of the very definite mental picture I had of Chet Poore: a huge tall grownup man standing over me and staring grinning down at me. And that feeling of intense smiling pleasure it always gave me.

I remember I had been out in the yard playing. It was an early summer morning, and the garage of our house was a double one, with a double concrete driveway that tapered down to a single one a car's length from the doors. This was my tennis court, and I was playing a championship match and that I was both Don Budge and the German, Baron von Cramm. I was not sure yet who was going to win today and the tension and excitement were tremendous. And that was when my mother had called to me to go uptown for her and get her a bottle of whipping cream, for some dish she was making.

I had to go, of course. There was no choice. I could sense at once with my child's sly knowledge that my mother was irritated with the cooking and the heat of the stove, and probably mad at my old man to boot, as she usually was, so I did not even try to argue but instead ran all the way uptown with the money and ran all the way back with the cream so that I might get on with my championship match. But then, just as I was lifting my racket for the first cannonball serve by Budge to the Baron, my mother came to the door and called to me angrily. The cream was sour. I must take it back at once, immediately, and make the shopkeeper exchange it.

Once again, of course there was no choice. I was her child, her property, and she had ownership of me, and was big enough to make me do what she said. I was about seven at the time. Or perhaps eight. Possibly I was six. Once again I took the little half-pint cream bottle in its little sack and started for town, but this time I did not try to hurry. I had given up all hope of ever finishing my championship match today. It was only in the second set, and the Baron had won the first. Hopeless, I went as slowly as I could. I was angry at the cream and at my mother, who was angry at the cooking and at my father, who was angry at all the bills he had to pay and at God. Actually, of course, we were all angry at life but I did not know this then and apparently, though they were much older than me, neither did they.

There was a little rise I had to climb which was a block long and which led up onto the square with the courthouse in its center. This same courthouse, in fact, it was. The grocery store was the second store around the corner. The first store, whose building ran all the way back down the rise to the other corner, was a furniture store then, but is something else now.

In the hot June sun which was already heating up the sidewalk and the street and beginning to make everything smell dusty, I started up the little rise which always looked to me like a long hill back then, though it has since dwindled, dragging my fingertips along the unevenness of the tan-painted brick wall. And it was then, as of course everyone has probably guessed by now, that I dropped the bottle of cream.

It crashed to the sloping sidewalk and smashed, and the cream began to run out of the mouth of the sack. I stopped and stared down at it, the enormity, the irrevocability of what I had done dawning on me slowly in a wind of terror. I stooped down to it on one knee, hoping desperately that it might be put back together again, but knowing beforehand that it could not; and of course it couldn't be. Kneeling beside it, and wishing desperately that it had not happened, oh if only it hadn't happened, as if the very force of my wish itself might cause the bottle to re-form and the cream to run back into it, I began to cry. And crying, I began to cast about in my mind as to just which lie I could tell that would get me out of it.

Terrified, I knew I could not go back to my mother and tell her the truth. Not only would she whip me and yell at me loudly all the while as she did so, but also she would accuse me of wasting money we could not afford to waste, which would disturb me even more, even though I knew we were not anywhere near poor enough that we could not afford a second bottle. On the other hand, I could not take the broken bottle on to the store and tell the storekeeper I had dropped it but that the cream was soured; he would never believe me. He would think I had carelessly dropped the bottle and was trying to get a free second bottle by saying it was sour so I would not have to tell my mother. Can you understand the terrifying implications of this? To tell the truth and not be believed? But then, what lie was there I could tell him? And the only other alternative left, to buy a second bottle, was impossible too because I only had seven cents of my own in the whole world, and I knew whipping cream was even more expensive than regular coffee cream.

Trapped, completely hopeless, terrified, I crouched over my broken cream bottle and merely continued to cry. I could go neither forward to the store, nor backward home to my mother. Casting about, I thought I might tell my mother that a little neighbor boy had attacked me and knocked it out of my hands. But I knew my mother well enough to know she would fly in a rage to the telephone and call the boy's mother; then she would find out the truth. And after rejecting this possibility I gave up entirely, and merely crouched, crying, and in a complete trauma, staring at my bottle and trying by force of will to make it not have happened, make it go back together and the cream to run back into it.

How long I remained like this, I have no idea because my time sense was distorted out of all reason by my fear, terror and guilt. Even today it still seems it must have been a very long time, hours; though I know rationally that it was not. Finally I became aware of two men walking down the hill on the other side of the street, and through my cascading tears of hopelessness saw them start across the street toward me. I didn't care. I didn't even care if they saw me, a boy, crying. Hell to them, I thought with my child's mind and true instinct, they don't know what it is to be little. Nevertheless I watched them approach until one man, huge, tall and grownup to my child's stature, stood over me and stared grinning down at me.

"What's the matter, kid?" he said. "You drop your bottle?"

Still today I have no recollection of the tone or timbre or quality of his voice. Such was the state of my collapse.

"Who're you?" I said cautiously, though still crying.

"I'm Chet Poore and I live in this town too," he said kindly. He must have been only twenty-four or -five, at that time, but he looked old, aged, to me.

"Who's he?" I said.

"He's my friend," he said. And I looked at the other man, but saw there neither the interest nor the kindness of the first face.

"Come on, Chet," he said. "Let's get goin'."

"Shut up," Chet Poore said and squatted down beside me and the bottle. "Come on, kid," he said. "Tell me about it."

So, inchoately, almost unintelligibly, stuttering with sobbings that tore at my diaphragm convulsively, I told him and poured out to him my terrible crime and what my guilty situation was, how I could not go on to the store because I would not be believed, how I could not go back home because I would at the very least be whipped.

"Well, now, that's not too bad," Chet Poore said. "What if I was to go up to the store with you and explain it to them."

I could only shake my head. "It wouldn't do any good." And I knew it wouldn't.

"Well, at least we can give it a try," Chet Poore said. "That won't hurt anything." And so saying, he picked me up and sat me on one arm, and picked up the wet sack of broken glass with the other, and carried me up the slope to the store, his friend following along disgustedly behind us.

In the store it proved that I was right, as I had known I would be. The storekeeper looked at Chet Poore strangely and said he was sorry for me, and said he really believed me, too. But he just couldn't give me a bottle of cream. He had to have back the bottle of sour cream to turn back to the dairy man before he could do that. And the bottle was broken, and the cream spilled. It was the fact.

"All right then, damn it, *sell* me a bottle of cream," Chet Poore said irritably, "you tight bastard."

"Sure," the storekeeper said agreeably, and Chet Poore, after he paid the storekeeper, set me down and handed me the bottle, slapped me on the bottom and started me toward the door, himself and his disgusted friend following after. It was as simple as that. I had my cream back and my problem, which had so terrified me, was gone. Just wasn't there, didn't exist anymore, and I felt the horrible nightmare of it had never happened. Outside the store I stopped to try and thank him again, effusive, over-eager, tongue-tied by my very gratitude and its inexpressibility.

"That's all right, kid," he said. "Run along home now."

And he and his friend turned and went off up the street.

They were going in a direction entirely different from their original one, perhaps to the poolroom across the corner of the square, and I realized suddenly that it had meant nothing at all to him, what he had done. Startled for a moment, but forgetting it immediately in my happiness over my reprieve, I started for home holding the new, unbroken bottle carefully.

Long years afterwards, when I was a freshman in high school and quite grownup myself, I got involved with another boy in stealing cartons of cigarettes from that same grocery store, though under a different management by then. We would steal them in the early morning after completing our paper routes and before the store opened, when the butcher who opened up would let us in to buy cookies and we would hide them in our by-now-empty canvas paperbags. Then we would sell them for a dollar a carton to another man who ran a little lunch counter. We lived very high for a while. Naturally, we were caught eventually— and were very nearly sent to reform school. Luckily, my father had a little influence and the chief of police was a kind man. But I had to pay back my share of the theft, and out of my paper route. It took me almost a year, and I am sure the storekeeper cheated me about how much I truly had stolen. He was that kind of a storekeeper.

At any rate, that was the only time I ever had anything to do with, or even said a word to, Chet Poore, and now I came back from inside my childhood to find myself still standing on the courthouse steps in the spring sun with my friend who had just been convicted of reckless driving but had been fined for drunken driving. For a moment, just for a moment, the square of my home city appeared to me as it had once looked in my childhood. But then, when I finally had to blink my eyes, it shifted and changed back to the way it looks to me today at thirty-one: shrunken, much smaller, much less exciting and romantic and adventurous. The lawyer was just leaving us.

I would like to be able to say something about Justice, whose concrete statue still reposed above the lintel of the door behind us. But I don't know what to say. I would like to be able to say Chet Poore and the episode of the bottle of cream changed my life in some way or another, but I do not honestly think it did. So I cannot say it. What did it do then? I don't know. I don't honestly think it did anything. And Chet Poore? What of him? I would like to know a great deal more about him. And about his life. But what is there to know? And if I knew it, what then? What would I do? I would continue to operate my tavern, that's what; and perhaps if Chet Poore who must be nearly fifty now ever came into it from time to time I would offer to buy him a drink, except that now he is back in jail again.

At any rate, standing in the warm spring sun on the courthouse steps with my convicted friend, and as we shook hands and separated to go each to our different cars, me to open my tavern in a different town, him to his own business, I still carried with me that definite sharp mental picture: of Chet Poore, huge, tall, grownup to my small child's eyes, standing over me and staring grinning down at me: as fresh, and clearcut, as on that day I had looked up at him through my tears.

And, today, now, as I operate my tavern in the middle of the twentieth century and try to keep my customers from drinking so much they get picked up for drunken driving (though I often don't succeed), as I watch my wife getting older and my children growing up and away from me and stand helplessly as middle age rushes upon me faster and faster and faster as it comes, I still have it, that picture. And that feeling of intense smiling pleasure it always gives me. I still cannot help feeling that Chet Poore ought not be in jail. Just as I can't help feeling that shopkeepers ought not to try and cheat on how much is stolen from them, and get off scot-free.

As it turned out, some time later the lawyer was in my place and informed me that Chet Poore was, after all, a three time loser. That means he is in for life.

Of course, in twenty years he can be paroled.

SUNDAY
ALLERGY

Unpublished. Just what it is, a diver-
tissement about New York girls and
their lives, which ain't all that romantic
all the time. I think it's kind of charm-
ing, cute, and rather poignant. But I've
alway liked that kind of gals. Nobody
ever wanted to buy it. One editor I
showed it to said, "My God, Jim! We
can't go around publishing stories like
that by you. You're supposed to be a big
tough he-man war-story writer. Send
me a war story." I took it and crept quietly away.

This particular Saturday afternoon Sidney Greene had thought she would go shopping for a new dress. The fall sales had only just started at Saks and Milgrim's, and if she bought it right away she could get several weeks' wear out of a summer dress before putting it away for the year. But by mid-morning (which, on Saturdays, meant almost noon) Sidney's first snifflings and sneezings had already begun to seize her, making it plain the shopping expedition was merely a hopeful essay into wishful thinking.

"I don't know what I'm going to do, Cott," she said in beginning misery around her handkerchief. "I really don't."

"You're going to have to make up your mind that it's all psychosomatic, that's what," Elena Cotrelli her roommate, who was a confirmed night owl and was just getting up, said crisply. "You know it is, and I know it is. Once you admit that to yourself, it'll just simply go away," she said positively.

Sidney stared at her fiercely, over her handkerchief. "I know it's not any such a damn thing. And *you* know I've had an allergy to cats all my life. Even when we were in college I had it. And you know it, darling." She sneezed, rendingly.

Cott tapped a long-nailed finger emphatically on the temple of her long flowing blonde hair, her fine-nosed handsome Italian face wrinkling with an almost motherly solicitude. "The mind," she said, continuing on longleggedly in her robe to the bathroom beyond the miniature kitchenette. "All in the mind. Do you think I majored in psychology for four years and don't know that? It's a simple, easy, direct, uncomplicated, almost classic, case history. Any fool could diagnose it. If you're allergic to cats, why don't you get it week nights then?"

"Simply because I'm not here long enough for it to take effect," Sidney said scornfully. "I'm working all day. But on the weekends— . . ." She let it trail off, and sneezed.

"On the weekends," Cott said, taking up the sentence crisply from beyond the open bathroom door, "on the weekends L. Carter Wright, the book reviewer, is off in the country with his three hundred pound wife and three kids, instead of in town. Really, Sidney." She came back out.

Sidney merely stared at her. "We simply have to get rid of Frederick, Cott," she said flatly, and looked accusingly over to the sideboard cabinet of the apartment's little living room where Frederick the Cat, a darkfaced handsome seal-point Siamese, was cleaning himself unconcernedly. "Larry Wright has nothing to do with it."

"You love Frederick as much as I do," Cott said confidently and not without amusement. "And you know it. And anyway, we couldn't kick Frederick out now, after we took his sex away from him when his children all died and it was discovered he had an Rh negative. That *would* be a dirty trick."

"Of course I love him," Sidney said, and sneezed. "Do you think I would have suffered this allergy all this time if I didn't love him?"

"And that son of a bitch Manny!" Cott said fiercely, suddenly. She flounced down into the single armchair.

Once again Sidney stared at her over her handkerchief, as if she had no comprehension of what Cott had said, or else had not even heard it at all. "I've been over Manny a long, long time," Sidney said coldly. "Months and months and months."

"Sure," Cott said. "Sure you are. But you're not over being unmarried. And neither am I, damn it."

"You," Sidney said plaintively, but without the slightest trace of rancor. "You, who are so beautiful, and have so many men chasing you around. How could you be expected to know what I feel?"

Cott did not answer her immediately. Indeed, there was no need to; at all. Rooming together seven years in the city, and the last three years of college before that, Cott could always be expected to know what she felt, just as Sidney could always be expected to know what Cott felt. After such long-term intimate close living you could almost believe you actually lived inside the other person's head as well as your own.

"Yes, and what kind of men are they?" Cott said in a voice of sudden thin, tired depression. "Never any kind that I can fall in love with." She spoke this last more to herself than to Sidney, in a low voice that not only did not require an answer but actively requested none be made, and the two of them just sat, staring at each other, Cott slumped down in the deep armchair, Sidney sitting up with her feet tucked under her on the day couch, all the knowledge and events of the past eight or nine months churning slowly around in both their heads simultaneously since each knew fully as much about the other as she knew about herself, so that in effect each was living the lives of both, a sort of concerted double viewpoint.

When the news had come about Manny, all Sidney had done was to simply scream. It was the worst sound Cott thought she had ever heard in her life, and Sidney herself thought it was the worst sound she too had ever heard; but that was what she had done. She screamed for two days; she did not go to work; she ate nothing but a little Crosse & Blackwell *Shrimp Bisque* which Cott fixed for her and lost six pounds, which looked good on her, or, rather, looked good off of her. Manny was the fourth man to have jilted her in eighteen months.

Sidney did not actually scream the two whole entire days; she screamed sort of intermittently. She would sit silent for long hours on the day couch in the little living room of the tiny apartment, either completely silent or weeping quietly into a handkerchief, looking out at Cott from those large brown beautiful injured eyes behind her slightly overlarge nose with the cleft in the end, and then suddenly (when the enormity, the sheer electric shocking fact of it would strike, smite, stab her again) would just simply begin to scream again, a high piercing senseless whistling shriek, of rage, and of indignation, at life, death, birth, breath, and any of the other basic human abstractions.

Actually, the news about Manny had not just "come". It was Sidney herself who had "brought" it. She had gone out alone to Idlewild in a cab, which she really could ill afford, in order to meet the plane bringing Manny back from his two weeks in Haiti. The irony of it, the terrible irony, was that it was Cott and herself who were responsible for Manny's two weeks vacation in Haiti "with pay". The two girls had vacationed there several times themselves—when they were flush from one of Cott's movie-acting jobs. Their Haitian friends who ran the hotel where they stayed had a young daughter in need of psychiatric care, and Manny was a psychiatrist. They had put him onto the job. Now he was flying back via Pan American with, although Sidney did not know it yet, the news that he had met a beautiful young Haitian mulatto, a singer, and was ditching Sidney to whom he had been engaged for three months, to marry this other girl instead. When he got off the plane he gave her a beautiful watch, which he had saved a great deal on by buying it in a free port like Haiti, then looking at her sheepishly, he had told her. Sidney had thrown his watch on the ground, smashing it; hit him as hard as she was able, which was never much, and even less under the present circumstances of shock; and had run for a cab. She managed to make it home and up the three flights of stairs to their apartment and to Cott, whom she sent down to pay off the cab she had not had the money for, before she broke down and collapsed.

Cott, of course, had stood by her, as she had stood by Cott's tragedies, as they both of them had always done for each other since they had become friends at Cornell and started rooming together their second year. Sidney had sent her over to his apartment in the middle of the night with all of Manny's shirts and underwear and ties he had kept in the apartment. Manny had been tearing his hair with distress, he didn't want to hurt Sidney he told Cott, but he didn't love her, had never loved her, and he did love this other girl. What was he to do. Cott had felt sorry for him but it was a dirty, stinking, cheap, gutless trick Manny had pulled, any way you looked at it, Cott had said. At least he could have written her a preparatory letter, couldn't he?

Sidney who thought as much herself, even if she couldn't bring herself to feel so much sympathy for him, and resented it in Cott, had spend most of the night walking around and around the block, making up and rehearsing her speech she was going to deliver to Manny. The total import of it was that she hated to see him ruin his life and career by marrying a girl he hardly knew, an honest-to-God real peasant, and a Haitian one at that, a schvartsa yet, but that if that was what he wanted, was what he had to do, she understood and would step down and he would not have to worry about her giving him any "trouble". She thought it a rather good speech, and early in the morning called him up and made him come over and spent an hour downstairs sitting with him in his car out in front of the apartment, delivering her oration. And finally, after that, and after those two days of intermittent screaming, she had been able to pull herself together and go back to work. Back to her familiar old job at Celebrities, Incorporated, Advertising Agency (on 49th just off Madison), which she had thought she would soon be giving up forever.

It had been just about a month after that that the first of her really serious attacks of allergy had hit her.

Sidney had had allergies before, of course; mild ones; and back in college she had suffered from asthma and hay fever especially around exam time it seemed. But never had she suffered anything of the magnitude of what hit her this time. This first attack, this first really *bad* one, had come on a Saturday night when Cott was going out for the evening with Eddie Maynar, the TV and short story writer. It started early in the day around noon and got progressively worse until by the time Eddie Maynar came for his date with Cott, it was already out of the question that Cott could go.

"Well, for Christ's sake," Eddie Maynar said disgruntledly and with chagrin.

"At least you could have called me. Can't you get a doctor or something?" He had sat himself down, still in his topcoat, in the single armchair across from the day couch where Sidney lay gasping for breath, her nose and eyes streaming.

"Well, I can't just go out and leave her here alone like this!" Cott said heatedly. "Do you think I'm some kind of insensitive animal?" And Cott, the beautiful Cott, had swept across the room indignantly to sit down by Sidney and feel her forehead for temperature. There wasn't any, but at midnight, long after Eddie Maynar had given up in disgust and disgruntedly gone off alone dateless, Sidney had reached such a state that she was actually turning slowly blue, slowly strangling before Cott's very eyes. And in the end there was no choice, even as late as the hour was, but to ring up their doctor and have him come over.

Big, shambling, perpetually rumpled looking, and elderly, a professional and acute psychologist as well as an expert diagnostician, a sort of combination spiritual father and nurse to both girls as well as their doctor, he came ambling disgustedly over carting his black satchel. He had been at a theatrical party given by another of his actress patients and had had to leave it. And after giving Sidney a shot of adrenalin that quieted her down and relaxed her enough so she could start breathing again, Doc Bernstein and Cott talked about it.

"But has she ever had anything like this before?" he wanted to know.

"I told you, no!" Cott said. "In school she used to get asthma around examination time. But never anything as bad as this! I'm sure it's all in her mind and she's making it up."

"Sure," Doc Bernstein said disgustedly. "Sure, it's all in her head and she's making it up. But that doesn't mean it couldn't kill her just as easy as if it was real. And I told her that. I told her if she doesn't stop playing these silly damned games with herself she's going to wake up someday and find it's for real and find herself dead. I've about run out of patience with her, Cott."

"Well, she just isn't happy," Cott said, and told him all about Manny's defection.

"Christ, can't you find her a husband around somewhere?" Doc Bernstein said disgustedly.

"Find *her* one! I can't even find myself one."

"There must be somebody around somewhere that the two of you could get married to."

"There is. Gobs of them. But what good is that? We've both of us turned down more chances to get married than you ever did when you were single, I'll bet. Would you have us just marry any damned body?"

"Well, it might be better than slowly choking to death," Doc Bernstein said sourly. "I get awful tired of hysterical women in my business. How far's a doctor supposed to go? Does he have to find husbands for his patients, too?"

"We're neither one of us getting any younger, Doc," Cott grinned at him. "I'm nearly twenty-nine, and Sidney's almost thirty." She paused. "They're either all slobs or else they're already married," she said thoughtfully. "And want only lovers."

"There're only about ten thousand girls like you two in this town," Doc Bernstein said. "And I guess every damned one of them is my patient. Why the hell don't you all go back to the Middle-west where you came from?"

"What? and marry one of the stupid middle-class slobs we all came to the city to get away from marrying?" Cott said. "Anyway, what would all the married men in New York do for lovers if we all went home? The business of the whole city would disintegrate. And with it, the nation."

"I guess you're right at that," Doc Bernstein said sourly. "Well, you better find her some kind of a man. Married or unmarried. I speak as your lay psychiatrist."

"Well, I'll try," Cott said.

And she did try. Sidney tried too, herself. And in the end it was Sidney herself who succeeded. Two months after the conversation with Doc Bernstein (which she recounted to Sidney who took violent exception to it) Cott got herself a job in a West Point movie, a bit part as the Cadet-elected Sweetheart of Flirtation Walk. She was gone six weeks to the Coast, and it was when she came back that L. Carter Wright, book reviewer and interviewer of female movie stars, had entered the scene. Sidney had found him herself, through having lunch with him in order to get an interview for one of her clients at Celebrities, Incorporated, Advertising Agency (on 49th just off Madison). But before that had happened, and during those two months, Sidney had had two more attacks bad enough that Doc Bernstein had to be called. Both of them hit her on occasions when Cott had heavy dates.

One, the first, (or second, rather, if Eddie Maynar was counted as the first) was when Hank Jeffer, novelist and script writer, flew in drunk from the Coast after a fight with his wife and put himself up for four days at their apartment, as he always did on such occasions. It was he who had first got Sidney her job with Celebrities, Incorporated (on 49th just off Madison), one of whose clients he was; and it was he who later got Cott the bit part in the West Point movie, which he had written. Hank had taken Cott out twice to El Morroco, but the third time was too much for Sidney and she came down with an attack which was even worse than the one Eddie Maynar had caused.

The third attack had occurred six week later when Cott was preparing to go off for a week to Connecticut to the ancestral home of a young CBS account executive, the latest in her series of prospective husbands. Cott had gone ahead and gone, anyway. But she might as well not have. It was a week which turned out to be one grand fiasco of misunderstandings, petty arguments, recriminations, and unhappiness; although the young man's family was nice. It succeeded only in her being forced to mark off as a total loss one more prospect.

But it was after Cott had come back from her six weeks on the Coast, to discover the advent of L. Carter Wright upon the scene, that Sidney's allergy appeared to have taken on its present form.

Larry Wright was, Cott thought, although Sidney violently disagreed, almost ludicrously typical of the available New York male. Tall, slender, sensitive-faced, impeccably dressed, married with three kids. Larry was miserably unhappy in both his marriage and his job because he had wanted to be a novelist, and he loved nothing better than coming over to the apartment late in the evening after getting done work and relieving himself of all of his troubles to Sidney (Cott of course always went out), before he made love to her and then drove out home to the country and his wife. Everything said, he was a nice, caught-in-a-trap, unhappy guy—who, nevertheless, did nothing about getting out of it; nothing that is, except talk to Sidney about it, and tell her he wanted to.

And sitting in the apartment any Saturday, just like the one today, Cott was convinced she could plot almost like on a graph—whether Sidney herself believed it or not, which Sidney didn't—the exact pattern of rise and fall that Sidney's allergy would take. And during the four months Sidney had been going with Larry Wright, that graph would not have varied a quarter of an inch.

Sunday was always the worst day. Friday night Larry Wright would be over at the apartment late after he got off work, as he was at least four nights every week, and Cott would get out and let them have the apartment. Luckily, she was still going with her CBS executive, (as Doc Bernstein advised: for God's sake at least keep a stud around), and she could go over to his place or else take in a late movie. Then around three Larry would leave for his home in the country. And then, late Saturday morning or at noon, the sneezing would start. It would get progressively worse until six o'clock, at which time it would abate and they would have a couple of drinks and eat and go out to a movie. But on Sunday Sidney would wake up sneezing, and it would stay that way all day—and generally half the night, until she could get herself to sleep. And the pattern never varied.

Sitting across from each other in the little living room, the beds in the tiny bedroom still unmade (the sight of which made for depression), and staring at each other while both their lives revolved slowly around simultaneously in each's head, it was all just suddenly too much. The remark, fatuous and untrue, as both knew, that Sidney had just made about how Cott could not be expected to know what she felt was still hanging over them in the air, and Cott suddenly, impulsively got up and went over to the day couch and put her arms around her friend.

"What are we going to do?" Sidney said brokenly, and sneezed. "What are we ever going to do?"

"I don't know."

Sidney sneezed again and leaned her head against her roommate's shoulder. "Who the hell wants to be a damned account executive in an advertising agency?"

"Who the hell wants to be a goddamned actress?" Cott said.

"Men!" Sidney said, and sneezed. "Why is it only married men that ever seem to like me?"

"Because the bastards know they haven't got anything to lose, that's why!"

"I'm going to have to break it off with Larry," Sidney said.

"Yes," Cott said. "I think you should. There'll never be anything permanent in it for you. We both know that. But remember what Doc Bernstein said: Always keep at least one man around. Don't break it off with Larry until you've found yourself another."

"No," Sidney said stubbornly, and sneezed again. "I've never been like that. I'm not going to start now. I'll tell Larry tomorrow."

"You have to be tougher," Cott said gently.

"Tougher!" Sidney cried, and sneezed. "Tougher! In two months I'll be thirty. Do you realize that? Thirty years old?

"I swear it to you," she said. "I swear it to you on my thirtieth birthday I'm going to put my head in the oven and just turn on the gas. I mean it. I swear it."

Her arms around her, Cott rocked her slowly back and forth. "You just have to believe," she said. "You have to believe there's a man somewhere. With your name on him. You have to believe it. I have to believe it."

"I believe it," Sidney said. "I believe." She straightened herself and sat back up and wiped her streaming eyes and nose. "And I'm going to tell Larry tomorrow." She sneezed again, rendingly, brokenly.

"We just have to get rid of Frederick the Cat, Cott," she said decisively. "We just simply have to, that's all."

THE TENNIS GAME

Esquire published this in January 1958. It refers directly back to the mention of the tennis game in "A Bottle of Cream," and in fact grows directly out of it. Certain phrases, such as those mentioning the boy's "peepee", his "pubis bone", the sentence "He wanted to play with himself.", which I had to agree to cut to have the story published in a magazine, have all been put back. I think it's an interesting study of male masochism of which there appears to be a great deal in my generation, brought on of course by mothers like the mother in the story.

Lying irritably and sweating between the rows of radishes in the hot humid air under the beating sun, he peered through the screen of tall grass and weeds that formed the boundary of the garden, at the man moving slowly under the shade trees beyond. A slow, warm, secretive pleasure crept over him replacing the irritation as he carefully got the man in his sights. He would never know what hit him. Slowly he cocked the hammer of his pistol and then squeezed the trigger, and the hammer fell upon the little red paper cap igniting it with a low splatting sound.

The man, who was colored and whose name was George and whom the boy's uncle had only recently brought up north from Florida to work for him, was too far away even to hear the sound and went on slowly pushing his lawn mower across the grass under the shade trees and the boy, whose name was John Slade and who was eleven years old, watched him secretively and with that wholly contained private pleasure that nobody else in the whole world knew about from between the rows of radishes in the garden he was supposed to be weeding for his mother. No, sir, he would never have known what hit him.

"Johnnn-y-y-y!" his mother's voice came from behind him, shrill, penetrating, nasal, demanding, insistent, rising in the air and going outward in all directions from the back porch of his house as if it were some kind of audible radio wave and himself the sole receiving set.

"I am!" he cried furiously. He holstered the gun, not really holstered, he didn't have a holster for this one, but jammed between his belly and the belt of his overall pants that he always had to wear when he worked in the garden to keep his better clothes clean. He hated them. And he hated her. And that shrill ear-shivering, penetrating, insistent voice of hers. In his mind's eye he could see her standing there in the shade on the back porch looking out at him through the screen and drying and drying her hands over and over on a dish towel from the kitchen. Without even bothering to look around he began pulling out weeds again from between the dirty damn radishes, the gun barrel he could feel pressed against his belly just above his peepee, his only hope, his only friend. Like Daniel Boone in the forest.

He had tried making a game of it, playing he was the army and the weeds the enemy and watching his hands which were his troops capturing more and more and more clean ground from them and killing them by the hundreds, infiltrating around the heavier pockets of resistance until they had them completely surrounded by clean captured ground and then uprooting the whole big bunch that died to the last man. But there was too much garden and too many too-big weeds, and in the hot humid summer air under the suffocating sun the game had just run down of itself. He had been at it over an hour, John had, if you counted too all the little bits of time he managed to sneak away from pulling.

Across the back-yard fence and screen of cover the colored man George under the shade trees had stopped pushing his mower when he heard John's mother's voice and looked up and grinned, his teeth flashing white in his dark face even at that distance. Now he called sympathetically, "Hot work, ain't it Mister Johnny, on a day like this."

John preferred not to answer and, pretending he had not heard, ignored him and went on pulling weeds lethargically. He would never tell him how he had got him dead to rights so he never knew what hit him. He would never tell it to anybody. Nobody in the world. And it would be one more thing he would have that his mother wouldn't know about, or his father, or any of the other grownups in the world. Or kids either, for that matter. The very thought of it, of having that to add to all the others, the secret, made the pit of his stomach whirl round and round inside him with excitement and he stopped pulling and lay down full length between the rows on the captured clean dirt and wallowed himself on it, all that dirty dirt, rubbing his hands in it above his head and grinding the gun barrel in his pants hurtfully, against his pubis bone, filled with a consuming luxurious hatred for himself, and for her, and for the colored man George, and for his father, and everybody else in the whole world. He'd show them. Let them all see him, wallowing here in the dirt. And just wait till she saw how dirty he got, too, boy, would she be mad, he thought with pleasure. Weeding her old damned vegetable garden.

"Johnnn-y-y-y!" his mother's voice came.

"I *am!*" he cried immediately.

"But what are you doing! Rolling around like that!"

"Working!" he cried with wild outrage, but frightened now, and guilty. "Pullin' weeds! I got to get hold of them, don't I?" Cautiously and slyly he raised himself partially onto his hands and knees and went back to pulling, pretending he had not stopped. After a moment she went back in. God, would she never leave him alone? Ever? Would he never be free of that shrill, insistent, constantly checking voice? Would it follow him around the world forever?

Right in front of him, but a couple of steps off to the left beyond the radish rows, and growing in and around and over the back-yard fence, was the big snowball bush his grandfather had planted long ago before he himself was even born, when grandfather lived in the house his uncle lived in now, the big house. The bush had grown until its branches had fallen back over and made a hidden cave inside it. He often hid in there when nobody knew it, or when he was playing Tarzan or just plain jungle explorers. It was even more secret and he liked it even better than his tree house he had built in the old hollow tree out behind the garage. He had sneaked out his father's pliers and cut away a large section of the wire fence beneath the bush so that he had a secret tunnel between his yard and his uncle's yard that nobody else knew about and could go from one yard to the other without being seen. And now for a moment, crouched on his hands and knees between the radishes, his heart still beating in his ears from her almost catching him, he debated making a run for there when she wasn't looking. The tickle of secrecy was still with him but now it was an angry tickle. He could sit in there where he could see out but nobody could see in and take down his pants and rub handfuls of the fresh dirt all over his peepee with his grubby hands. The thought of doing that excited him because he would be getting even with her. And she would never catch him provided he could get to the house and in the bathroom and wash himself first. And he thought he could. Because she'd never think to make him take his pants down. But he wisely decided against trying to make the run for it. She would surely be looking out again in a minute and see him gone, and anyway if he didn't get the weeding done he would be out here all day and not get to play at all. She would see to that. And after this, there was still the front half of the yard to mow. And of course he would have to go to the store for her too, for something she'd forgotten.

Furiously, in a violent if momentary burst of vigorous energy, he attacked the weeds because it was the only way out of this that he could find. And he had been wanting to play his tennis game today, ever since early morning.

Johnny Slade wasn't any damned fool. And he knew enough to know that he didn't *have* to weed the garden, or mow the yard. They didn't even have to *have* a damned old vegetable garden. His mother said it was to save money, and then would put a sad look on her face, but he knew better. He had watched his father shopping at the A&P store, and he knew the money they saved by putting out a garden was not enough even to count. He knew there was a Depression on, and had been for five years ever since the President had closed the banks when he was little; but he also knew the money his father made in his dentist's office downtown was enough that they could afford to hire a man to mow the yard, and weed the damned garden if they had to have one, just like his uncle who was a lawyer had hired the colored man George in Florida. But they were just too cheap to do it. That was the truth. That, and because his mother wanted something to hold over his father when he got drunk. And because, as she said when she got mad, her son was going to learn to work because it built character and was good for his soul—and he was going to learn it if it killed the both of them. But the real truth was she couldn't stand to see him outdoors playing and having fun while she herself had to clean house and cook. She just couldn't stand it, he could tell by the look on her face, and so the whole thing was no more than one damned big lie. One of those grownup lies, that grownups told each other and pretended to believe, and that children because they were little had to accept and pretend to believe too, because they could not argue back.

Thinking about it, and the whole entire huge conspiracy of it all, in which a kid as long as he was little had no chance at all, depressed him so his violent burst of energy dwindled away inside of him leaving him feeling only weary, and defeated, completely beaten, and lethargic. He had, in his burst of activity, cleared two feet of ground. There was at least twenty more to go. How would he ever get it done in time to play the tennis game? Or anything at all, for that matter.

As it turned out, he didn't have to finish it, although it was after lunch before he was finally allowed to quit. His mother called him in and made him wash for lunch (exclaiming over how dirty he always managed to get, to which he of course said nothing) and fed him and then sent him back out to work on it another hour. But then she let him quit and made him take a bath because this afternoon she was having her Wisdom Club bridge ladies that she had to entertain once every two months, and she didn't want him coming in the house all messy and dirty while they were there. So he was free to play, reprieved, and the rest of the garden as well as the yard to mow was put back until tomorrow. Happy just simply to be free, and willing to let tomorrow take care of itself and not even think about it, he ran outside through the kitchen and the back door after he had dressed and across the driveway to the playhouse his father had bought for him and his baby sister a year ago, wanting only to get away and out of sight before she changed her mind maybe, as she often did.

Listening to the Wisdom Club bridge ladies as they began to arrive, and feeling like a rich man, he sat in the little chair on the porch of the playhouse and went over in his mind the various games he could play. The tickle of secretive pleasure had come back into his stomach again. He knew of course what he was going to play. The tennis game. But he enjoyed going over his possibilities and pretending he was making his choice. For instance, there was the tree house and Tarzan, for which he would have to take off his shirt and put on his hunting knife, and he could carry her there, Jane, and make her play with his peepee. Or he could get out his sun helmet and play jungle explorers and how they found the lost tribe of naked white women Amazons who captured them and tortured them. He could, if he wanted to, go on with the lead-soldier battle he had in progress in the playhouse. He sat on the porch of the playhouse luxuriously, and thoughtfully studied all of these.

The playhouse where he sat was a regular little house with a regular roof that sloped two ways like a real house and a front door and back door and windows that opened; it was very realistic, and the floor of the single room interior was the scene of the lead-soldier battle. It had been going on almost three weeks now. First he had fixed up the floor with pillows for mountains and piles of Big Little Books for hills and long strips of blue paper for the river, and then later two lines of Big Little Books for the trenches in front of the big plaster fort. From one end of the room the bad side was advancing upon and trying to capture the good side who were gradually being forced back to take refuge in their fort. At present, the good side had had to abandon two whole lines of trenches. Trenches which the bad side, naturally, had taken over to use against them. With it arranged this way, and the attack moving from one end of the room toward the other, he could shoot for both sides through the open windows at either end of the playhouse. Only just yesterday he had killed a colonel of the good side who was leading a counterattack against the steadily encroaching trenches in an attempt to break through and split the line. The BB had struck the colonel's horse, breaking off both of its front legs, and that particular soldier was ruined forever, which made John feel curiously and pleasantly sad, and the colonel's force had been driven back in confusion, losing two more killed before they could get back to their own lines. The counterattack had failed. It was a bad blow for the good side. The colonel had been one of their best field commanders and they had counted a great deal on that attack and now things didn't look good for them at all. Steadily they were being forced further and further back, ringed in into a smaller and smaller maneuvering space. It gave John a strange delicious feeling of tragic fatalisticness, to see them fighting so hard and bravely and being gradually beaten back. On the other hand, as the bad side steadily advanced into the good side's territory, they came more and more into dead range of the BB gun in the window, and consequently were now losing a great many more men than they had before. It even appeared at times that they might not have sufficient forces to capture the fort once they got there. Also, John had contemplated putting a relieving force of reinforcements in the field behind the bad side to aid the beleaguered garrison. He had the men. And if he did that, it would turn into a real blood bath, a regular rout, for the bad side. And in fact John was not sure yet just which side was going to win. Sometimes he could hardly wait to find out.

The deciding factor of course was himself, and he knew this, and understood it fully and completely in all its implications, and accepted the responsibility. Just as he accepted the responsibility of destroying his own soldiers, which he loved and valued, every time he levered his BB gun against his leg and shot a big ugly hole in one, or knocked off its head, or broke it off from its stand. He understood this too and it made him sad when he had to do it. But there wasn't any choice. It was necessary in the cause of reality. Otherwise the battle wouldn't be real or realistic at all. And every time he got one of his better soldiers he particularly loved in his sights, the old sad fatalistic secret tickle of almost hurtful pleasure would arise in his stomach. Of course, he didn't shoot these better ones very often, like the colonel, and saved them back for special occasions.

Nevertheless, though he knew what the deciding factor would be, in other words himself, and it was a great responsibility, he still didn't know which side would win. Naturally, he wanted the good side to win, because they were the good guys. But in some ways he wanted the bad side to win too, and tear the good side all to shreds and kill them to the last man like the Arabs did at the fort in BEAU GESTE when he read it, or like at the Alamo. So he could not be sure which side would win because he wasn't sure which side he *wanted* to win. His opinions changed with his moods. He was not above cheating a little, either, and making a greater percentage of his shots miss one side or the other depending upon what mood he was in and who he was for at the moment, but he didn't really feel that that was really cheating. One day, in a fit of mood, he had organized an all-out attack by the good side which in an hour had the bad side in full retreat and which before it was done had swept away and destroyed almost all the gains the bad side had so laboriously built up since the battle started, and in fact the only thing that saved them from complete defeat was a last ditch stand by a small group of French Foreign Legionnaires, tough fighters all, who were fighting with the bad side this battle. That time almost all the shots the bad side made either missed or went astray, and when it was all over and he looked around at the carnage and havoc and the ruptured plans he felt half sick and strangely astonished, although he had known all along what he was doing and was going to do. Why had he done it? Now they would have to start all over.

Sitting on the little porch and hearing the high-pitched cackling chatter of the Wisdom Club bridge ladies in the house, John looked in through the window at the battlefield of the floor. The bad side had by now of course regained all of the lost ground that the good side's attack had wrested from them and were once again encroaching upon the fort. Maybe tomorrow he would start a feeling attack by the bad side with the objective maybe of driving a salient into the good side's line and breaking it. If it did, if it succeeded, did break the line, it would be nearly the end. The good side would have to retire into their fort, the fort would be invested, and from then on it would only be a matter of time. There wasn't anywhere behind them to fall back to; the fort was right back against the end wall of the playhouse. It gave John a strange excited sad feeling. And now would be a good time to start off such a feeling attack, while the good side was still shaken up and in distress over the failure of their counterattack, and the loss of their fine colonel. Yes, that was what he would do. But not today. Today he was going to play the tennis game.

Getting up from the little porch, excited, and tingly all over at the prospect, and with the high-pitched cackle of the Wisdom Club bridge ladies still irritably in his ears (the boobs), he went to the garage to get the racket and balls. The playhouse which served as battlefield for the lead-soldiers also doubled as grandstand for the tennis game, and he brought the equipment back to where the umpires waited, to be introduced to his opponent. Although, of course, they knew each other, and had in fact played against each other many times at Wimbledon and Forest Hills and in many other tournaments. The introduction was only a formality.

But first, before beginning to play, he laid the equipment on the little porch and went around to the side of the garage to pee, and suddenly for no reason, but with his heartbeat rising in his ears frightenedly and causing his excitement over the game to dissipate and leave him feeling hollow and empty, found himself thinking of that day a month or so ago when Alice Pringle from the other side of town had been here to play.

He knew, of course, why he suddenly thought of Alice, whom he hardly knew; it was because of what had happened right here around the side of the garage, right where he was standing now, when Alice had been here. It was a secluded spot here, out of sight of his house, and the spot where all the guys came to pee when they played here or in the vacant lot behind the playhouse. A neighbor's garage which faced the other way from his own toward the other street was built right alongside John's garage, so close their eaves were only a few feet apart and you could jump from one garage roof to the other and there was almost like a tunnel between them, a sort of passageway between the yards, from one side of the block to the other, and right at the back end of it a big young locust tree that partly shaded the playhouse. This was where he brought Alice to pee too, when she had asked him to take her some place. He had offered to take her in the house, first, but looking at him with a funny strange grin that made her eyes seem to get littler, the same kind of grin he could feel beginning to come over his own face, she had said no she would rather go somewhere close outside instead of in the house.

Alice was just exactly his own age, but he didn't know her very well because she wasn't from his town and was only visiting here for the summer with her mother. She did every summer. And her mother had brought her by for the afternoon because she had to go somewhere. So feeling strangely scared and embarrassed, though he didn't want to, he had taken Alice in between the garages where all the guys always went, and then had turned to go away until she was through, as he knew he was supposed to. But she had said in a funny voice didn't he want to stay, maybe he had to pee too, and it was all right as long as he turned his back and didn't look, and then she would turn her back and not look, that was the way the boys and girls all always did in her town where she came from.

And so that was what they had done, and the sequence they followed—except for one thing: when she asked him if he was done and he should have said no he said yes instead and she turned around and saw him still peeing, while his heart was beating in his throat like a triphammer. Alice had giggled and slapped his arm, and then she frowned and looked angry and turned back around and said in an angry voice that he shouldn't have done that, that was bad. It was not exactly the reaction he was expecting. Or even why he had done it, really. Anyway, it didn't matter because that was when his mother's voice, shrill, strident, demanding and insistent, like some all-seeing all-knowing powerful dark angel of God, had come out sharply at him from the upstairs bedroom window over the back porch where she was supposed to be lying down taking a nap. *Johnnnnyy! What are you children doing? Where are you? Come here!* Hastily buttoning his pants, his mind fumbling and balking on him frightenedly, he walked slowly around from between the garages to stand looking up under the upstairs bedroom window, feeling like a criminal caught in the act and brought before the high bench of the stern judges of the bar of justice. And when she asked him again what they had been doing, he simply told her, his mind floundering and fumbling so badly that there wasn't even any question of thinking of an excuse. Later he would wonder why he hadn't lied; she couldn't prove anything. Alice wondered why he hadn't lied, too.

"What did you do that for? What did you tell her the truth for?" she whispered furiously, while they waited for her to come down. "Now you've got us both into trouble."

He didn't know what trouble Alice got into, when her mother came to take her home, but she had certainly been right about him anyway. His mother had separated them and made Alice stay in the livingroom and him in the bedroom upstairs. Then she had, first, washed his mouth out with soap on a wet washcloth (although he didn't know why she had to do that to him; that was usually his punishment for lying, not for telling the truth) and then, second, she had given him a whale of a whipping on his bare bottom while she glared at him with angrily narrowed eyes and made it plain to him in no uncertain terms what a filthy, dirty thing it was he had done.

He never did find out what happened to Alice when she got home, because she never came back any more and he hadn't seen her since.

Standing there between the garages to pee, where it had all happened, his heart beating dully with fright and fear again in his ears just as it had that day (although at least he didn't have to listen to the high-pitched cackle of the Wisdom Club bridge ladies around here where you couldn't hear it), he finished and then went back to the little porch, the enthusiasm for the tennis game all gone. And it was quite a while, sitting there hollow and empty and dandling the tennis racket lethargically, before he could work himself up to starting to play it.

The tennis game was a new one, one that he had invented only a few weeks ago, when he read a story about a championship tennis match in a *Collier's* magazine that his mother had brought home. The idea for the story obviously came from Don Budge's victory over Baron von Cramm in the Davis Cup and the Wimbledon, which John had followed in the sports pages with interest. The writer had taken that for his starter, and then had made up a story about this championship match, and these two men both of whom *had* to win it. It was a real battle of wills. Everything both men wanted from the world was at stake. The young American would lose his girl he wanted to marry and the big job her father had offered him if he lost the match, and the German Baron had been told by the Führer that if he did not win for Germany all his estates would be confiscated and himself imprisoned. All this came out in the story as the two men played the match, and you could read it tensely, liking both men, hoping both could win, but knowing only one could. In the end, in this great test of wills, the young American had won over the older German sportsman, and the Baron, rather than return to Germany and what he knew waited there, had shut the garage door and turned on his car motor, thinking he had been an adventurer all his life and now he was embarking upon the greatest adventure of all. It was a gripping story and John, who would be twelve before too long, in some strange way that he couldn't describe was able to sense out and associate with the German's sad but strong feelings his tragic courage. And in fact, in the story, he had liked the Baron much more than he had liked the young American who won.

And that was the story of his tennis game. Sometimes, when he played the match through against the garage doors, he would become so involved in it and its struggle that the play of emotions which ran through him became unbelievably intense, almost unbearable, exquisitely powerful. He *became* the German, and the young American too. Of course, he never played it when any of the other kids were around; and he never told anybody about it. He would have felt silly and embarrassed. So to all intents and purposes he was merely practicing tennis strokes against the garage. But the very secrecy itself added to the excitement of it, and even before he would begin to play out the match that secret, completely contained, private pleasure which caused his stomach to spin, would steal over him, as he marched out onto the court.

He had arranged it all so it would be very realistic. The playhouse was the grandstand, and the concrete driveway which was double for two car-lengths back from the double doors was the court. The garage doors, which were on rollers and slid from side to side one behind the other, were made with two-by-four braces that framed their edges and crisscrossed from corner to corner and were painted white, and the brace that ran across them cutting them in half horizontally across the middle was the net; every shot that hit below that was a lost point. And every shot that went off the concrete was an "out," and another lost point. The crisscross braces themselves, as well as the offset door joint, gave an added element of chance to it since at times the ball would hit one of them and squirt off out of bounds to the side, or else hit the concrete where he could not possibly get it back. In spite of this element of chance, however, the deciding factor was once again, of course, as with the lead-soldiers' battle, himself. He could make whichever one win he wanted to, and could *be* whichever one he wanted whether winning or losing, according to his mood. Usually he chose to be the Baron and to lose.

And today, after getting over the upset of the memory of Alice Pringle, that was who he was. After getting himself worked into it and beginning to get involved by the end of the first set (the Baron took the first one, building his tragic hopes unnaturally high), the cackling conversation of the Wisdom Club bridge ladies coming out to him from inside the house added a strange, new, exciting element. They were the crowd, chattering and talking excitedly among themselves as they sat happily in the grandstand. What did they know about the tragedy that was being enacted out here on the court as the Baron fought desperately to win? What did they know of his desperate effort to keep all his estates and keep himself from being put in a Nazi concentration camp? It was only a game to them, an exciting match to be enjoyed while they drank Cokes and ate sandwiches. Just for spite, as if Fate itself were playing nasty tricks on the plucky German, he let the Baron take the second set too. Now he was all set up. Just one more set to win, out of three, and he would have the championship and all it meant to him. But then, just as the German thought he had it, thought he was safe at last, he switched sides to the young American and really began to go to work.

Cold, calm, collected, the young American (he had always been noted as a pressure player) began to play tennis like he had never played in his life before. Ferocious drop shots, sizzling volleys, high lobs in the very corners, everything. He, and John with him, was everywhere on the court, growing steadily and relentlessly stronger in confidence and power. Even the crowd hushed and became quiet at such a brilliant exhibition. And slowly the score crept up on the weakening German. The American, playing brilliantly, took the third set 6-4. Then came back to take the fourth set 6-2.

And then, as the two of them stood staring implacably at each other across the net after their rest, John switched back to the Baron for the fifth and final set and the climax. The Baron already knew it was a lost cause now. Several years older than his opponent, weakening, tired, winded, his knees shaky, he fought on grimly, the handkerchief tied around his forehead to keep the sweat out of his eyes. Several times he, and John with him, staggered on the court going after impossible placements. But he did not go down. He lost the first two games without even a deuce. But then, almost completely exhausted, in actual physical pain almost, he rallied and took the next three straight games, all of them with at least two deuces, making one supreme effort, which was his last. Then, with the game score 3-2 in his favor, the American broke through his service, and on the last point he, and John with him, staggered and fell, trying to reach an impossibly brilliant drop shot, and he knew it was all over. Lying stretched out on the court, his racket still reaching across the concrete after that irretrievably lost ball, breathing convulsively, he rolled over, then got wearily up to one knee and looked across the net at the man who had defeated him. There would be no going back to Germany for him now. There was almost a luxury in knowing it, in knowing it was over, in embracing his defeat he had fought so hard against, a real happiness and pleasure almost. And, his stomach spinning almost sickly with excitement and emotion, John climbed back slowly to his feet.

The rest was an anticlimax. Everybody, even the crowd, knew it was over. For the next three games the Baron played grimly. Several times he staggered and nearly fell, and twice he, and John with him, went down on one knee. But it was all only a formality. And then it was finally over. Knowing what he must do, now, he walked slowly over to the umpire's stand on the little porch in front of the grandstand to congratulate his opponent. And almost physically sick with excitement and emotion, the nerves in his arms and legs tingling with it, John dropped the racket and balls on the porch in beaten defeat and started around the garage to where the tree house was, out in back of it, to do what he always wanted to do when he felt like this. He wanted to play with himself. It was then that his mother's voice followed him from out of the kitchen, where she was fixing the refreshments.

"Johnny! Johnny! What are you doing out there, falling around like that?"

"Playing," he said grimly, his face a mask of German iron control, as became a Prussian.

And as he went on to the tree house, his peepee throbbing in his pants, behind him he heard his mother say laughingly to the Wisdom Club bridge lady who was helping her:

"Playing! Oh, well, you know how children are. They're always playing some little game or other when they're by themselves."

THE ICE-CREAM HEADACHE

This one's really a bonus. Not even conceived except as a vague brief note when the Introduction for this collection was written, it was intended originally as simply another of the fairly uncomplex childhood stories mentioned earlier. Then it got away from me. The "near-but-not-quite-incest" thing, a much commoner experience in America than commonly admitted, got taken over by the failed-family theme and an attempt to understand the curse of family alienation and where it came from to so many of us in those years. And that, of course, changed everything. I think it's better for the change. It was begun several months after "Go to the Widow-Maker," that much misunderstood novel, was finished and handed over: ten years and three novels later than the last group of four stories, three of them also childhood stories; and it took a little over two months to write.

ThereT was nothing so Faulknerian about the town, but there was sure something very Faulknerian about the family. Tom Dylan thought this gloomily. He was sitting on his stopped bike with his empty paperbag down his back and looking across a wide lawn through the faint predawn light of another summery day at the dark un-lived-in shell of his grandfather's columned old colonial mansion on West Main Street. The house was a part of his paper route, but where lights would soon be coming on in the other big houses on West Main no lights would be coming on in there. Well. He was meeting two girls in there at around three o'clock this afternoon. One of them was his sister. The thought made his heart pound. Almost seventeen, tall and lanky, with a hawk's nose, he pushed off with his right leg and rode the bike on in toward the middle of the town.

It was one of those Middlewestern villages in western Indiana which, in this modern age of 1935, liked to call themselves cities. Tom grinned. It had a courthouse with a square of grass around it from which the old trees had been cut down and around that a square of business buildings variously labeled 1880 or 1904 or some such year to indicate their date of construction. It all looked Faulknerian enough. But the town had not suffered in the Civil War as Faulknerian towns had suffered, because Indiana was Northern. This particular town had not suffered since the Campaigns of Mad Anthony Wayne for the Indiana Territory which meant, since the town had not even existed then, never.

The family was different. The family had suffered. Or thought it had. Which was almost as good. Certain members of it like his mother believed certain members of it, themselves, had suffered greatly. And that was about as good as real suffering and might even, in a pinch, be taken for real suffering. What the Dylan family had suffered from was, mainly, pride. Good old *human* pride, the stuff that made the spheres revolve and the world go round, as *humans* liked so much to say of it. But which also caused more stubborn bitchery, hardheaded meanness, hate, destruction, murder and organized mayhem than could be found anywhere else in the animal kingdom all put together. Good old old-fashioned American, Middlewestern, kill-me-but-I'll-never-budge pride.

Tom stood up on his pedals and began to pump up the short steep hill to the town square. He figured he was the only person in town, except for the librarian, who had ever even heard of this guy Faulkner. Certainly there were no other return dates stamped in the books the librarian had suggested for him. On the square he turned right toward the newsstand.

That house. Tom could barely remember his grandfather as he had been in life. What he really remembered were the pictures and old tinplates of him as a younger man that they had in their house and in the old albums, and these became confused with the real old man. The grandfather, dead now in the 1930s, dead in fact since September 1929 just a few weeks before The Crash which would have ruined him had he lived but which instead ruined only his heirs, whom he left extremely well-provided-for, could be traced as the source of the Dylan pride and a lot of the Dylan suffering. Of course, both might have extended back into the past beyond him and so have been carried forward through and after him into the future like relay runners carry and pass a baton among them, Tom thought. But in 1935 nobody in the family knew or remembered or cared about anyone before him, so they were not equipped to say. If they had been, it would not have helped them. As far as they were concerned, it had begun with him. Even the two grandchildren knew that much. He loomed over them all like stern, giant, frock-coated apparition, waving—or perhaps signaling—to them from back there, back there in the past from on the other side of that Big Crash he had been unable to save them from.

Tom checked in at the newsstand, turning over two extras to the proprietor, a mealy-mouthed little man who was nice in spite of himself. He had been a tall, dark, ramrod-straight man, the grandfather, with heavy dark eyebrows, a long flowing black mustache, hard black eyes, (but that was those pictures, now, wasn't it?) and long sleek black hair which he wore long to the nape of his neck and only had trimmed in the dark of the moon, which accounted, he said, for why it stayed black, which it did, up to and after his death at the age of 72. He looked in fact not unlike, looked extremely *like*, the photos of Wyatt Earp taken in Tombstone at the time Earp had shot and killed the terrified Mexican horse-handler after the famous full count of three, Earp the great Earp, whom the grandfather almost certainly had admired, Tom suspected, at least in his youth and younger married years. Which were the only years that counted as far as his four sons were concerned. If he had perhaps mellowed later, that could be of no damned help to the already warped family.

It was rumored in the town that the grandfather was a quarter Indian, a rumor he enjoyed and did nothing to dispel. The story was that his father's father as a young man, while on a staples-buying trip to Evansville for the family farm in the lower backwoods riverbottom part of the county, had come upon a young and near-dead Cherokee squaw in a ditch by the side of the road during the time of the Removal and had brought her home in the wagon with the staples, later to marry her after she healed and grew up a little. Unfortunately, this was not recorded in the family Bible since the family Bible was only begun with the grandfather's father, after the old family Bible was burned with the old family farmhouse. But the grandfather, always a somewhat secretive man, never denied it. Certainly the burning of the old family Bible was a fact. Certainly the grandfather looked Indian. And this, plus the fact that he had twice been Sheriff of the county before turning to the Law as a profession, had caused him to be looked at with a certain amount of awe and respect and even fear in the town, as he, quietly and ramrod-straight right up into his seventies, walked its streets tall and stern and reserved and stately. The town had grown modern in The Boom of the 1920s and by then even sported a Country Club, but its moderns still could not entirely forget the town's raw wild wide-open days in the 1890s when it had been an oil-boom town and the grandfather had been its Sheriff. In his later years, when he "had perhaps mellowed," he maintained and cherished a considerable collection of brass knuckles, bowie knives, pepperpots and pistols which he had taken away from roustabouts and drunks during his two terms as Sheriff. The town, even from the deep-porch, bungalow-style veranda of its modern 1920s Country Club, could never quite forget that. Neither could the two grandchildren forget it, since in his elder years he had used to take the collection out and let them play with it. Tom wondered what had ever happened to it. Probably his lawyer uncle had it. Or rather, his uncle's widow—his lawyer uncle's latest, last widow. He—and through him she—had wound up with just about everything, including the old house.

Outside the newsstand it was full summer daylight now but almost nobody was out and moving yet. Tom grasped his bike's handlebars with indecision. He didn't want to go home now. His mother would just be up, and slopping up the breakfast in her sloppy robe in the kitchen. His father would be climbing out of bed coughing, with the slow movement and huge paunch of a dedicated drunk, getting ready to go down to his tiny veterinarian's office. And Tom didn't want to see his sister now, this morning, under normal home breakfast conditions. When he thought of her, and her friend, his heart pounded again. He would see her later in the morning when his mother was busy with her eternal, and complaint-ridden, housecleaning.

The other boys who had had to come back to the newsstand for something or other were dispersing on their bikes toward their homes. About the only thing open this early in the morning were the two jerrybuilt little shack restaurants on North Street behind the bank. They opened early for the five o'clock shift at the chemical plant. Tom headed his bike there. After he had eaten a hot greasy hamburger and drunk a half-pint milk bottle of chocolate milk, he left his bike leaning against the brick of the bank building and after looking around sneaked in between the two shack restaurants to a high weedgrown wooden wall. Pulling out two seemingly solid planks he slipped behind them and was under a head-high wooden truck ramp that belonged to the lumber yard which occupied the interior of the block. Closed in on three sides by wood and on the fourth by the poured concrete beginning of the ramp, just enough light filtered in through the planks to make it possible to see. He called this his thinking place. He had four others scattered around town. Putting his back against the concrete and squatting on the gritty cinder and earth floor, he pulled his knees up to his chin and sat looking at a smooth white stone he called his spitting stone. Thomas Wolfe had the same kind of crazy nutty family in his two books but he didn't get the same kind of sense of doom in his family that this guy Faulkner got into his. After a minute a truck rumbled up the ramp shaking cinder dust down on him and he began to practice spitting at the stone. That house. Mansion. He couldn't get that big rich empty mansion out of his mind. Today. Usually it didn't bother him. For some reason it did today.

But it was his own four stalwart sons who were most unable to forget the grandfather's days as Sheriff, Tom thought. As small boys they had used to watch from hiding places as he would walk sternly up to some drunken oilfield roustabout, take from him his pistol he had just fired in jest down the crowded Saturday night street and pistolwhip him over the head with it before escorting him to the jail. They couldn't forget it because he had employed the same style and methods to raise and educate his sons. He was Protestant, sternly religious, and a teetotaler. And like any proud, serious man of his generation he meant to bring his sons up the same way. To spare the rod was to spoil the child. It was a common enough philosophy in America in 1900. It was practically universal. Sternly, like any of the twenty other most successful men of his period in the town who now owned the large homes with the big lawns along East and West

Main Streets, he applied it. Why, then, hadn't it worked? With his sons. It had worked with the sons of his friends. And they still had the big houses to prove it. What was the fatal flaw? Where the error? Four sons, and four failures. Tom could almost feel himself feeling the grandfather's horrified thinking. Four sons, four drunken weaklings. A hundred percent reading, that. It seemed highly unlikely that anyone would have four failures out of four sons simply by accident. Perhaps unfortunately, he did not live to see the total working out of their collective failed destinies, but it was almost certain that he had already suspected and anticipated them. That almost surely was why he put so much of his hard-earned life's savings at the Law into Insul stocks for them, to take care of them the rest of their lives. Having—he believed—rectified, or at least covered up for, whatever the mistake was he had made in raising them or the fatal flaw he had transmitted to them in his seed, he could die peacefully. And in fact the last words he was supposed to have said were, "I've left you all well-provided-for." Then he turned on his side with his face to the white hospital room wall and tiredly, even almost blissfully as one of his sons was to say, sighed his last. Some people were just lucky, another, more bitter of his sons was to say, later; because The Crash was not long in coming.

The two little grandchildren were not in on any of this, since they were hustled outside by their weeping mother and not allowed back in the white room until "It" was over, on the theory that the sight of death might scar their precious little souls. But they had speculated and whispered between themselves, and of course they heard all the endlessly repeated family stories about it all, that were told over and over. Their father maintained that had grandfather lived he would have anticipated The Crash it and sold all his "Instul Stocks" for lots of money. They knew that this disease and demise had to do with his "prostrate."

It was Tom's own personal theory that he, the grandfather, was almost certainly very highly oversexed, had frustrated and stifled that part of himself in him, and so instead had just taken it out on his four sons, in meanness. People did that. Only, how did you know with people like that from a generation like that that was all so stuffed up shut and ignorant. He doubted his grandfather had ever even heard the word oversexed. And yet there was something very sensual about him, especially in those older pictures of him, when he was younger. Anyway, whether he was or not, all of his four sons were, and so were his two grandchildren. Tom did not think it unreasonable to assume the old man had passed it on—from wherever *he* had gotten it.

So there they all were: the four brothers—now—and no longer the four sons, and the wives of the three of them that were married, and the two small grandchildren, brother and sister, all crowded together around the deathbed in the white room in the town's doctor-owned "Sanitarium." It was just about the last time that they would all ever be together again at the same time. The last time would be after The Crash itself.

Even without the upcoming Crash, Tom mused, and their sexual heritage whatever it was, they were perhaps ill-equipped to be on their own. He worked his mouth for a minute and then jetted spit at the white stone and hit it dead center. Perhaps the grandfather should never have insisted they all become veterinarians. But in the 1900s who could have guessed that the horrible smoke-belching horseless carriages of that decade would turn into the beautiful, stream-lined, carbon-monoxide-producing Stutz Bearcat of the 1920s. The grandfather was a lover of fine horseflesh and in those earlier decades kept a beautiful pair of beautifully trained carriage horses as well as his own fine saddle horse in his own carriage house behind the big house and wide lawn on West Main Street. The four boys had been taught to take care of horses since early childhood. What could be a better or more honorable profession for them. The grandfather refused to believe that fine horses could ever be replaced by unthinking, unfeeling mechanical monstrosities. It just simply wouldn't happen. And since it wouldn't, the idea was that after their training as vets he, the grandfather, would lay out the capital to set them all up in top-flight, very high-class livery stables in various county seats across that part of the state. And of course back then, in the 1900s, the strict social hierarchy which places lawyers first, doctors second, dentists third, and veterinarians fourth and last, so that no one would invite a dentist or a vet unless nothing else was available—that unbreakable social structure had not yet been constructed and imposed upon Middlewestern America. How, in 1907, could the grandfather have anticipated that.

The rest of it was done by the cars. As, in the 1910s, the automobile industry grew and as large, elaborate and expensive livery-stable establishments dwindled and finally disappeared in the '20s, it was one thing to be the rich fashionable owner and sole proprietor of a big livery stable, and quite another to be the little man who doctored people's cats and dogs and was without the necessary training or permission to doctor people and whom nobody invited. In a way, Tom mused, spitting morosely and hitting off center this time, in a way an era had ended in America then: When the grandfather had "read Law," he had not been required to go to any school or college and had merely apprenticed himself to a local judge; and the local doctor in whose *Sanitarium* the grandfather died had learned his trade by simple trial-and-error practice, while his wife sat with him in the operating room on a stool and from a Surgeon's Manual read to him where he was supposed to cut. By the 1920s such easy going methods were finished. Still, in the 1920s with the grandfather ladling out the money from his apparently inexhaustible supply and having no necessity to do anything but drink at the Country Club and flirt and maybe play a little golf, it was not so bad being a vet with a dwindling livery stable. But The Crash would take care of that, too.

They had not all four actually become veterinarians, in fact. Just the first son and the third son, Tom's father. The first son didn't really give a damn what he became, since all he really cared about was gambling, drinking and whores. Tall, ramrod-straight like the grandfather and ice-faced, he was the unmarried one, the bitter one who later had called the grandfather smart, or at least lucky, for having died when he did. He and the grandfather hated each other with cold implacability. He had wound up with his own dwindling—and neglected—livery stable in another county seat over near Evansville, while spending all his serious moments gambling in Evansville or Cincinnati. But the second son had rebelled. He did not like animals, and never had. Especially horses. When presented with his older brother's tools, instruments and textbooks and ordered off to vet's school he had run away from home and apprenticed himself to a drunken carpenter and cabinet-maker in a nearby town and become a drunken carpenter and cabinet-maker himself. Though he was still underage the grandfather did not try to bring him back. Instead he publicly disowned him as his son and disinherited him. A lean, gnarled, twisted man, bent from leaning over his cabinetry and carpentry tools, he and the grandfather loved each other as implacably as the grandfather and the oldest son hated each other. But this did not help make it possible for them to speak to each other during the next twenty years, and he did not get reinstated to his inheritance until the last weeks of the grandfather's final illness, so that he had very little time to get used to it or enjoy it before The Crash wiped it out and forced him back to being a drunken carpenter again. But it was the fourth son, the "baby"—whom the other three insisted had been "babied," all his life—who was the lucky one. By the time he was old enough to go off to vet's college, inheriting from the third brother, Tom's father, the tools and textbooks the third brother had inherited from the first, the grandfather had seen his mistake—if not about the low position of the veterinarian in the emerging social scale, at least about the emergence of the automobile. He was shipped off to law school, from which he graduated to become the grandfather's law partner. After the grandfather's death he inherited the law practice. But even that could not help him when The Crash came and everything was in Insul stock. After getting involved in a bootleg liquor deal while running for District Judge the very next year, he was forced to leave town. He went, leaving his wife behind him, but this did not stop him from taking with him everything else left of the family inheritance that was not nailed down, including the grandfather's pistol collection, ownership of the family farm in the riverbottoms, and ownership of the big house on West Main Street, just how nobody ever quite knew. Mainly it was in fees for having done the legal work of the inheritance for all of them.

What could have flawed them all so? the four of them. Within five years of the grandfather's death in 1929 the three of them, the uncles, would be dead of some violent death or other, each connected with some woman in some way or other. The eldest, the gambler, would be found sitting in his car with a knife in his chest on a back street in Henderson, Kentucky, and without his customary large roll of bills in his pocket; although the claim was that it was the irate husband of some enamored wife. The second son, the carpenter-cabinet-maker, would be found dead, burned, in the remains of his concrete-block workshop, where a gasoline stove—apparently—had exploded and caught fire while he slept in a chair with a whiskey bottle between his knees—this, after having found out two days before that he had gotten pregnant a young countrygirl distant cousin from down in the bottom part of the county near where the old family farm used to be. And the fourth son, the "baby," after settling in Iowa and remarrying, then moving on from there minus his second wife to California, where he became a somewhat shady scandal- and divorce-lawyer on the periphery of Hollywood, would die at the wheel of his own (unpaid-for) Cadillac convertible in a drunk-driving accident with the wife of another man dead beside him.

That left the one. Tom's father. The third son. Who might just as well be as dead as the rest of them, as far as his son was concerned. He had probably never argued with the grandfather once in his life. And he was a goddam veterinary today to prove it. A drunk veterinary. It was pretty obvious he hated his work. And what kind of life was that. For a man. Tom jetted spit at the white stone again, morosely, and hit it center. He knew a bit more than he was telling, too, about his father's women. This was back when there were still any of them who would still have anything to do with him. He secretly suspected that in about five years his father would be dead too, a suicide maybe, dead of a pistol shot in the heart, or an overdose of pills, and without even having the prestige of the courage of having killed himself sober.

Tom was tired of sitting. And he had solved nothing. What was there to solve? That house. That damned big old house. He stretched out his legs in their cor-duroy pants in the cinder dust. There was a pissy smell in here, due to the work-ing men taking a quick leak against the boards of the truck ramp inside the lumber yard, but he didn't really mind it. After a moment he looked at his five dollar Bulova watch. It was barely eight o'clock, and he did not want to go home this soon. He didn't want to go home at all. Except that he had to. He had to be-cause he had to confront his sister about their date with her friend this afternoon in the deserted old house. The thought made his heart jump again despite his depression. But he wanted to wait to do that, to see his sister, until his idiot mother was busy.

But what could he do? He decided to ride out to the depot and watch the 8:53 go through. That would do it, that was it. Gingerly he crawled out of his sanctuary and after looking all around to make sure he hadn't been seen, got his bike from against the yellow brick of the bank building. *Sanctuary*—that had been a good one. And he bet he was the only one in town who had read it, except maybe the librarian.

On the bike, riding out Main Street toward the tracks, his thoughts came back to his father despite himself. It had been Tom's father, the grandchildren's father, who had more or less emerged as the new family leader there in the white hospital room of the grandfather's death, largely by default. He had become the grandfather's favorite when he had fathered two children. None of the other three had had any children. And the grandfather cared a great deal, after the fashion of his time, about his family continuity. So he bought his third son a large fine family house— his reward—directly in back of his own big place with its Corinthian columns and huge old lawns on West Main, so that their backyards adjoined and he could be near the kids. Then he remodeled it for him, put it in his name, and installed him in it with his family; although of course, naturally, he could not stand the wife—the mother—who could not stand him either. Probably it was this being the old man's favorite that had caused his father to step into the role of leader, Tom mused. But more likely it was that none of the other three wanted the job. At any price. In any case there wasn't much of anything that needed leading at that moment. They were all "well-provided-for." In Insul stocks. Even the two children appreciated that. Ha.

Tom remembered that outside the hospital under the stone and brick carriage porch of the *Sanitarium*, on the newly curving and richly planted driveway which the old self-taught doctor had just had redone commemorating that his one son had just graduated from Harvard Medical School, the men had shouldered into their topcoats in the chilly September night and got into their cars, switched on their lights and pulled away. His father had been the last to pull away, in his brand-new Studebaker. As he did, his wife, Tom's mother, had begun to sob and cry again. She had hated the old man, the grandfather, ever since she had first met him; and he had equally disliked and detested her. Tom and his sister had whispered together in the backseat about this new state of things where they were no longer grandchildren. They knew all about the active dislike between their mother and the grandfather, since she had told them over and over how miserable and unhappy he made her life having to live so close to him, so they did not put too much stock in her weeping and grief. They were much more interested in where people went when they died.

Strangely enough, Tom thought, or perhaps not strangely at all, the grandfather although he had been quite hard on his own sons had gotten along remarkably well with his grandchildren. Maybe he was trying to undo with them what he felt he had done wrong with his sons? During summer vacations he would invite them over across the two backyards to drink heated milk in coffee mugs with him, while he himself had his morning coffee. He kept boxes of chocolates hidden around the house from which, if the children could find them, he would allow them to have one or two chocolate creams. He loved to feed them large doses of ice cream on summer afternoons, would laugh at them gently when they got the terrible sharp headaches from eating too much too fast, and then give them a gentle lecture on gluttony. He took them for walks around the big lawns and grounds and showed them trees, shrubs and flowers he had planted and nurtured. Did he ever look at them and wonder, Tom wondered now himself, study them and try to discover if the "Mark of Cain" he had somehow passed on to his sons had also passed on to them? "Mark of Cain" was certainly what he would have called it, Tom thought. By this time he must have been convinced he had failed them all. His guilt must have been an enormous felt mat, blanketing everything. "Mark of Cain" was almost what Tom would call it himself. Now. If he believed in things like "Marks of Cain." But back then the children had known nothing of this. They knew only that their mother hated for them to spend so much time with grandpa, was jealous and complained that he gave them candy. All their spare time was spent whispering about ways to outwit and lie to her and get back to the grandfather.

At the railroad station four old men had taken over and apportioned among themselves the two benches on the station platform. Their knotty hands clasped and leaning on their creaky knees, these relics of another age, two of them chewing tobacco and spitting quietly down between their feet off the platform onto the gravel roadbed, sat and chatted while they waited for that same 8:53 Tom had come to look at. He did not go near them but backed off slowly and simply stood in the shadow of the depot, leaning against the wall. He had no use for the old-timers in the town except to be contemptuous of them. They were almost always mean and teasing all the kids, as if being old gave them certain special rights, and at the same time as if they were in some way jealous of the young. He certainly did not want to wind up spending his whole life in one town like them, to end up at the railroad station watching trains go through.

A sort of bleak despair of total hopelessness took him, making it unworth the effort it took to breathe, at the thought that that was probably just about what would happen to him. With no more money—and no more desire than his family had to educate and set up well their children, it was almost certainly what would happen to him. *And* his sister Emma.

The Crash, The Crash, always The Crash. The Crash and the Depression. Would his grandfather really have had the foresight, had he lived, to get out from under and save himself—and them? Other families had saved themselves, at least partially, and still lived in their big family houses. But Tom saw no reason to assume the old man would have. He had already made at least two serious mistakes in thinking. The future of the automobile was one, and the social status of the veterinarian was another. And what about the Insul stock itself? having so damned much of it? Total despair came over Tom Dylan again. They had done a hell of a lot for him and Emma, hadn't they? He owed them a lot. He and Emma owed them an awful lot, didn't they?

He did not even wait for the train to come through, but got on his bike and left. The encapsulated old men horrified him and at the same time scared him. The livery stable of course had been the first thing to go. It was going downhill all through the 1920s, and only the grandfather's money kept it going. The man who bought it for a little of nothing was a mechanic and immediately turned it into a garage, a money-making garage, and his father was immediately reduced to a grubby one-room office and the taking care of people's pets. The grandfather's house could not be sold. It was a white elephant; nobody had money to lay out for a mansion of an earlier, wealthier time; everyone was retrenching. Anyway the lawyer uncle—and then his widow—wound up owning that, and she didn't even live in the town. And then they, Tom's family, had lost their own house.

It was about then, Tom remembered grimly, that all the party invitations and come-to-play requests had stopped coming in from the old family friends still in the old, once-familiar big houses along East and West Main Streets.

It was true the house had been in their name, his father's name. But he had had to mortgage it almost at once, for the money to set himself up in a new vet's office after giving up the livery stable. Then, when they could no longer keep up the payments, the foreclosure came. Since then they had been living in a rented house, an old inelegant place, given them—allowed them—at a very low rent, like poor relatives, by a rich old crony of the grandfather. The only thing at all nice about it was that it had three huge hard-maple trees in its small front yard. That was where he was going now.

He could tell the moment he walked into the darkly shaded old house that his mother was down in the basement washing. He could hear the washing machine motor hum-chugging away down there, and the house had an unanxious, unpreoccupied feel; the late-summer air outside sucked gently at the curtains at the windows. His sister lay on the divan in the tree-darkened livingroom, her favorite place, reading a book. For a moment he stood in the doorway motionless, studying her. If the grandfather had ever wondered about that "Mark of Cain" of his in his family, Tom thought suddenly, that flaw in the blood passed on in his seed, then he ought to see the two of us now. And yet he knew nothing would deter him. An earthquake might. They had done a hell of a lot for him, hadn't they, and Emma? And their damned town had too, for that matter. His heart was pounding in him again, so hard it seemed to cut off half his breathing in his throat. Not as if she had just seen him, but as if she had been aware of him all the time, Emma lowered her book and looked at him and smiled. "Hello. You're late getting home."

Tom didn't answer for a moment. He had been her hero all her life. Obviously for his benefit, but as if she were alone in the room, Emma stretched herself luxuriously, seductively in her shorts, raised her arms up over her head, yawned prettily. For her age she had nice breasts, fine long legs below a flat belly and a noticeable mound. Tom had been born in 1919, nine months almost to the day after his father's return from The Great War, and Emma a year after that. That made her fifteen and a half. More. Fifteen and ten months. Practically sixteen. Tom continued to stare at her from the doorway. She continued to stretch out her body, teasing him.

All his mother's precious furniture, her precious proofs that she had not always lived like this, were crowded into this one small livingroom. Back in the other house they had had two livingrooms, a Main Parlor and then an Everyday Parlor they actually used, and now almost the entire furnishings of both rooms were crowded into this one room smaller than either. Beside him at the doorway stood a woven wicker floorlamp which had a huge umbrella-like shade of faded, discolored pink silk which had been red with three-inch, faded pink fringe dangling around its circumference, one of the few items she had managed to acquire from the grandfather's mansion and she loved it. Tom hated it. Still looking at his sister, he reached out and combed his fingers through the hated fringe, and six or eight faded fringe strings came away in his hand or fell to the floor. This fringe had always fascinated him as a little boy with the fragile, half-rotting way it came off to the touch, and he had gotten more than one whipping when his mother had caught him standing by it in complete and fascinated absorption, touching it to watch the fringe fall. This time, however, he did it totally cynically, and grinned.

His sister Emma tittered. "You'll get caught."

"Nobody's ever going to lick me again in this house," Tom said. Just the same he bent and picked up the two or three telltale fringe strings which had fallen to the floor and pocketed them.

"I said you're late getting home," Emma said from the couch.

"I meant to get home late," he said gruffly. "Is our date all fixed up for this afternoon?"

"Yes. I think it is," Emma said. She put her arms down at her sides and looked at him in a totally different way. "I talked to her about it yesterday."

"How did Joan feel about it? What did she say?"

"She was—excited," his sister said. "She wants to do it." Her voice had gotten heated, and almost as choked-up sounding as his own, and her eyes had a deep almost red color in the dim light. But then she looked at him a long moment and then sat up nervously on the couch. "But Tom really I don't think—"

"Never mind," Tom said sharply. "I told you I'd tell and I mean it. You'll do it or I'll tell. Anyway," more softly, "you know you want to do it."

"Yes, I want to," Emma said in a small breathy voice. A hush fell in the room. She stretched out on the couch again.

"Okay. Hadn't you better call her up on the phone and check and make sure?"

"I'll be having luncheon with her down there at her house anyway today," Emma said. "What's the point?"

Luncheon, Tom thought. Haw!

"Anyway, she wants to do it. She said so. And she said she'd be there. And I'll be with her all afternoon. And we'll be right next door." Joan's house was right across the street from their own old house which they had lost and whose backyard connected with the backyard of the grandfather's mansion. She had been their childhood neighbor all their lives until they had had to move.

"Okay. Then I'm going upstairs. I'll meet you both there, in the house, at three o'clock." He straightened in the doorway.

"But why did you think to pick on grandfather's old empty house?" Emma said.

"Do you know any better place for it?" Tom said thinly. "I mean—there's probably no place else in the whole town that's as safe, is there?"

"I guess not," she said in a hushed breathy voice. Upstairs in his room he locked the door. A dull heated excitement in him made it nearly impossible for him to think. He went to the bookcase and got down the library copy of *Sanctuary*, intending to reread the part where that guy used the corncob on that girl Temple, but he found he could not concentrate enough to read. He put the book back and lay down on the bed and clasped his hands behind his head.

It had all started a week ago, exactly one week ago, when he returned from CMTC camp at the Army fort Fort Harrison in Indianapolis. He had brought home with him a brand-new pornography collection.

There had been no chance that his father would spring with the money to send him—or Emma—to summer camp this year, just as he had not done last year either, or any of the four years before that. So Tom had signed himself up with the Civilian Military Training Corps, taken the physical exam and gone to

Indianapolis at government expense. It was the first time he had been away from home on his own and he had learned a lot, mostly from the older boys in CMTC, who were all quite happy to break him in to life in Indianapolis. One of the first things he learned was that downtown in the low dive section where the whores were were certain shops, usually disguised as antique shops, which specialized in selling pornography under the counter. This pornography was not like the badly smudged photos and comic-strip books you could buy at the shoeshine shop in his hometown. This pornography was real modern-day glossy photographs, of real live people, well composed and well focused. You could see everything, and the people were doing just about everything. Since he did not go to the whores himself (he had never been with a woman yet and anyway he was afraid of catching a disease) he had spent every dollar he had, and every dollar he could scrape together or get his father to send him, on the pornography.

It was Emma who had found it. How, he didn't know. She had come into his room and lain on his bed while he was unpacking, but that had not bothered him. The stuff was all in a plain brown paper envelope, and he had put it quietly into his handkerchief drawer to wait until he was alone to hide it. He had already picked out his hiding spot even before he got home. In this rented house the never-used trapdoor to the attic, papered over the same color as the ceiling, was in his room; by pushing that up he could slip the brown paper envelope up onto a couple of rafters. This he had done, after Emma left. Two days later when he went to look for them again, three of his best pictures were missing. Furious, he had scoured her room and found them. And that was how it all had started. She had put them down among her lingerie in her underwear drawer, a stupid place to put them.

When he accosted her, she confessed and then she started to cry. She herself did not really know how she had known, either. Something about the way his back looked as he so quietly put the envelope in the drawer had told her, given her a hunch, that whatever it was it was something sexy, something dirty. Later when she looked and found the envelope gone, she had gone automatically to the little attic trapdoor as the hiding place.

It had never occurred to Tom that girls might have dirty thoughts, sexual thoughts, too, the way boys did. Girls to him had always been objects of desire, basically anti-sexual creatures, and therefore unattainable objects of desire, after which he chased eternally and never reached. Almost all the boys he knew played with themselves, and quite openly, and sometimes even in groups. It was understood that it was dirty and therefore fun, that if parents or grownups caught you, you would be given a whipping or punished, but they all did it anyway. But it had never occurred to him that girls might.

Such, he soon found out, was not at all the case, or not Emma's case. Caught, and in his power, she went further and confessed she and Joan had been doing things like that, looking, and touching themselves, for years. Then, stopping her crying and looking at him shrewdly, she had offered to arrange a meeting with Joan. Or, failing that, if Joan balked, to arrange for him to come upon them unexpectedly and catch them. But she hadn't had to. Joan had agreed quite readily enough.

On his bed Tom felt flushed all over. They had done nothing together yet, he and Emma, only looked. But Tom had some ideas about things he wanted to do, scenes out of his new pictures, when he got the two of them together. Feverishly, he fell asleep.

When he woke it was after lunchtime, Emma had clearly already gone, and he was still feverish. Still on the bed, he stretched himself. He felt hot all over. His face was flushed, and even his eyes felt hot behind their lids. If that was the way sex made you feel, then it was not at all all that pleasant. But when he thought of what was in store for him this afternoon, he felt hotter still. He got up a little woozily and unlocked the door.

As he did, his eye fell on the letter lying on his working table, his study table, and he paused. It was a letter of commendation from the General commanding the Army fort in Indianapolis. The night before breaking camp to go home Tom had been on guard duty, and there had been a cloudburst. The General's two small children had taken refuge from the downpour on the ring platform under the roof of the fort's boxing arena, and when the cloudburst filled the natural hollow waistdeep with water that couldn't run off fast enough, had become marooned there. On the second or third tour of his ten o'clock shift Tom had heard them calling and, flashing his light down there, had found them. The little girl was crying. Not knowing whether to call the Corporal of the Guard for such a thing—afraid to really, embarrassed to—and already soaking wet anyway, he had waded out to them and, feeling both magnanimous and a little heroic, had carried them both back, first one, then the other, through the cold waistdeep water to the safety of the bleachers. The boy of ten, who already had about him the authority of at least a Lieutenant Colonel, had asked him his name. Next day the letter had been delivered to the Captain of his company for him. More important, he had slept the rest of the night, if you could call it sleep, in his wet clothes on his bare cot under his one blanket, shivering and shaking, since there was no provision for the Guard to change its clothes. He had been sure he was going to get a bad cold, but there had been no after-effects at all.

That had been exactly eight days ago, Tom mused woozily, looking at the letter. He knew it didn't really mean anything, but even so he had thought of having it framed. It was his only trophy he had brought home from Indianapolis. He had been runner-up in the boxing tournament, and he had been second choice for a scholarship to a military academy. If the damned letter had arrived two or three days earlier, he might have—probably would have—won the scholarship. But if he had, his damned father in his total inertia would never have come up with the minimum tuition money for him to accept it. He turned and went downstairs.

His mother had gone out to one of her club meetings. He had not had any lunch. He had ten or fifteen minutes to kill before three o'clock. He went to the refrigerator. As heated-up and excited as he felt, he did not want to eat anyway. In the icecube freezing compartment there was a square quart bucket of strawberry ice cream and he sat down with it at the silent kitchen table. In three minutes he had eaten so much of it so fast he had a piercing headache, exactly as if somebody had struck him between the eyes with a sharp-pointed hammer. He had to quit and let it subside before he could finish the rest of it. It made him think of his grandfather. How the old guy was always feeding them ice cream like that, when they were little, and then laughing at them. He chuckled. Maybe the old son of a bitch did it on purpose, some kind of sadism. "Mark of Cain." "Mark of Cain" was right, all right. Tainted blood!

He was surprised to find that the ice-cream headache did not go away when he went out and got on his bike to ride across town, instead it got worse. Never had he felt like this before. He had been pretty excited and hot at times, but never like this. But then never before had he ever had a prospect like this before him, two whole girls, who would do anything, or practically anything. His ears felt fiery. His eyes felt like two hot burning coals in their sockets. And he noticed that when he exhaled through his nose, his breath actually burned his upper lip. When he rode in and out of the shade into the hot September sunshine, it actually made him feel faint. But he felt faint all over with excitement anyway.

It was a long ride, ten minutes, from where they now lived back across town to the high-class section where they used to live. This seemed symbolic to Tom and he snorted. He did not try to go through his own old driveway and backyard where strangers lived now, but rode on around the block and came to his grandfather's deserted house from the front, up its driveway which ran across the porticoed front, but which also ran around to the back. He half-hid his bike by wheeling it up the two steps and inside the latticed backporch. The girls' bikes were not there, but that didn't mean anything. They would have left theirs at Joan's. Maybe they were already there, he thought secretly, cozily, already waiting for him, whispering and rustling and tittering and touching themselves. He went around to the basement window he knew was not locked.

It was while he was sliding up the sash of the basement window that he realized he had a bad stitch in his side. He had not thought he was riding that hard or that fast, but every time he took a deep breath now it hurt him. Once inside the window, which opened onto the cellar stairs, the column of air that flowed past him from the depths of the cellar cooled him off a little. He shivered twice violently. His head still throbbed with that damned ice-cream headache which would not go away. Slowly he climbed the stairs into the kitchen.

Here it all was: the old high-ceilinged elegant rooms with their moulded plaster mouldings and their mirrors still fastened to the walls behind their wooden or plaster columns or above the fireplaces. The cut-glass chandeliers still hung from the middles of the rooms. Only the furnishings, the rich old rugs, the wall tapestries, the elegant old furniture, were missing. Tom went from the sunroom with its wall of glass windows to the east to catch the winter morning sun, through the diningroom whose long hand-waxed table was gone with its twelve chairs, through the parlor itself into the hall where the big winding staircase was. Across the hall from the parlor was the old music room, empty too.

He leaned his hand against the huge carved newel post. They would almost certainly be upstairs. One of the five bedrooms on the second floor still had an old bed in it intact with mattress. Emma knew where it was and that was where they would be. Excitement ran all through him. He had never been so hot. He started up the curving stairs and then stopped. He was so excited he was weak, and his knees were shaky. His breath was coming in short panting gasps, and wherever his breath flowed against the skin of his face it burned. He hesitated a moment and then sat down on the stairs and leaned back against the wall to catch his breath. Could sexual excitement, just plain sexual excitement, do all that to you? make you weak in the knees and out of breath? He guessed it could. He listened hard, and was sure he heard whispering and movement upstairs.

After a minute he got up again. He had to get up there, and right away; now. He had never been so excited and so hot in his life. This time he made four steps before he had to stop. Then he sat down again. His breath coming in short gasps, he rested his head back against the wall and stared at the huge wall painting two floors tall where it leaned above him at the bend of the stairs with its 18th century colonial figures in their knee britches and long dresses. He remembered how he had used to believe, even though you could feel with your hand the plaster of the wall under the painting, that the painting was a secret panel which opened onto a secret corridor and rooms in the middle of the house. It was when the cock-hatted, high-coiffured figures in the painting seemed to move, and then to actually change places in it, that he realized he wasn't just only all excited and sexually hot, he was sick. Tom Dylan was sick.

He blinked, and the figures seemed to sort of move, reapportion themselves and go back to their original places. He felt woozy and half-drunk all over, and when he stuck out his lower lip and exhaled his hot breath up across the plain of his face, it actually seemed to sear his nostrils and lower lids. And when he shook his head the headache was still there, even stronger although the ice-cream which had caused it had long since been ingested. So was the stitch in his side still there, but now it was on both sides at once.

Somewhere, he did not know just where, the sexual heat and sexual excitement he had felt had ceased to be sexual excitement and become something else, a raging fever apparently. How could that have happened? It confused him. The two seemed to have fused in him, run together and into each other, so that he did not know when he was feeling sexual excitement or a fever, or both. He was as weak as a kitten. And the weakness wasn't excitement weakness, it was sickness. *Oh, no!* he thought with a kind of silent inward wail of despair, *Oh, no!* There they were, up there, waiting for him. He was sure he had heard them. Two girls, ready to do anything he wanted. So near. He had waited for this a long time. He had waited for it all his life!

He struggled to his feet, took two more steps up the stairs and had to sit down quickly. How could this have happened to him? How could it have? Could it have been that cold wet night in the shivering Guard tent? But that had been eight days ago. Should he call to them? But what good would that do? Could they help him up the stairs? and place him on the bed between them? They wouldn't. And by some adult instinct in his boy's psyche he knew that if the opportunity was lost now, it would never come again. Girls were notoriously fickle about their sex. The chance was here and it had to be seized now. And yet he couldn't.

God. Was it going to go on like this forever? Runner-up in the boxing tournament? Second choice for the scholarship? Always a bridesmaid and never a bride? Was it some kind of punishment? Sitting on the stairs, he shook his drooping head, and noted that his ice-cream headache had gotten even worse.

Besides, he was scared now. He wanted to be home. He was really sick. Slowly he stood up, and looked up at the fortress heights of that second floor which he had not been able to scale. Then he looked down the length of the staircase, and began to beat his retreat back from the high point of his advance. He had made it up ten steps. The staircase, and the bannister which he clutched, as if they were made of flexible materials seemed to sway back and forth weirdly with each step down.

He made it to the basement window and out and around to his bike. Maybe it was a punishment, a bad punishment. Maybe he was going to die, as a punishment. Pictures of his grandfather in his youth rose up around him, those old tintypes, with the hard eyes, and the mustache which hid the mouth so you could not see if it was gentle or stern. But you knew it was stern. Because in the movie his grandfather striding down Main Street on Saturday night in his Western hat had begun to pistolwhip over the head a roustabout who, bleeding, turned out to be Tom's father while Tom, a very little boy, hid behind the bank building beside the filling station and watched. All he wanted now was to be home, as fast as possible. Home with his mother. Yeah, a lot of help she would be. A lot of help.

The white cardboard placard said in bold black letters below the stern eyes, Wyatt Earp mustache and long black hair, EDWARD DYLAN FOR SHERIFF. Across the top in smaller letters was printed TRUST YOUR LAW. The right eye and eyebrow turned slowly into one of the women's crotches from one of his pornographic pictures. Slowly it winked at him. The woman's face smiled at him from above it. Then it began to revolve. Then the left eye and eyebrow turned into another one from another picture. The widow's peak at the hairline became a third, the mustache over the mouth a fourth. Then the entire picture became covered with them, revolving, revolving.

The bicycle seemed to be driving itself. Breasts, crotches, delicious shaved armpits, delicious unshaved armpits, sixguns, mustaches, Western hats all revolved around each other now, turning, merging, separating, disappearing, reappearing, glaring and then dimming as great lights flashed. Tom shut his eyes, but the pictures did not go away anyway. His grandfather's placard had faded away somewhere. Then it came back, zooming to hugeness with a screaming noise. Punishment! Punishment! Tom kept his eyes closed. The bike pedals felt light as feathers. Then he heard Doctor Sachs's voice say somewhere, "I think it's passed." He opened his eyes and saw Doctor Sachs's haggard face staring down at him in the bed. It appeared to be his mother's and father's bed, in their bedroom. His mother, haggardfaced also, was standing down at the foot of it, looking at him too. He could see them, but he could not understand them.

"You've had several pretty bad days there, boy," Doc Sachs said with a tired smile. "A lot of people don't get over double lumbar pneumonia."

Tom did not understand him. He could only breathe in the very top part of his chest without it hurting him. But he felt he had to try to explain it to them anyway. "It's not that," he said clearly. He knew what he was saying, but his mouth did not feel as though it was working right. "Nothing's that bad. Nothing is ever that bad. There's nothing in the world that's ever that bad. And they should never have let him do it to them. Guilty like that."

"What's he talking about?" he heard his mother say.

"Don't know. Mumbling something about guilt," Doc Sachs said. "He's still pretty delirious, with the fever."

Tom looked at his mother. She was so awful. The poor thing. She had cared, he guessed, from her face. Suddenly the woven wicker floorlamp with its faded pink shade appeared in front of and over her but he could still see her through it like the two images in a double-exposed photographic negative. "And I'll fix it for you," he babbled. "I promise I will." He made a claw of his fingers and clawed the air with them, as if combing something. "I'll buy you a new one. A whole brand-new one if you want it. When I make the money."

"What's he talking about now?" Doc Sachs asked.

"I don't know," his mother said.

Tom found he didn't know himself. "A new one," he insisted. If only she would understand. Or anybody. Guilt? Guilt?

"He'll be all right now," Doc Sachs said, and sighed, getting up. "He's a tough kid. All the Dylans are tough. He's probably got a helluva headache, right now. That fever and all."

STUDY GUIDE
by Dr. Judith Everson

This brief study guide suggests questions and activities designed to enhance the reader's understanding and appreciation of James Jones's short stories, both individually and collectively. Discussion questions follow for each of the thirteen stories. A subsequent series of exercises is intended to illuminate connections between certain stories and to foster comparative analysis. Finally, a list of recommended primary and secondary sources is provided to encourage further reading and independent research.

"The Temper of Steel"

1. As Jones's preface indicates, he debated whether to make his main point directly (at the risk of sacrificing subtlety for clarity) or indirectly (at the risk of being misinterpreted). He chose the latter approach in marketing the story initially, but reverted to the former by adding a challenge to the reader—followed by his solution—in this edition. Do you agree or disagree with his original decision to imply rather than state his message outright? Could you identify his intended point on your own, or only after consulting his explanation? Did you find other possible messages in the story?

2. Like most good literary titles, "The Temper of Steel" is a brief phrase that is also richly resonant. Examine how it operates both literally and figuratively to foreshadow the story's focus and enhance its meaning.

3. From their similar-sounding names to their mutual knowledge of knives, Lon and Johnny are systematically and revealingly paralleled. How are they compared and contrasted as the story unfolds, and what does this add to the development of the theme?

4. For an apprentice effort, this story features an ambitious design. In your opinion, how well does Jones integrate the major parts—the veterans' postwar cock-

tail party encounter and the central flashback to Johnny's combat experience it triggers—into a unified whole?

"Just Like the Girl"

1. In the familiar song from which the title comes, a young man plans to follow in his father's footsteps toward marital bliss by winning a wife who resembles his mother. Although the lyrics sound innocent enough, James Giles points out (p. 105) that both the song and Jones's story carry Oedipal overtones. How does Johnny's problematic relationship with his parents render the title ironic? In answering, pay close attention to mother and son's reliance on romantic language, consciously or unconsciously, in their references to each other as they conspire against Johnny's father.

2. The story's third-person narration confines itself to Johnny's perspective while presenting the dynamics of his dysfunctional family. What advantages and disadvantages does this storytelling strategy entail? To what extent are the resulting portraits of father, mother, and son relatively simple or complex? Sympathetic or unsympathetic?

3. An important motif that recurs throughout the narrative concerns Johnny's active imagination, which often conflates fact and fiction to create fantasies about sex and violence. In your view, did this motif increase or diminish the story's poignance and power? Why and how?

"The Way It Is"

1. In a letter to his editor Maxwell Perkins on June 23, 1947, Jones expressed pride in this story because "it has a sense of action in it, a sense of this happening now instead of being a story about what happened then" (George Hendrick, pp. 95-96). How does Jones try to achieve the desired effect of immediacy rather than retrospection? Why might Jones have considered this effect such a vital goal? Did he succeed in reaching it as far as you are concerned? Why or why not?

2. Setting proves crucial to the impact of "The Way It Is." The relentless roar of the wind on the remote stretch of Hawaiian beach does more than merely particularize the locale and reinforce its realism. Gradually, the wind assumes a growing symbolic significance. Like most effective symbols, it is capable of suggesting different things to different people. What deeper meaning(s) did it suggest to you?

3. Jones's fiction generally and this story specifically reflect a keen awareness of the persistent class conflict in contemporary American society and its painful consequences. Consider the relationship between Sgt. Mazzioli and Cpl. Slade as a microcosmic case study of such tensions within the army, an inherently hierarchical institution. Then analyze the dramatic role reversal between the civilian suspect and the road guard detail. How does this power play further illustrate the potential costliness of America's internal divisions in the aftermath of Japan's attack on Pearl Harbor, when greater national unity will be required to win the war?

"Two Legs for the Two of Us"

1. With its twin references to duos, the title announces a focus on pairings as well as unpairings. Many of the story's couples have been formed or transformed since George and Tom each lost a leg in the service. How does their shared disability status affect the linkages between George and Sandy, Tom and his last wife and, finally, George and Tom themselves?

2. Steven Carter claims that George, Tom, and Sandy all avoid personal responsibility by blaming external circumstances for their present plight, thus falling into "the trap of self-pity based on the idea that their lives would have been happier if the war had not interfered with them" (p. 147). From your reading of the story, defend, modify, or reject this argument.

"Secondhand Man"

1. "Can This Marriage Be Saved?" is a popular feature in *Ladies' Home Journal* magazine. Each month, a wife, her husband, and a counselor successively analyze where the union in question has broken down and whether it can be repaired. After summarizing how Mona and Larry Patterson each perceive their relationship, assess their situation in your own words as an outside observer. In your view, can/should this marriage be saved? What course of action would you recommend to the partners, and why?

2. The third-person narration employed here presents the personal perspectives of individual characters while also qualifying or challenging their viewpoints at times. The doctor, for instance, can be seen as offering either good or bad advice to the Pattersons, depending on our weighting of the evidence. Likewise, Larry's faith in the healing power of nature is both upheld and undercut at different

points in the narrative. Explore these examples of intentional ambiguity in depth, and explain your interpretation in each case.

3. Although Jones is best known and most respected for his war fiction, he also devoted several long novels and short stories to gender politics—the challenges men and women face in defining themselves and relating to each other within a society that stereotypes sex roles and represses sexual expression. The Pattersons embody this struggle because their problems—including his recent illness, possible alcoholism, and past adultery—require not just a change of scene but also a reassessment of their respective roles as well as the future of their relationship. How does their early discussion about strength and weakness, independence and dependence, reflect the representativeness of their difficulty and anticipate the downbeat conclusion?

"None Sing So Wildly"

1. Jones experimented here and elsewhere in his fiction with "colloquial forms," a controversial attempt to reproduce what George Garrett calls "the living, spoken American idiom" in dialogue as well as in first- and third-person narration (p. 116). The story's semi-autobiographical writer-hero also likes to hear the vernacular and "to reproduce it on paper." Review Jones's use of such devices as contractions without apostrophes, misspellings that replicate informal speech, and vulgarities or obscenities. Did you notice these stylistic features on first reading the story, and—if so—did they help or hinder your initial response? Upon reflection, do you think this kind of language experimentation strengthens or weakens the story?

2. The power struggle between Sylvanus Merrick and Norma Fry dooms their engagement, but it also juxtaposes their sharply differing notions of sex and work, propriety and security. In their failed attempt to convert rather than communicate with each other, we find a classic case of "he said" versus "she said," with little room for genuine dialogue or compromise. Outline the main points at issue between the mismatched lovers, then discuss whether both sides are treated fairly, if not equally, within the narrative.

3. Although Van and Norma dominate the action, secondary characters also appear at pivotal points to advance the plot. Taking either the arrival of Russ and Arky in Part II or the incident involving the young couple at the beach in Parts IV-VI, explain how these support players help to reveal the story's major conflict and accelerate the crisis that resolves it.

"Greater Love"

1. This story offers a meditation on brotherhood, both concrete and abstract. On a literal level we encounter two sets of biological brothers—Al and Vic Zwermann, and Quentin and Shelby Thatcher—who are separated by death in battle. In a broader sense, however, war redefines the meaning of brotherhood, extending it from the biological to the sociological by making blood brothers of comrades and by making mortal enemies of fellow human beings with different nationalities or ideologies. How does "Greater Love" illuminate these distinct but related notions of fraternity?

2. "Greater Love" can also be considered a rite-of-passage account of Quentin's baptism by fire in combat. How does the nameless First Sergeant try to mentor the young clerk before and during his first battle? What has Cpl. Thatcher learned by the end of story, and what must he still absorb?

"The King"

1. Jones's long-time interest in jazz emerges in "The King," which counterpoints the up and down career paths of the title character, aging jazz legend Willy Jefferson, and a small-town band of his admirers with big-time aspirations of their own. Jones called these double plotlines "almost unrelated but spiritually connected." What do you think he meant? How would *you* describe their connection?

2. Steven Carter contends that Jefferson's suffering develops and expresses his spiritual growth, while the narrator's band lacks the courage to risk genuine pain and loss in the pursuit of their artistic dream (p. 85). What textual evidence supports Carter's contention? Is there an adequate basis for an alternative argument?

3. "The King" is one of only a few stories in the collection featuring a first-person narrator, who lacks the omniscience available in third-person narration. Because of this inherent limitation, first-person narratives generally reveal perceptible gaps—places where something important is missing because the narrator doesn't know or tell it. In such cases the reader is left to ponder, perhaps even to try and fill, the blank spaces in the text. From the various narrational gaps in "The King," select one to consider closely for its implications and impact.

"The Valentine"

1. The subject of this story, unrequited young love, is difficult to treat without lapsing into sentimentalism (overindulgence in excessive emotion of the mawkish kind). In your view, does Jones manage to avoid this literary offense? If so, how? If not, why not?

2. The dimension of time is foregrounded here in several ways, some more obvious than others. The time of year is stressed, for example, by the romantic holiday celebration; furthermore, the hero's youthful idealism underscores his vulnerable stage of life. On a subtler level, though, Jones also exploits John's—and the reader's—rising sense of urgency by conducting a veritable countdown to the purchase and delivery of the candy. Take a scene where you shared John's awareness of the ticking clock, and—with it—the approaching deadline. Isolate the details and devices employed to foster your identification with John's impending comeuppance.

3. Even if the reader misses the author's introduction, where the story's outcome is previewed, the narrative itself furnishes many clues to the disastrous disparity between John's expectations and Margaret's response. List as many of these hints as you can. Why do you think John misses or misreads them, setting up a textbook example of dramatic irony, where the reader knows more than the character about a major matter at hand?

"A Bottle of Cream"

1. Beginnings and endings tend to be privileged places in literary texts. Sometimes, as is the case here, the opening and closing of a story even work together to bring the reader full circle. With this in mind, discuss how from its first line to its last, "A Bottle of Cream" seems determined to unsettle or complicate common notions of truth and deception, innocence and guilt, justice and injustice. How would you summarize the point of this deconstructive exercise?

2. Because of its comparative brevity and compression, the short story genre tolerates less excess than its more capacious fictional relatives, the novella and the novel, making it in some ways a more demanding form. Jones's prefatory comments show that he held this story in particularly high regard, an opinion shared by some reviewers and critics (like Frank MacShane, p. 168). Praise has not been unanimous, however. James Giles accuses Jones of attempting "too much" here

(p. 112). Revisit "A Bottle of Cream" in light of this disagreement. If you were Jones's editor, would you suggest any cuts in order to tighten its focus? If so, where and why? If not, how might you explain and address Giles's concern that the story tries to do too many things in too brief a space?

3. Jones regarded the adult narrator as a great addition to the story, though one so integral to its confines that he could not be transferred elsewhere. What does "A Bottle of Cream" gain from the narrator's grown-up reflections on his childhood encounter with Chet Poore? Contrast this mode of narration with that used in "Just Like the Girl," in which young Johnny's perspective is maintained throughout.

"Sunday Allergy"

1. Despite a persistent reputation as a "man's writer" whose best work addresses masculine issues, Jones was also interested in creating credible, complex, and sympathetic female characters when his storyline required this. His inability to sell "Sunday Allergy" may help to explain why it is the only woman-centered story in the collection. How successful or unsuccessful do you find the portrayal of Sidney and Cott when compared to other (male) protagonists in surrounding stories?

2. The narrative skillfully contrasts the co-heroines' apparent freedom and independence on the one hand and their actual sense of entrapment and dependence on the other hand. In what ways are Sidney and Cott seemingly more privileged and liberated than many other women of their time? Alternatively, in what ways are they revealed to be dysfunctionally dependent—on their lovers, their doctor, and each other?

3. As in "The Ice-Cream Headache," Jones inserts an official medical diagnosis for the "Sunday Allergy" into the story while leaving room for alternative speculation by the reader. How would you label the source of the allergy, and what cure—if any—would you recommend?

"The Tennis Game"

1. As its title implies, Jones builds the story around a game of tennis; yet as the reader discovers, it is far from a conventional contest between two players. First, summarize the various ways this natural expectation is contradicted; then de-

scribe how Johnny's solo recreation of the historic match functions not only as play (escapism) but also as work (therapy).

2. A thread running through this story and connecting it to others in the collection concerns the parentally transmitted attitude that sex is dirty and forbidden, which only heightens its allure for the young and compounds the pain of their maturation. Examine how Jones links sex and dirt both literally and symbolically here, and explore the effect of this association on Johnny's developing identity as well as his attitudes about females.

"The Ice-Cream Headache"

1. Jones privileges this final story in two ways—by giving it the climactic position in the volume and by borrowing its title for the entire collection. What specific aspects of "The Ice-Cream Headache" (characterization, theme, setting, plot, etc.) might explain this special emphasis? Having read the other stories, how appropriate do you find his choice?

2. In correspondence with Burroughs Mitchell, his editor, on June 19, 1963, Jones bragged that he'd already written the first sentence of the story and it was "good" (George Hendrick, p. 300). He reinforced the opening line's evocation of William Faulkner's fiction by repeated references to the Nobel Prize winner in succeeding paragraphs. In what ways is Jones's story overtly reminiscent of Faulkner? What risks and rewards do you see in such an opening gambit on Jones's part?

3. The title refers to a familiar phenomenon of childhood—the brief but intense discomfort caused by overly rapid indulgence in eating ice cream. In what ways does this early link between the pursuit of pleasure and the punishment of pain presage Tom's fate?

4. In just three generations, the Dylans have risen to prominence, then suffered serious reverses. While this dramatic decline in their family fortunes is painful for each generation, it can also be considered a fortunate fall if they gain compensatory knowledge from their individual and collective loss. To what extent do the patriarch Edward Dylan, his sons, and his grandson Tom appear to have learned or failed to learn a valuable lesson from the family's downward mobility?

Overview Questions and Optional Exercises

1. As his introduction states, Jones arranged these stories not by their content but by their order of composition, from the mid-1940s through the mid-1960s. As you read the stories from first to last, did you detect signs of the author's artistic evolution over time? In your judgment, might the collection have benefited from another structure—for instance, one that grouped certain stories by their overlapping subject matter? Overall, do you believe the volume gains or loses by its present organization?

2. In his editorial comments throughout *The Ice-Cream Headache*, Jones acknowledges what contemporary readers might have suspected and subsequent scholarship has confirmed—that the short fiction collected here is often autobiographical in nature. Indeed, this personal dimension may help to explain much of the volume's appeal. As John Thompson notes in the *New York Times Book Review* (April 21, 1968): "Jones is incapable of anything but total loyalty to his experience as a man, as an American, as a Middlewesterner, as a child of the Depression and of WWII; as the son of an American mother and, may Heaven help us all, of an American father." Satisfy your own curiosity about this convergence and divergence between fact and fiction by researching the author's life, using relevant materials from the accompanying bibliography, and crafting an essay on your discoveries.

3. Because several stories feature a character named John (ny) Slade, it can be tempting to read these as a continuing treatment of one character's growth from childhood to adulthood. Write an essay in which you analyze this hero's gradual development not only in his own right but also as a representative of what *Nation* reviewer Sara Blackburn calls his generation's experience of growing up (206: June 17, 1968).

4. Like Ernest Hemingway, to whom he often alludes, Jones left the Illinois of his birth and boyhood after high school, went to war, and became a writer who often returned obsessively to the Midwestern landscape as a setting for his fiction long after he had ceased to live there. Also like Hemingway, at his best Jones not only described the Midwest's physical terrain and related social environment but also evoked their emotional effect of the region's inhabitants. Select for close reading a passage from one of the stories that in your view captures this profound sense of place, and justify your choice as fully as possible.

5. Readers of these stories are often surprised and moved by Jones's powerful portrayal of a problem less openly acknowledged in his day than ours—the damaging effects on a sensitive child by emotionally abusive parents. Discuss this recurrent theme in "Just Like the Girl," "A Bottle of Cream," and "The Tennis Game."

6. *The Ice-Cream Headache* was widely, and for the most part favorably, reviewed when it appeared in March 1968. If you were reviewing the book today, upon its republication, how would you characterize its virtues and shortcomings? To whom would you recommend it, and why?

7. Because Jones's reputation as a novelist preceded the collection's initial publication, and because the book was out of print for many years, Jones's short fiction remains unfamiliar to many readers. If one of these stories could be chosen to appear in an anthology of modern American short fiction, which do you find most deserving of this attention, and why?

Additional Related Works by James Jones

Most critics regard Jones's greatest literary legacy as his fictional trilogy about WWII from prelude to aftermath: *From Here to Eternity* (New York: Scribner's, 1951), *The Thin Red Line* (New York: Scribner's, 1962), and *Whistle* (New York: Delacorte, 1978). *From Here to Eternity*, which won the National Book Award, treats a company in the regular army that is stationed in prewar Hawaii before the Japanese bombing of Pearl Harbor, an event which concludes the novel and which Jones witnessed. *The Thin Red Line* covers the same infantry company's combat on Guadalcanal, where Jones was injured and where he killed a Japanese soldier. *Whistle*, written while Jones was dying and completed by his friend Willie Morris, depicts the return stateside of wounded survivors from the company.

Jones also wrote a highly regarded novella, *The Pistol* (New York: Scribner's, 1959), about a private's struggle to retain the weapon he wore during the attack on Pearl Harbor. In addition, Jones's nonfiction narrative titled *WW II: A Chronicle of Soldiering* (New York: Grosset and Dunlap, 1975) contains interesting personal reflections.

Of Jones's remaining fiction, *Some Came Running* is probably of greatest potential interest to readers of the short stories. In this epic novel about a veteran's return to his Midwestern hometown and desire to become a writer, several characters and themes from "None Sing So Wildly" are reprised at greater length.

Recommended Works about James Jones

Carter, Steven. *James Jones: An American Literary Orientalist Master.* Urbana: University of Illinois Press, 1998.

Garrett, George. *James Jones.* San Diego: Harcourt Brace Jovanovich, 1984.

Giles, James. *James Jones.* Boston: Twayne, 1981.

Giles, James, and J. Michael Lennon, editors. *The James Jones Reader: Outstanding Selections from His War Writings.* New York: Birch Lane, 1991.

Hendrick, George, editor. *To Reach Eternity: The Letters of James Jones.* New York: Random House, 1989.

Hopkins, John, compiler. *James Jones: A Checklist.* Detroit: Gale Research, 1974.

James Jones Literary Society Web Page at http://JamesJonesLitSociety.vinu.edu

Lennon, J. Michael, and Jeffrey Van Davis, producers. *James Jones: Reveille to Taps.* Springfield, Illinois: Sangamon State University, 1984. PBS Television Documentary.

MacShane, Frank. *Into Eternity: The Life of James Jones, American Writer.* Boston: Houghton Mifflin, 1985.

Morris, Willie. *James Jones: A Friendship.* Garden City: Doubleday, 1978.

Shepherd, Allen. "James Jones." *Dictionary of Literary Biography.* 143: 51-70.

Dr. Judith Everson
Professor Emerita
English Program
University of Illinois at Springfield

Photo by Bruce Dale, © National Geographic Society, 1967

T H E   J O N E S   F A M I L Y
James,   Gloria,   Kaylie,   and   Jamie

James Jones (1921-1977) became internationally famous with his first novel, *From Here to Eternity,* a classic portrayal of Army life in WWII, which won the National Book Award. Over the next twenty-five years, he wrote ten more books, both fiction and nonfiction.

Kaylie Jones, daughter of James Jones, is the author of four novels, including *A Soldier's Daughter Never Cries* (also a major film) and *Celeste Ascending.*

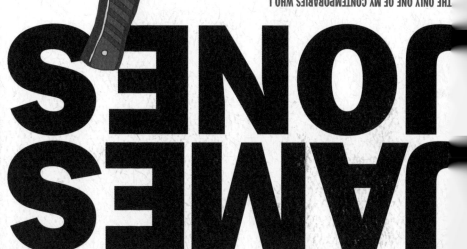

THE ICE-CREAM HEADACHE AND OTHER STORIES

WITH A NEW PREFACE BY KAYLIE JONES

JAMES JONES

"THE ONLY ONE OF MY CONTEMPORARIES WHO I FELT HAD MORE TALENT THAN MYSELF WAS JAMES JONES, AND HE HAS ALSO BEEN THE ONE WRITER OF ANY TIME FOR WHOM I FELT ANY LOVE."
—*NORMAN MAILER*